A Lion Named Rollo

Carol Livramento

PAUL ANTHONY PUBLISHING

clivramento@earthlink.net

Copyright ©2024 by Carol Livramento

All rights reserved including the right to reproduce this book in whole or in part. For reprint or permission information, contact Paul Anthony Publishing at: clivramento@earthlink.net

Cover illustration by: Evelyn Thorsness
Cover design and interior design by
Toby Cowan, Performance Design Group
Sebastopol, CA 95472

Print ISBN: 979-8-3302-0461-8
eBook ISBN: 979-8-3302-0462-5

This book is a work of fiction. Unless otherwise indicated, all the names, characters, businesses, places, events and incidents in this book are either the product of the author's imagination or used in a fictitious manner. Any resemblance to actual persons, living or dead, or actual events is purely coincidental.

Dedication

Dedicated to Paul, my best friend and husband
of forty years.
Thanks for the love and support.

Chapter 1

"Bob!" Sarah screamed. "Look out!"

Bob slammed on the brakes as a beast dashed in front of their Land Rover. He swerved to miss the animal when a second tawny shape flew over the truck's hood. The resounding thump jolted them hard enough to throw the Aimtrees against their seatbelts. Bob stopped the vehicle as Sarah watched the second animal tumble end over end and land on the verge.

Leaning his forehead on the steering wheel, Bob gasped, "Thank God the windshield held or that beast would be in our laps." He pulled the truck round and trained the headlights on the motionless animal. Sarah activated her phone to call Dr. Malcolm Curry, their vet and good friend.

She was halfway out of the vehicle when Bob, rifle in hand, joined her. "Oh no, it's an adult male lion. Damn and blast, I hope I don't have to put him down."

Sarah was sure Malcolm rarely slept. No matter the time, he always picked up on the first or second ring. The only exception was when he was treating his reluctant and usually enormous patients. True to form, Malcolm answered immediately. He was, by pure chance, near them.

"I'll be there in thirty minutes," he promised.

Not quite a full moon, there was enough lunar illumination to bathe the African grasslands with light. That silvery light lit the clifftops of the Northern Escarpment. The enormous rock structure resembled the back of a huge dragon. After a dinner meeting with a group of fellow South African cattle ranchers, Bob and Sarah Aimtree were headed home to their ranch east of Karoo

National Park. They were engaged in a spirited discussion of hybrid cattle versus purebreds. Sarah liked her purebreds while Bob was pro hybrid. That discussion was now the last thing on Sarah's mind as she glanced at the inert animal.

"I'm not sure he's alive," she told Malcolm. "What should we do? Try to interact with him to see if he is still breathing?"

Sarah winced at Malcolm's reply. "Okay, okay, I got that. We'll see you soon." She turned to Bob. "He wants us to stay far away from him. Mal is afraid this beast will waken and decide you and I are his next meal. He also said this lion may get up, shake himself and disappear into the brush."

Sarah gnawed on her lip. Desperate to see if the animal was alive, she picked up two egg-sized stones. Turning to Bob she said, "What if I toss these rocks at him? I can do it from the Land Rover. If he comes for us, we can jump in and slam the door."

Bob nodded. "Okay, even if he does attack, I doubt it'll be at normal speed. Go ahead, I'll hold the door."

Sarah bounced both rocks off the animal's rib cage. In response, he produced a weak, wheezy groan but didn't move.

"Bob! He's alive. We need Malcolm. Where is he? He said it would only be thirty minutes."

Bob glanced at his watch. "Sarah, it's been five minutes since you called. We must wait for him. Malcolm doesn't have a teleporter."

She paced and fretted. Malcolm had come to South Africa on vacation and never went home. The magical continent captivated him. Even when he returned for a visit to his hometown in California, he barely lasted two weeks before returning to his practice in nearby Snowtown She knew it was selfish thinking on her part, but she was glad the man had remained single. It gave him more time for patients.

Malcolm pulled onto the verge and made a quick stop. Dust spurted from under his wheels and swirled like smoke around the unconscious lion. He flew out of his truck, went to the rear of his vehicle and threw supplies into a bucket.

"Not sure what I'm going to need," he told them. "Better dart this big lad. If I get close enough to inject him, he may waken and lunge at me. Bob won't have time to shoot him."

"Oh Mal," Sarah cried, "we couldn't miss him. We barely missed the antelope, then plowed into this guy. We know he's alive because he groaned when I bounced two stones off him."

Malcolm looked at his two friends and said, "Look, I need to say something before I examine him. I've worked on big cats, but most of my wildlife work has been on hooved animals. I can look at him, but he's a large apex predator. We don't know how badly he is hurt. He might simply have a bad whack to the head but could also have broken bones, internal injuries, and maybe a bleed into the brain." He ran fingers through his hair. "He could have a combination of all the things I just mentioned. Even transport is an issue. My truck's modified to serve as a makeshift ambulance, but I usually transport weak, young animals like zebra foals and sick calves. One more thing. Those critters have been diagnosed so it is reasonably safe to sedate them. I can't transport this lion without sedation. If he wakes up in the truck, he might injure himself further and possibly destroy the back of my vehicle. I might also be running for my life. On the other hand, sedating him without evaluating his injuries might kill him."

Sarah narrowed her eyes and asked, "Malcolm, what exactly are you saying?"

"Sarah, I'm suggesting euthanasia now is a fair option."

"Ach! Mal, I want to help him. We hit him, and I feel responsible. Bob, what do you think?"

Bob said, "The same, I'd like to help him, but I understand you. If he's severely injured, we should put him down now."

In addition to their cattle raising business, Sarah and Bob worked with local sanctuaries and wildlife rescue organizations. They were repeatedly called upon to provide temporary shelter for sick or injured animals. Bob had built enclosures and paddocks for hooved animals and had a few areas that would house indigenous predators.

Both Sarah and Bob were born in South Africa, their parents were ex-pats from England. As children, they had been exposed to every species of animal that lived in the region. Both felt a responsibility to help wildlife in need and dedicated a portion of the ranch to that purpose.

Malcolm glanced at Sarah, then turned to Bob. "You two are sure about this decision? Once this big fellow is sedated it will take the three of us to load him. He's so heavy, I hope the three of us can load him. We can't use my sling, he's too big for three people. We'll use the gurney."

Bob sighed. "Hell no, I'm not sure this is a great idea, but you know Sarah. She has the bit in her teeth. If we don't help her, she will sling this beast over her shoulder and walk home."

"Alright, without a scale, I'll guess at how much sedative to give. Jeez, I bet he weighs two hundred plus kilos." He returned to his truck for more supplies. Loaded dart gun in hand he joined Bob and Sarah at their truck.

Malcolm smiled and said, "This will be like shooting fish in a barrel. My patients are either running away at top speed or they're attacking me." He fired the dart. The animal jerked as he felt the needle, rolled to his chest, and swung his massive head around to peer at Malcolm. This sent Sarah, Bob, and Malcolm scrambling into the Land Rover. Safely inside, they watched and waited. The lion, still on his chest, gazed back at them with a benign expression in his amber eyes.

Bob heard it first. "He's growling, isn't he? Is that noise growling? Mal, what is that noise he's making?"

"Ah, I'm not sure. It doesn't sound like growling, more like rumbling, deep in the chest. It's not a normal sound for a lion. He may have fluid in his lungs from the impact."

"He's purring," Sarah declared. "He sounds like a big domestic cat."

Malcolm frowned at her. "Lions don't purr. Don't be making this beast into something he isn't."

"Purring," Sarah huffed. "He's purring. Listen to him."

The object of the discussion blinked, yawned, put his head on his paws, and went to sleep. The vet got in his vehicle and drove close to the sleeping animal. He and Bob pulled Malcolm's makeshift gurney out of the back. The wheels dropped and locked in place. Once Malcolm was satisfied it was close enough to the lion, he collapsed the wheels.

Malcolm said, "Look, let's do this. I'll do a quick exam before we load him. If his heart rate is abnormal, if I hear fluid in his lungs, feel fluid in his belly, or fractures in his limbs, let's re-consider euthanasia."

The Aimtrees agreed and Malcolm went to work. He thumped and prodded, felt all four limbs, and listened to vitals. He sat back on his heels and said, "His heart rate is surprisingly normal. Lungs are clear and I don't feel any obvious fractures. Let's load him and get to your ranch."

All three worked wide bands under the lion, secured them and with considerable effort slid the animal onto the gurney. The hardest task was pulling the transporter upright to lock the wheels. Once done, it was a moment's work to push it into the truck.

Sarah turned to Malcolm. "Where do you want him? Where's the best place for us to keep him? I'm calling Obert, He can have lights on and gates open."

Malcolm thought a moment. "Well, sure, someplace with lights and plenty of room."

"We can use the enclosure on the west side of the house. It's about half a kilometer from ranch traffic yet close enough to easily monitor him," Sarah said.

"Okay Sarah, just to clarify and I know I'm repeating myself. I can't do much. No X-ray capability, no way to do soft tissue scans. I'll take blood samples, repeat what I did here to see if there are changes. It's primitive medicine but the best we can do."

"That's fine Mal. Let's see if we can care for him until he can return to the wild."

Sarah waved her phone at Bob, signaling she had Obert on the line. "Obert, we're bringing a lion home. Can you have the gate to the side enclosure open? We should be there in half an hour. Yes, correct, a lion. What? Yes, full-grown. Obert, I must go. I'm riding with Malcolm. Talk to Bob about the details." She handed her phone to Bob and jumped into Malcolm's truck.

Thirty minutes later, Obert hurried out of the side yard, a look of disbelief on his face as Sarah and Malcolm pulled into the Aimtree driveway. Bob was right behind them. Obert opened gates and had the front yard ablaze with lights. With an extra pair of hands, the lion was quickly moved to the secure area.

Malcolm drew blood samples and rechecked the animal's vital signs. He secured the samples in his truck and spoke to the group. "His vitals are unchanged, a good sign. Leave him be. Let him sleep off the drugs. I'll get this blood on its way to the lab. Call me first thing in the morning and let me know if he's alive."

The South African dawn, shot with gold from the rising sun, found the mighty simba still snoring from the drugs that had been administered. That same South African dawn found Sarah standing in front of the lion's enclosure, impatiently waiting for him to wake up. At least he's still breathing, she thought. She decided not to call Malcolm until the lion was conscious.

Bob sauntered across the lawn holding two cups of coffee. He handed one to his wife and asked, "How is our patient?"

"Still sleeping."

Husband and wife stood shoulder to shoulder, sipping coffee, and observing the lion. A few moments later, the beast opened his eyes and turned to look at them. He was a rich golden color with a darker-hued mane. Like most of his kind, his paws were the size of baseball gloves. He began to rise but toppled over. A second attempt brought him to a sitting position. He stared at Sarah and Bob with a placid expression in his amber eyes. An odd rumble rose from his chest.

Sarah frowned, "That's the same sound he was making last night. Have you ever heard anything like it from a cat his size?"

"Nope, not a clue as to why he's doing it. You heard what Mal said. It's not a normal sound for a lion. I agree, it sound like purring."

"Geez, he looks so calm, he must still be goofy from the drugs."

"Again, I agree, but remember, he's an enormous predator. For all we know, he thinks we are the antelope he was chasing. We can't assume anything and must treat him with caution."

The lion yawned, exposing his lethal ten-centimeter-long canines. His gaze drifted back and forth, first on Sarah, then Bob.

Sarah took a step forward. "We're going to help you get strong enough to return to your home."

As if to answer her, the lion hauled himself to all fours and wobbled to the front of the pen. Startled, Sarah took a prudent step back. "He's disoriented, maybe he thinks we're lions."

Bob nodded. "God only knows what's on his mind. We both know he can't habituate to people. If there's a chance for him to recover and be released, the less contact with people, the better."

"I know, I know, you're right. Let's call Mal. This animal is waking up but clearly disoriented. Let's see what he wants to do."

A cloud of dust crossed the driveway, accompanied by the roar of a well-used truck. Obert Ntutu hung his head out the window and waved a jolly hello. The Aimtree ranch foreman for several years, was a Maasai. He was tall and rangy, with the long flat muscles of an endurance runner. Like the Aimtrees, Obert had been raised caring for indigenous cattle and he'd attended the university to learn more about the bovine species. The lanky African hopped out of the vehicle and laughed, "Looks like he is following a tennis match, that big head bobbing back and forth. Glory! He is huge. Is Malcolm coming? How the heck is he going to treat him? Will he have to resedate him? Are we going to—?"

Bob held up both hands. "Obert, my answer to all your questions is, I don't know."

"Hah!" said the foreman. "Well, let's hope he doesn't get too frisky. That pen wasn't exactly built to lion specs."

Bob nodded. "Yes, I've been thinking about that. All we need is to have him escape and chase our cattle."

The potential cattle chaser laid down and stared at the three. His gaze would fix on one, then the other. After a few moments, his head sank to his forepaws, and he returned to sleep.

"Oh boy," Sarah said, "maybe he does have a head injury. Can't you be groggy with a concussion?"

"Well," Bob replied, "Mal did mention that was possible. If

you recall, he also mentioned there's nothing to be done, other than wait." Bob pulled out his phone. " I'll call our favorite vet."

Malcolm's voice boomed through the phone. "Is he still alive? Is he on his feet? Have you seen him—?"

Bob shouted back. "Malcolm, you sound like Obert. Yes, our patient is breathing and trying to get on his feet. He's still wobbly, I'm not sure he could even get to his water trough."

"Okay, I'm at the Von Berg's, just finished vetting Fluffy. I'm packing up my stuff and will be there in less than an hour."

"Who the heck is Fluffy?"

"He's that Beefmaster bull Brandon has been leasing for a year. The first calf crop is on the ground and Brandon is satisfied with them. He is going to put some real money down to buy the bull. He wanted my veterinarian seal of approval.

Bob asked, "Fluffy? How did a massive, mature bull get a name like Fluffy?"

Malcolm laughed. "Samantha named him. The bull has curly hairs on top of his head, it's unusual for his breed, I wouldn't call them fluffy, but Samantha did. The name stuck; this enormous, macho animal now has a goofy name."

"Leave it to Samantha. I'm curious, what is the bull's registered name?"

"Oh," Malcolm answered, "something like 'Baron von Hasting the Fourth."

Bob laughed. "Almost as bad as Fluffy."

Samantha, Felicity and Brandon Von Berg's four and one-half-year-old daughter, was a tiny dynamo. Barely a meter tall, she was already passionate about animals. She had brown eyes and a mop of curly brown hair. Constantly in motion, she questioned everything that came into her world. Bob and Sarah were considered her second parents, but even patient Sarah could be frazzled by Sam's energy.

"Hey Bob," Malcolm said, "speaking of Samantha, Felicity would like a word. I'm handing her my phone while I finish loading my stuff. I'll see you shortly."

Felicity Von Berg took the phone, "Bob, we understand you have a new pet. Sam's favorite toy is that stuffed lion you both gave her. For reasons known only to her, she named him Rollo. Samantha heard Malcolm talking about your close encounter with the real thing and is driving everyone mad. She wants to see the real Rollo right now. You know Sam. No patience. Brandon and I want a peek at him as well. Shame on us blaming our child for our nosiness. Can we follow Malcolm? Ach! Speaking of Malcolm, he wants his phone back."

"Oh Filly, of course, you can. We will brew more coffee and find something for lunch."

"Excellent, and thank you, I'll pack up my family."

✸ Rollo ✸
Chapter 2

Oooof! Holy hyenas, my head hurts. Everything is blurry. Where am I? What happened to me? What is this place? It's a large flat space, cool and dim. There's a barrier that goes round it, solid on the sides and back, wire in front, and a raised area behind me. It would make a fine sleeping spot. I'd inspect it if I could get up. I'm thirsty. I can smell water, but there are no ponds or streams in here. Is it coming from that tiny round thing in the corner? It's too small to be a water hole.

I remember chasing an antelope. Why would I be chasing an antelope? Were there two-legs involved? I hope not, Mum always told me to avoid them. She said they have long sticks that shoot invisible bees that harm us. My uncle Sid had an encounter with the two-legs and their long sticks and none of us ever saw him again. Drat, two of the creatures are walking toward me. My mum was right, they are magical because they just changed into twins. Could there be four of them? Or is it my fuzzy vision? At least these two, or four, don't have any long sticks.

I'll lie here quietly, maybe they won't notice me. Galloping zebras, no such luck. One of them is in front of me. I'm glad there is a barrier between us, I'm frightened of them and too groggy to run away. How do you tell the males from the females? This one seems female, but like me, has a mane. I'm male, so, is this one male or female? Well, it's making sounds, but I can't understand them. Here comes the other one, they turned themselves into twins again. I'd better get up but my legs are too weak. Bah! I lost my balance and am sprawled in front of the maned one. How embarrassing! I'm almost positive this one is female. If I'm hearing correctly, the other one is calling her Sarah. That must be her name. What is she trying to tell me?

I'll sit here a moment until I feel stronger. The Sarah creature is approaching the wire, she's talking but makes no sense. If I can keep my legs under me, I'll walk to the barrier and greet her. These two-legged creatures are so unpredictable I wish to appear friendly. This may be a bad idea. The other two-leg is, maybe, a male, even with no mane. He's joined Sarah at the wire. She called him Bob.

Oh, leaping leopards! What is that awful noise? Some sort of contraption with round things on the bottom. I remember Mum saying the two-legs ride in them to observe us. Sure enough, another two-leg is getting out of it. How odd! This one is a darker color than the other two. Oops, he just turned into two, now there might be six of them. If they all gang up on me, I am surely doomed.

Wobbly and desperate for water I stagger to the corner of this space. I've never seen water held in such a fashion. I give it a careful sniff. Fresh and cool, it's in a high-sided container. I take a huge drink. Exhausted, I collapse for a rest.

My head is so sore. I have an odd memory of striking a hard object. I can't remember anything else until I awoke, here. Well, my balance is abnormal but all my limbs, while sore, appear to be intact.

Chapter 3

Later that morning, Obert, back from chores, returned to the Aimtree yard. His older brother, Michael, accompanied him. The two brothers shared DNA but were very different. Michael was shorter and stockier than his brother. He had none of his brother's outgoing personality. Reserved, he thought carefully before asking a question or giving advice. Michael's primary interest dealt with plants that contributed to successful cattle raising. He had gone to university to study specimens that were drought resistant and nutritious enough to be used for fodder. He also studied water irrigation systems and crop rotation. This part of South Africa was semi-arid. Michael's knowledge was a huge asset to the farm.

Hands in pockets, he walked to the front of the pen and studied the lion. The beast gazed back at him with the same sweet expression he bestowed on all humans. Then he began to purr. Taciturn Michael burst out laughing and said, "Sarah, do we have a big house cat here? Has he eaten? And how are we going to clean the pen if we can't shift him to the outside yard?"

Sarah said, "Michael, leave it to you to think of something no one has considered. You're so right. I like this animal but wouldn't walk in there with a wheelbarrow and shovel. Malcolm is on his way; he'll help us sort this. Our patient did wobble over to the trough and drink. Michael, isn't there an old bench in the shed? We need something for people to sit on. The Von Bergs will be the first of many visitors."

With Sarah supervising, all four trooped to the shed. Sarah waved cobwebs away and sent the men into the gloomy interior.

Michael, in one corner called, "Found it, under some tarps and two elderly wheelbarrows. I could use some help here." Loud coughing punctuated by several sneezes followed this remark.

All three obliged and the bench was carried outside, hosed off, and inspected.

Sarah frowned. "Where did this come from? I don't remember."

Bob replied, "Didn't it belong to your parents? I recall taking it when they sold their farm."

Sarah, hands on hips, replied, "Yes, exactly right, we put it in the shed when Mum and Dad moved. Now, where to put it? It should fit on the lawn between the shade trees. We can't have people sitting in the blazing sun, so parking it between these two trees will be perfect, and a safe distance away from the pen."

With minimal maneuvering, they positioned the wooden bench between the two shade trees. Laughing, Sarah plunked herself down. "Let's see if it's still sound. Hmm, a bit damp but seems sturdy.

Obert and his brother sat, then Bob. All four bounced up and down.

"Testing, testing," Obert said between bounces. "Very strong. It will do nicely."

The old bench, constructed of mahogany was two meters long with scrolled armrests and two supports in the middle. The wood had a matte finish.

Malcolm Curry arrived to find the four sitting on the bench. "What the heck are you doing? It looks like you're at the movies." He strode to the fence, squatted, and scrutinized the lion. Over his shoulder, he called, " The Von Berg tribe is right behind me. Blast! He's still making that odd rumbling noise that Sarah thinks is purring."

"Mal," Sarah asked, "We need instruction on his care. Food,

activity, and a safe way to clean up after him. Michael pointed out that we must be able to shift him outside so we can clean this area. He did take a drink. I've been thinking about the logistics of this. That big sliding door on the right leads to the paddock. There is also a small door into this area on the left, near his water trough. I'm thinking we can put meat over the fence and lock him outside. We can then safely clean his pen." She paused. "Also, this outside fence needs to be inspected and strengthened. It was never meant to hold a big cat but I can't see a different choice. Your thoughts?"

"Okay, you're right about moving him back and forth. It's a safety issue. Let's hope he cooperates and goes outside. Have you offered him food? And ... er ... has he shown signs of stress? Or aggression?"

Sarah grinned. "Could purring be a sign of stress? Ah, no, Mal, sorry to disappoint, he continues to behave in a very un-lion-like fashion."

"Humph, he just got here, don't drop your guard and take no chances when working round him. This fence wire is not exactly for lions. What is it? Eight-centimeter squares? It's strong, heavy wire though. That's good. Like you say, there isn't a choice. Let's hope we can release him soon. Feeding him may be a problem but since there are doors on each end of this covered enclosure, I suggest putting a small amount of meat in the left corner. When he goes for it and let's hope he's interested in food, two people can be at the sliding door, with about five kilos of meat. One person opens the door, the second can toss the meat inside. I can't say it's entirely safe but should work short-term.

"Okay, Mal, it's worth a try. Can you give us advice about a proper feeding station in case he is here longer than expected?"

Malcolm said, "Let's think about that. I've seen some simple but safe ways to feed cats at some of the sanctuaries."

The five of them were discussing this problem when Sarah heard an approaching vehicle. She rightly guessed the Von Bergs had arrived. The four men walked down the fence line, heads together, working to solve the feeding problem. Sarah rose to greet the newcomers. She could hear Samantha's whoops before the car stopped.

"Rollo! Rollo! I want to see Rollo now!"

Sarah thought, not for the first time, how can such a tiny being make such a racket? Sam's parents exited the vehicle, admonishing their daughter to stay put until she was safely undone from the car seat.

Brandon opened the car door and looked his daughter in the eye. When he was sure he had her attention, he said, "Sam, Sarah wants to speak to you about this lion. He's not a large version of your toy. You'll sit here and listen. Your mother and I expect you to follow Sarah's instructions, if you don't, we'll go back home."

Sarah knelt next to Samantha. "I know you understand animals. I know how much you love them so it will be easy for you to be quiet around this one. He has been injured. We can't be running, shouting, or waving our arms about when we approach him. Can you do that?"

Samantha, unable to take her eyes off the lion, nodded. "I'll be quiet, I want to see the real Rollo."

"Okay, good. We shall all go over and sit on the bench, that is the closest we get to him."

Under the shade trees, Samantha scrambled onto the bench, turned around, and looked imploringly at her mother. "Can I pet him?"

Felicity sighed. "Sam, what did Sarah just tell you? This is as close as we get. Remember, we can't upset him."

The little girl nodded, crossed her arms, and scrunched her face. The two women began to catch up on gossip while Brandon joined the problem solvers at the fence.

Sam turned to Sarah. "Is Rollo sick?"

"Well, not exactly sick. He has a sore head. Dr. Malcolm feels we should let him rest until he gets better. Oh, and thank you for naming him. We now have a lion named Rollo."

Sam fell silent. Sarah looked over her head at Felicity. "Filly, I swear the wheels are turning so fast in that little head I believe I see smoke coming out of her ears."

Sam turned to her mother and crowed. "Rollo can come home with us. I'll make him all better. He can stay in my room."

Felicity, a patient look on her face, said, "Sam that lion won't fit in our car, he's way too big."

Sarah watched Sam frown at this news. The little girl stood up and pointed to Malcolm's truck. "I know! Dr. Malcolm can bring big Rollo to our house." Obviously pleased with herself, she sat down and beamed at her Mum and Sarah.

"Malcolm, could you come over here and explain to Sam that Rollo can't be moved?" Sarah called out.

Malcolm gave Sarah an exasperated look. He wasn't kid savvy and the first to admit it, but he came to the bench and spoke to the child in his official veterinarian voice. "Samantha, I'm this lion's doctor. I tell you, as his doctor, he must stay here and rest until he can return to his home with other lions."

"Okay, Dr. Malcolm," Samantha whispered, then folded her hands over her toy and stared at Rollo.

Sarah saw Sam fidgeting, the little girl swung her legs, looked right and left, and pushed her toy down the front of her overalls.

Turning to Felicity, Sarah resumed their conversation. "So

what exactly did Danny DeGroot do in the Safari Club last Saturday?"

"Well, what I heard—"

The men walked further down the fence line. Snatches of their conversation drifted toward the bench. A metal sliding tray … perhaps a small safety fence here … as Sarah listened with rapt attention to Felicity's description of Danny DeGroot's escapade.

Sarah gasped as Samantha leaped off the bench, sprinted to the fence, and began to climb the wire. The adults heard her shouting. "Rollo! Rollo! You're coming home with us. I'm coming in there to take you home!"

For a few seconds, the group was paralyzed. When they began to move, it was a performance that would have put the Keystone Kops to shame. Sarah and Felicity lurched off the bench and tripped over each other's feet. At the fence line, Bob and Obert did the same. Malcolm made an end run around them and smacked into Brandon, knocking both off balance. Michael, after what seemed an eternity, plucked the child off the fence by her overall straps.

Samantha, furious, arms flailing, tossed her toy through the wire squares. The lion didn't retreat. He stood, nose against the fence as the toy bopped him in the face and rolled under his front legs.

Michael handed screaming, dangling Samantha to her father, and collapsed on the bench.

White-faced, Brandon clutched his shoulder and said, "Thank you, I thought she was going to be injured. He could have taken her arm off."

Michael, unable to speak, waved a hand in answer. After a few breathes, he looked at Brandon and asked, "How are we going to get her toy?"

Malcolm hurried toward his truck. "I've a tool with a grabber, not meant to pull objects out of a lion's den, but it just might work."

Red-faced and sobbing, Samantha shouted for her toy as her parents moved her briskly toward their vehicle, putting more distance between their daughter and the big cat.

Sarah approached the wire and got on her hands and knees. She determined the toy was several meters out of reach. Rollo backed up and sniffed the object. He picked it up in his huge jaws and gummed it several times, then dropped it and carefully prodded the toy with first one forepaw, then the other. Sarah, fascinated, remained still. The animal looked at her and used his nose to roll the stuffed lion in her direction.

Sarah heard Malcolm returning. "Sarah, I finally found this bloody thing!"

Sarah put her hands behind her. "Shhh! Malcolm, stop, stop, don't come any closer."

Hearing concern in her voice, Malcolm complied. "What is it? What's he doing?"

Sarah whispered, "Good, Rollo, can you do that again?"

The animal gave an explosive snort, landing the toy against the wire. Sarah reached in and grabbed it.

Malcolm threw his hands in the air and declared. "Geez, Sarah, you're worse than that howling kid. You know better. You know how fast and strong these cats are."

Ignoring Malcolm's diatribe, Sarah got up, waved the toy, and headed toward the Von Bergs. "Look, Sam, here's your Rollo, safe and sound."

Grim-faced, Brandon and Felicity were buckling their daughter into the car seat.

Brandon looked at his wife. "Filly, do we have any rope? I'm thinking of wrapping several meters around her and the seat."

Badly shaken, Felicity replied, "What do you think? Grounded until she is eighteen?"

"At least, maybe longer. Thirty sounds a more appropriate number."

Felicity asked her tearful daughter, "Sam, what were you thinking? You know that animal could have clawed you through the fence."

"I wanted to take Rollo home so I can make him well. I could take care of him at our house. I love him."

Sarah handed the toy to Samantha and looked at her friends. "Are you all okay? Oh Filly, looks like lunch is a wash."

Brandon rolled his eyes. "Yes, I don't know how our daughter still has all four limbs intact. She's very lucky. The three of us will recover although Filly and I will be stone deaf if Sam doesn't dial down her volume."

Sarah rubbed her forehead. "I don't know why he didn't react more aggressively. As much as I hate to think it, maybe Malcolm is right. Maybe this poor animal is brain damaged."

Sarah walked back to the men. "Let's try to feed him. Lord knows he deserves a good meal after all that excitement. Bob, can you get a slab of meat from the outside kitchen? Mal, what do you think of me going to the far corner with a small portion of beef? If we're lucky, he will get a whiff of it and follow me. Then one of you can open the slider and a second pair of hands can toss the meat. Boom, we shut the door. He may be fast, but he can't be in two places at once."

"Bravo, Sarah," said Malcolm. "That's a good plan. Let's hope he's hungry enough to follow you."

Bob returned with a huge chunk of beef. He cut off a small portion and handed it to Sarah.

She held the meat near the wire and spoke to the lion. "Come on, big boy, are you hungry? Come with me and have a snack."

Rollo tossed his shaggy mane and paced alongside her. Sarah shoved the meat through the wire and signaled Obert. He opened the slider; Bob threw the meat inside and Obert shut the door.

Malcolm punched his fists in the air. "Yes! That didn't take fifteen seconds. Well done, everyone."

The lion ate the snack in one bite and followed Sarah back to the men. He picked up his meal and stepped onto the wooden raised platform in the middle of the pen. He settled and began to eat.

Sarah turned to the group. "Good, he's eating and speaking of food, I don't know about the rest of you, but I could do with a spot of lunch. I know it's early in the day, but I wouldn't say no to a good, stiff drink."

A chorus of approvals was her answer. They drifted toward the house. At the foot of the stoep steps, Malcolm stopped and cocked his head.

"Mal, what is it?"

"Sarah, how long is your driveway?"

Perplexed, Sarah said, "About one kilometer, why do you ask?

Malcolm cocked his head again. "I believe I can still hear Samantha."

✹ Rollo ✹
Chapter 4

I'm learning the two-leg language. Like us, they have names. There's Sarah and Bob, a mated pair. Two unmated males, Obert and Michael are part of the pride. They don't look alike, but I'm certain they're littermates. Obert is tall and thin. Michael is shorter and has a calmer temperament than his brother. I remember one of my siblings looked nothing like me, but we were always in trouble with our pranks. My Mum said we drove her crazy, trying to keep us out of trouble. One day she hid us to go hunting. We were supposed to stay under the thick bushes, but we got bored and went exploring. We found a termite mound and were rampaging up and down the sides when a pack of hyenas scented us. We were too young and stupid to know we were in trouble. The ugly brutes waited to see if Mum was near. They soon decided we were alone and surrounded us. We screamed and screamed. Fortunately, Mum was returning and heard us. She tore through the hyenas, killing one and wounding several others. We learned our lesson and stayed where Mum hid us after that experience.

Four more of these odd creatures arrived this morning. I'm glad they have left. This was a quiet place, but I'm getting ahead of myself. In this new group, were Brandon and his mate Felicity. Their cub is called Samantha. The last of this group is Malcolm. He's a mystery to me. Another solitary male, he's well tolerated by the others. He appears to have status. In our pride, the three unattached males would be driven off. They must have different rules. They're so primitive compared to us. Another strange thing, these creatures have coats that don't appear to be part of their skin. I know this sounds impossible, but their fur blows and flaps in the breeze. The cub, Samantha, has a coat with straps that hold up the bottom of her fur. I can't understand it. Maybe it's because they walk on two legs. But monkeys can walk on two legs and their fur sticks to them. Oh, the oddest thing of all, Samantha had a tiny object that looked like me. It can't be her cub. Can it? It's so small. I wondered if it was a tiny dead lion. A strange thought crossed my mind, perhaps it was never alive. How silly, that makes no sense.

This morning they talked about food for me. I wished they would do more than talk. I'm clear-headed now and very hungry. The lot of them were discussing how much to feed me and how to put meat in here. Are they daft? Instead of wasting time talking about food, why can't they open the door and toss meat into my space? They'll have to bumble along until they solve this simple problem. They were nattering on about a tray with a lid when Samantha arrived. Things took a turn for the worse when she was loose in the yard.

Sarah, Samantha and Felicity were sitting on the long flat log. The men were at the fence, still talking about food. My stomach rumbled. I was too hungry to purr. The cub couldn't take her eyes off me. I'm magnificent and understood her fascination. I tossed my mane and looked regal. After all, we're kings of this land.

Moments later, Samantha leaped off the log, raced toward me, and scooted up the wire. How could this short, stubby creature climb so quickly? And noisy! Trumpeting elephants could take lessons from her. Startled, and unsure what to do next, I stood. Watching. She shouted 'Rollo'! 'Rollo'!

Rollo? I thought, who's Rollo? These dimwits think my name is Rollo. I do like it. It suits me and rolls off the tongue in a pleasant manner. Besides, I'm sure they are incapable of pronouncing my real name, so Rollo is acceptable. The naming ceremony was the least of my worries. Samantha climbed so fast, she was above my head in seconds. Michael rushed over and yanked her off the fence by her coat straps. Ow! That must have hurt. If he'd tugged on my coat with such force, I would have been angry. I'm glad he caught her. She might have gotten into my space. If she can run and climb, maybe she can fly. That would be the last straw, some noisy creature flying round in here. In all the excitement, she tossed the tiny lion through the wire. It smacked me in the face and rolled underneath me. My goodness! What a commotion. The big two-legs dashed about yelling and running into each other. Sarah approached the fence and looked so frightened, I felt sorry for her. She knelt in front of me and whispered my name.

Here was a chance to examine this odd, little object, so I ignored her. First, I took several deep sniffs. I know what dead stuff smells like but this thing didn't smell like anything. Then, I checked to see if it was edible. Everyone had lost interest in feeding me, so I gave it a little nibble. Yuk! It tasted like fuzzy straw. I can't eat it. Last, I gave it several paw pokes, just to make sure it wasn't alive. No response. Sarah was still there, and she was interested in the worthless thing, so, between snorts and shoves, I put it against the fence. She can have it and grab it she did.

Things calmed down and, finally, the talk of food resumed. These animals are so dumb. They ran here and there, placed food in one door, then another. I finally tucked into a delicious meal. Once alone, and ready for a well-deserved nap, I considered the cub, Samantha. She's a puzzle. So fast. Could she have cheetah blood? All the cheetahs I know are sleek, with long legs, and quiet. Malcolm gave me a clue about her climbing. He told Sarah that Sam was a holyterror. I don't know what that word means but I'd bet my mane it's a monkey.

Chapter 5

Three weeks later, as the sun peeped over the horizon, Sarah hurried down the stoep stairs. A glance toward Rollo's enclosure, what she called his night area…told her the lion was sitting next to the closed sliding door.

"What a good boy! Patiently waiting for breakfast. Just a moment, I'm coming." She pushed a small wheelbarrow into the outside kitchen and selected a robust slab of beef. "This would feed Bob and me for several days," she mused. Once across the driveway, Sarah opened the slider to release Rollo into the yard. The lion ambled outside and sat in front of his food tray.

Sarah smiled. "You really are Mr. Manners. Alrighty here's your meal." She marveled at the simple device that fed Rollo. Malcolm's idea, a metal tray slid back and forth on a one-meter-high stand. It went from Rollo's side of the fence to the human's side. Sarah placed the beef onto the tray and slid it back to the lion. She exited the safety fence that was constructed around the tray. "Brilliant idea," she told Malcolm. It's safe for man and beast. A second feeding station was installed on the opposite side of Rollo's indoor enclosure. He could now be safely fed if he was confined or outside. Malcolm repeatedly stressed there be minimal contact between Rollo and his caregivers. Habituation to humans could be fatal when they released him.

Later that morning Sarah stood on her stoep and surveyed her plants. She was waiting for Malcolm and used the time to inspect her favorite flowers.

From hanging baskets, white alyssum cascaded down to the

railings perfuming the air with their other-worldly, sweet fragrance. Twin spur, in yellows, reds, and oranges, kept the alyssum company. Tucked on the far end of the stoep was a huge Boston fern in a meter-tall stand. Its lush fronds brushed the floor.

Satisfied with her stoep specimens, Sarah moved down the stairs to the two rock beds that flanked the stoep. Succulents rioted in the beds. She had a word with them and walked to the bench, well shaded this morning by its two flanking trees. She sat and reflected upon the activities of the last few weeks. Mid-January, she thought, and this beastie has been here a month. She looked at the lion's covered area and fence, pleased with the upgrades and repairs.

Much work had been done on the original enclosure. The paddock was a rough rectangle, two and one-half hectares. Weak spots in the fence were repaired, and a water trough was installed in a corner of the den. Several sections of fencing were raised. The paddock hadn't been used for several years. Full of weeds and brush, it could easily hide a lion. All his caregivers agreed Rollo would be more comfortable in tall grass, but it made him impossible to see. He could escape with no one the wiser. Thus, the raising of low spots in the fence.

She marveled at the speed at which the work was accomplished. An army of volunteers appeared to help with the project. Family, friends, and distant acquaintances showed up to dig, pound nails, saw boards, and stretch wire. None of them fooled me, Sarah thought. They all wanted to gawk at our Rollo. The object of all the gawking behaved beautifully. He sat for photos, purred, rolled on his back with paws in the air, and solemnly paced the fence keeping an eye on the workers.

She remembered coming down the stoep stairs one morning to find three strangers digging postholes for the safety fence. Bemused, she could still recall the entire conversation.

"Good morning. I'm Sarah, it looks like you three are hard at work. Did Bob hire you?"

"Oh no, ma'am. We don't know Bob."

"Ah," Sarah replied, "so it was Obert? Or Michael that hired you?"

"No ma'am, we don't know them either. Crikey, forgetting our manners, I'm Bernie, these other two lads are Billie and Stan."

"Happy to know you. But if no one hired you, how can we pay you?"

"Oh, no, ma'am, we're volunteers. We heard about this big fellow and as ashamed as we are to admit this, we didn't believe he was here. So, when the word in town went round, about needing a little help with his living space, why we just had to come by and see him for ourselves. The lads working on the fence told us they needed post holes dug."

"Well," Sarah replied, "I thank you for your hard work. Can I get you a cold drink? Or perhaps some coffee?"

Bernie shook his head. "No ma'am, we best be getting back to these post holes. Thank you just the same."

Stan shuffled his feet, stared at his shoes, then glanced shyly at Sarah. "Ma'am, could I be askin' a question?"

"Of course, Stan what it is?"

"Well, we heard he got a rap on his noodle and you nice folks are trying to get him better so he can be released. Is that true?"

"Yes, my husband and I were on our way home, and he ran in front of us. He was chasing an antelope. We missed the antelope but couldn't avoid him. So, yes, we're trying to get him better, so we can release him. His vet is afraid that rap on his head may have affected his prey drive."

Stan turned a startling shade of red before speaking. "Ma'am, I surely don't mean to be tellin' you, your business, but that lion don't look to me like he wants to bite a loaf of bread, never mind chase down his dinner."

"Stan, you're right again. We're worried he's too damaged to hunt."

Stan once again had trouble finding words. He peered at Sarah. "Ma'am, if you can't help him, you wouldn't be puttin' him down? Would you, ma'am?"

"Don't worry, Stan, we've talked about it and as long as he stays calm and doesn't seem too stressed by this confinement, we'll look after him."

"Ah, ma'am, that's champion! By golly, he seems a good sort."

The good sort sat by the fence and produced a booming purr, then stared at the three men.

Bernie threw back his head and laughed. "Why look at that. He's supervisin' the job! Lads, we best get our backs into this project."

And work they did. This strange animal had made three more friends that day. Again, Sarah worried about the lion's future but consoled herself that Rollo was getting excellent care and seemed quite content.

She thought back to the Aimtree annual Christmas braai. A Bar-B-Que according to her American friends! Concerned Rollo would be frightened or stressed by the unusual number of people and noise, she and Bob fretted about whether to leave his door open so he could escape the crowds and sleep in his outside favorite corner. Malcolm was consulted. He was also unsure of the best course of action. All three recognized there was a risk with either plan. If the lion were locked inside, all the festivities might upset him. If his yard door remained open, he could retreat into the paddock. But at night, were he to escape, no one would know it. Though Rollo had been allowed out during the day, he was confined at night. After much discussion, all of Rollo's caregivers decided it was best to give him an escape route to the outside.

Sarah couldn't believe the amount of time wasted discussing this problem. In the end, Rollo happily sat on his small knoll near the perimeter fence until the last guest had gone home. Then, he got up and went to bed.

All during the party, parents had given strict instruction to their children. Ronald do not go near that animal! Ronald, did you hear me? Stay away from the fence. Five minutes later, Ronald would be towed back to the lawn by a sputtering parent. Sally, if you don't come away from the fence, there will be no presents and no dessert. Sarah reflected that the 'no presents and no dessert' worked for all the kids. And poor Samantha, Sarah had felt so sorry for her. Either Felicity or Brandon, sometimes both, always had a firm grasp on at least one of Samantha's limbs.

At one point during the evening she saw Malcolm, drink in hand, standing near the fence. She joined him. "Don't you think our boy looks calm? I think he's enjoying himself."

Malcolm sighed, "I wish I could disagree with you but he looks ready to sign autographs."

It was Sarah's turn to sigh, "Mal, what are we going to do with this big, beautiful animal? We can't release him if he doesn't change his behavior. He wouldn't last a week in the wild."

"Agreed, I'm going to talk to some big cat sanctuaries. I'll also consult with Professor Bainbridge at the university. He's an expert on lion behavior."

***

Sarah's reverie was interrupted by the sound of an approaching vehicle. Obert pulled to the side of the yard and hopped out of his truck. He waved hello to Sarah and began rummaging in the bed of his vehicle.

"Good morning, Obert, what have you got back there?"

"Ha! A surprise for our favorite simba. Wait til you see."

Intrigued, Sarah approached the truck. "What on earth is that?"

Obert hauled a long object out of the truck bed. Made of wood and a meter long, it had two chains fastened on the top board of each end. The chains had two large U-shaped hooks on their free ends. With a flourish, Obert held it up so Sarah could see the wood. 'ROLLO'S BENCH,' the sign proclaimed. The words were stained a dark color that stood out against the light shade of wood.

Sarah clapped her hands in delight. "Obert, it's perfect! Where did you find someone to make it?"

Well pleased with himself, Obert said, "You remember the Indian fellow that made our pet's tray? Sinbad Patel? Well, turns out he dabbles in woodworking. When I asked him about a sign, he was happy to create one."

"How much did he charge? I'm afraid to ask, it's so professional-looking."

"You won't believe it. Naturally, thanks to our bush telegraph, information about this beast is all over town, ha, probably over the whole Western Cape by now! Sinbad asked if he and his family and Lord knows how many friends could come and see the lion. They all came over the day you and Bob were vaccinating cattle. Our simba performed beautifully for the lot of them. He sat right by the wire and purred his shaggy head off. Sinbad's kids went nuts. They all brought cameras and took a million photos. Mr. Patel was so amused by the whole experience he offered his services for free."

Sarah grinned at the lion. "Rollo, we owe you an extra slab of meat. Obert, hand me one end of that sign and let's install it."

The U-shaped hooks slipped over the top of the bench and proclaimed to all visitors that this was, indeed, ROLLO'S BENCH. The two were admiring the sign when Malcolm drove into the yard.

Malcolm took one look at the sign and proclaimed. "So glad you're following my advice and not humanizing this lion."

"Oh, Mal," replied Sarah, "it was a gift, we couldn't turn down a gift? We can't hurt people's feelings."

Malcolm grunted a non-committal reply, then turned to the problem at hand. "Okay, I think we all agree that this lion has somehow lost his prey drive. Something happened to his brain when he got rapped on the head. It must have loosened his wiring."

Obert said, "More like disconnected his wiring, you saw him at the braai. He reminded me of a huge, hairy Golden Retriever."

"As much as I hate to admit it, you're right," said Malcolm, "if you're amenable, I've got a couple of ideas that might get him interested in catching his own food. Do you want to hear them?"

"Yes, of course, Malcolm," Sarah replied. " We can see he's getting too comfortable around people."

"OK, good, let's try the simplest thing first. Your paddock gate is wide enough for a truck, correct?"

"Yes," Sarah replied, "we must be able to get vehicles into all our pastures and paddocks, there's a four-meter gate at the far-right corner of this one."

"Okay, good, here's the plan. Can you hook a piece of meat behind a truck with a quick release rope?

"Sure," Obert replied, "but I'm lost, why would we do that?"

"Well, some sanctuaries do this, they tow the meat behind the truck, then release it when the cat pounces on it. It can stimulate hunting behavior. Maybe it will trigger something in his brain and jump-start his prey drive."

"Okay, Mal, it might work," Sarah said, when do you want to try it?"

"Well, the sooner the better, I can't be here tomorrow, but if someone could video this, while two people man the truck, that would be great."

Sarah thought a moment. "I'll do the video on my phone. Bob and Obert can be in the truck, one driving and one in charge of the rope."

"Excellent," said Malcolm, "I'll be looking for the video. In the morning, drive the truck in front of the door. Toss the meat out. Open the door and let's see if he will chase it. If he does, release the rope when he grabs his breakfast."

Chapter 6

The next morning, Sarah waited for Bob's word to release Rollo. Her husband positioned the truck in front of the door. Obert jumped out and tossed the chunk of meat behind the truck and re-entered the vehicle. Sarah pulled the big door open, Rollo ambled out, saw his breakfast, reached down to grab it, only to see it glide slowly away. When the chunk of meat stopped moving, several meters from him, he walked toward it. Again, when he reached for it, breakfast bounced along the track. The animal shot Sarah a reproachful glare. Bob stopped the truck. Once again, Rollo padded toward breakfast. Breakfast, once again, left. The little procession was now in front of Rollo's favorite resting spot, a small knoll near the fence. The animal stalked to this spot, turned, and sat, facing the truck and breakfast

Sarah offered a suggestion. "Bob, why don't you drive to the end of the paddock, make a U-turn and drive by him, maybe, if he sees the food passing in front of him, he will pounce. Maybe the truck noise and fumes bother him."

"Okay," Bob said, "it's worth a try."

Bob made the turn and drove the truck past Rollo. When the meat was in front of the knoll, he stopped and waited. The lion gave Obert a suspicious look, then slowly got up and approached the vehicle. When he started to pick up the food, Bob drove away. Rollo walked back to the knoll and sat down.

"Try it again," Sarah called.

And try they did. After four passes, the animal was still sitting and watching them with a very bewildered gaze.

Bob pulled to the fence, passed a weary hand over his forehead, and asked, "Sarah, can we stop now, because if we don't, Obert's laughing so hard he's going to injure himself."

"Yes, this experiment has been an abysmal failure. I just sent the video to Malcolm, why don't you release the meat in front of Rollo and drive to the gate. As soon as he grabs it, I'll open up for you."

"Very good, I think Obert can just about manage that."

Sarah predicted correctly. Once the bothersome truck was gone, the lion carefully picked up his breakfast and went to the olive tree in the far corner of the paddock.

Moments later, Sarah fastened the gate and turned to find her husband and foreman falling about the yard in hysterics. I shouldn't do this, she thought, it is mean-spirited and un-Christian-like. There is a small devil on my shoulder. He is stabbing me with his tiny pitchfork. She activated her phone, took a video of the two men, and sent it to Malcolm.

Twenty minutes later, the three were sprawled in the comfortable stoep chairs.

Obert looked at Sarah and asked, "Do you think Malcolm will have another prey drive plan?"

"Yep," said Sarah, "I'm sure he'll contact us when he sees the video. Shame on me for sending the one of you two, acting like circus clowns, but I just couldn't help myself."

Five minutes later, Sarah's phone chirped. "Yes, Mal, we know, I agree, not much of a reaction from our boy. Uh-huh, I see, looking forward to hearing about it, see you soon. Bye for now." She turned to Bob and Obert. "Mal will be by after he sees his last patient, late this afternoon. He wants to explain his next plan to the three of us."

"Glory!" Obert mumbled, wiping tears from his eyes. "I don't know if I can stand another event like this."

Bob looked at his friend and agreed. "You and me both, that was one of the funniest things I have ever seen."

Sarah said, "You have to wonder what Rollo thought about this bizarre experiment, I'm glad we can't know what he's thinking. He must think we're as mad as hatters."

✹ Rollo ✹
Chapter 7

These people have lost their minds. That Malcolm is the ringleader. This craziness was his idea. Three weeks ago everything was perfect. One day Sarah left my door open. I thought she had made a mistake, just forgotten to close it, but she was being thoughtful. That evening, humans and their cubs came for the braai and it was nice to sit on my knoll and watch the festivities. And what a celebration it was! The human cubs kept coming close to my fence, only to be hauled away by their mums and dads, sometimes both. I guess nobody wanted a repeat of Samantha's high-wire act. I could agree with that. It was scary. Samantha was at the celebration, but her parents wouldn't allow her to cross the yard. She could get as far as the lawn, then one or the other parent would have her in tow. She wanted to visit me, but that wasn't allowed. Just as well, Samantha can be best appreciated only when she is far, far away.

After the lovely party, there was work done on my living quarters. I had to be indoors for a few days, but it wasn't so bad. I was soon released and could closely observe the work.

One day, three men were building a fence to hold a small metal apparatus that went from my side of the fence to the human side. Perplexed, I couldn't understand what function that metal thing could have. So, I sat close by to watch their work. I learned it's called a tray and what a clever idea. Sarah can put my meal in there and just slide it in front of me. Very handy! I was happy to see another feeding station constructed on the opposite side of my enclosure. It meant I could be easily fed while confined indoors. I'm not sure the second tray was necessary. Really, whoever fed me could open the door near my water trough and toss my meal onto the ground. I can't imagine why these two-legged creatures are reluctant to be near me. Perhaps they think I'll try to escape.

Anyway, the three men would pause and point little flat things at me. Those flat things are another mystery. The big humans have them. They talk to them! No wonder these creatures are slow-witted. It would be like me talking to a tree branch. Those flat objects never talk back. And yet these silly people talk to them much of the time.

I got off my subject. I watched the fence building. The men were so serious and focused on their work, I thought I would purr my loudest in recognition of their efforts. That was a splendid idea, they worked even harder. They would laugh and exclaim about my size and beauty. Well, of course, as I've said, we're kings here.

I remember Sarah came round that day and spoke to the men. She told them I had lost something. She was wrong. I haven't lost anything. Something about a prey drive. After I overheard that conversation, I looked everywhere, inside, and out. I'm not sure what a prey drive looks like, but there was nothing in my area that looked like it belonged to me. Besides, that may have been why I was chasing that antelope. If the antelope stole it, well they can all forget about finding it. Everyone knows those creatures are fast. They are speedy, like cheetahs. That antelope is likely halfway across the Sahara Desert by now, carrying my prey drive. None of us will ever find it. But I've been around these silly humans long enough to know they can't see what's right in front of them. I remember thinking I haven't heard the end of this prey drive business.

It wasn't long after the building projects that Malcolm came to see Sarah and Bob. In my wildest dreams, I could not have imagined what came next. All was normal that evening, dinner as usual and Sarah closed my big door for the night.

The following morning, Sarah stood near my tray, but put no

food in it. Where's my breakfast? Next, Bob and Obert drove the truck into my paddock and turned round in front of the door. I thought, what are they doing? Obert hopped out of the truck and threw a delicious looking chunk of meat out of the back. He rejoined Bob and Sarah opened the door.

Mystified, I thought this might be a new way to feed me. I can't keep up with their antics. Sarah opened my door and released me. Well, I was hungry, so I went to the meat, reached for it, and watched it move slowly away from me. My word, what are they doing with my food? The truck and breakfast stopped. I went forward, reached, only to see it glide away again. After the third or fourth round of this nonsense, I gave up and sat on my little hill. Bob and Sarah conferred, the truck turned, maneuvered past, and stopped in front of me. I was suspicious but very hungry, so I stepped off my knoll and reached for the meat. Bah! The same thing happened. The only difference was the meat traveled side to side instead of in front of me. I'd already learned my lesson and retreated. I sat! Surely, they can't expect me to grab it while it is moving. I might break a tooth or injure my neck.

Another Bob and Sarah conference. For some reason, Obert thought this was funny, he laughed and laughed, but he did something to my well-traveled breakfast, and it remained in one spot. When they drove out of my yard, I finally got my food and found a quiet place to eat.

Chapter 8

The fierce African sun was releasing its hold on the day when Malcolm hurried up the Aimtree stoep stairs. Working their way through cold beers, he found his four friends on the stoep.

Sarah rose from her chair and greeted Malcolm. "Mal, can I get you a beverage? Iced tea? Coffee? A cold beer?"

Malcolm laughed. "I'm sure I swallowed all the dust in South Africa today. A cold beer would go down a treat."

"Coming right up," Sarah replied, as she went into the house.

Malcolm turned to the three men. "Well, I guess the meat-dragging experiment was a spectacular failure, although it was heartening to see that you two got some pleasure out of it."

Bob and Obert began to protest.

Malcolm waved his hands. "Oh, don't bother to deny it, I saw the video and can't blame you for laughing. As you know, I've been worried about you humanizing this wild animal but, I must admit, he was looking at you with the oddest expression. It must have been the quality of the video, after all, he's a lion, not a human. Anyway, I've been thinking maybe he needs a live creature in there. Maybe the meat wasn't enough like real prey."

Obert straightened in his chair. "Malcolm, if you think I'm going to get in his enclosure and run round, you have another think coming!"

"Me neither," Bob replied, "but Sarah probably would."

"Sarah probably would what?" Sarah asked as she returned to the stoep. She handed Malcolm his beer. "What would I probably do?"

"No, no, of course not, no people in there, it's far too dangerous. You keep hens, don't you? Laying hens? For the eggs?"

"Sure," Obert said, "we keep between twenty and thirty laying hens."

Sarah added. "We all like fresh eggs, Bob and I, the workers. If we have a surplus, friends are always happy to take them."

"So, is there any way to know which hen is past its laying prime? Do you cull them at a certain point?" Malcolm asked.

Michael answered, "My kids know more about those hens than any of us. They take turns feeding and gathering eggs. They make sure the birds are locked in the coop at night. Now and then there are chicks. The children love that. As to culling, no, they just go to the Big Chicken Coop in the sky. Nobody knows which hen is laying any given number of eggs, but the kids would know which birds have been in the flock the longest."

Malcolm looked at Sarah. "Can you spare two or three hens? I want to put them in there with the lion. The birds will be terrified. They will fly and squawk, maybe all that motion will wake his predator instinct." He stood up and flapped his elbows, a credible impersonation of a chicken.

Bob burst out laughing. "Mal, can you get a little footwork going? Maybe stand on one leg?"

Droll Michael added. "There are bugs under the plants, maybe you could hunt for them."

"Ah," Sarah said, "well, as ghastly as it will be for the hens, I can see the logic. Sure, let's try it. You're right in observing that Rollo is getting more comfortable with humans"

"More comfortable?" Bob exclaimed. "He's been comfortable since he arrived. Malcolm, you should see him at mealtime, most cats would be pacing and snarling, waiting for their food. This big oaf sits in front of his tray like a diner at a restaurant. All he needs is a napkin tied round his neck and a knife and fork in those big mitts of his."

"Mal," Sarah asked, "what if he ignores the birds? What do we do? When should we remove them?"

Malcolm waved a dismissive hand. "I don't think there's much chance of that," he replied primly. "I'm confident this will wake him up."

Michael said, "Well, if it takes a while for his predator instinct to arise, we can put a feeder and waterer in the far end, near Rollo's water."

"If you want," Malcolm replied, "but this should do it. I can be here tomorrow morning, round eight, can you have the hens here?"

Bob answered, "Sure, we'll cage two or three tonight and bring them in the morning."

"Excellent," Malcolm said, as he bounded down the stairs. "See you then."

Chapter 9

Eight AM the following day found Bob and Sarah sitting on Rollo's bench. Bob turned to his wife. "Sarah, do you think this is going to work? Do you think Rollo is going to have these old hens for breakfast?"

"Nope."

"Why not? I'm not disagreeing with you, I'm just wondering why you think he won't attack them."

"Husband of mine, have you ever seen this animal show any sort of predator instinct? Or just plain old aggression? Remember the braai? He sat there like the guest of honor, which he turned out to be. He could have left anytime and retreated to his spot in the far corner, but he didn't. I don't think it will be any different than the meat-dragging business. He'll probably ignore them."

Their conversation was interrupted by the sound of two trucks coming into the yard. From the rear of Obert's bakkie came a chorus of outraged squawking. Three incarcerated hens were yelling their displeasure at the confinement and the bumpy ride. Malcolm jumped out of his vehicle and hurried to help Obert and Michael with the cage. They placed it on the far side of Rollo's enclosure and signaled to Sarah. When they were in place to release the hens, Sarah walked to the opposite corner and pushed a small piece of meat through the fence. Rollo strolled to Sarah and ate the snack. Bob, standing midway between the lion and hens, signaled three men. Obert released the birds.

One hen was a speckled black, one a dark red, and the last pure white. Once released, they began to do what all chickens do. They scratched and pecked in the dust. An astonished Rollo turned to stare at the birds. He took a few careful steps toward them.

Malcolm rubbed his hands. "This is it; he's going to attack."

The black hen looked up to see an enormous lion padding slowly toward her. She sounded her best chicken alarm and the three birds went berserk. Dust flew. Feathers flew. Bomblets of chicken poop flew. Blackie zoomed under Rollo's nose and caromed into the wire. The white hen ricocheted off the fence and banged into the lion's side. The red hen was the most vocal, as she flew into the solid walls and wire, she managed a continuous, desperate, braaakkkk. She bounced off the wire, landed on Rollo's head long enough to poop, and flew on. The lion shook his head, retreated to his platform, and sat down.

"Oh boy," Sarah muttered. "I've a bad feeling about this."

The black hen, realizing sideward flight was futile, looked at the top of the enclosure and, missile-like, went straight up.

"Oh no," Bob said, "that's wood up there, not sky."

Five humans and one lion craned their heads at an ever-increasing angle. The hen hit the ceiling with a tremendous bang and, like Icarus, made a speedy and undignified trip back to earth. She somersaulted several times on the way down, hit the platform, bounced, and sprawled on her back, mere centimeters from the lion's front paws. Rollo leaned forward and gave her a careful sniff. He turned to look at the humans and then back to the unconscious hen.

Malcolm seized two handfuls of hair and tugged in frustration. "The great bloody oaf, she's right there, she might as well be on a plate."

"Ahem." Bob cleared his throat. "Well, maybe he does need a napkin, knife, and fork. Perhaps one of us could pop in there with a nice glass of wine!"

Sarah glared at her husband. "Bob Aimtree, you hush!"

"Mal, do you think she is dead?"

"Well, she just tried to remodel the ceiling with her head, so she very well may have brained herself."

The black hen, feet still spasming, flopped to her side and opened her eyes. She managed a feeble croak, then hauled herself onto her chest. With beak and both wingtips on the ground, she attempted to get her feet underneath her body.

Bob, spoiling for another rebuke, said, "Looks like one of those planes that can leap into the air. What do you call them? A haraffe? giraffe? hare?"

"Um," Michael replied, "I think they are called Harriers."

Obert peered through the wire. "Nope, not a plane, she looks like one of those kitchen things. You know, tripod? No, trivet."

The dazed bird raised her head and peered at Rollo. Rollo peered back. A determined effort brought her to her feet. Five fascinated people and one fascinated lion watched as she put her left foot forward, propped herself on her left wing, repeated with her right foot and right wing. In this fashion, she tacked back and forth across the platform, right, left, right, left.

Obert remarked, "Looks like the old biddy has had one too many martinis."

Bob, ever helpful, cried. "Margaritas! Margaritas always do that to me."

The bird flopped off the platform and tottered over to rejoin her sisters. The white and red hen had forgotten about their large hairy roommate and were industriously pecking and scratching in the dirt. Ten minutes later, the black bird was back to normal, carrying on a conversation in chicken language and chasing bugs round the enclosure.

The white hen fluttered onto the platform and gave a happy cry of delight at the sight of Rollo's bedding. The other two birds joined her. All three were soon flinging straw and shavings in all directions.

Blackie pottered close to the lion. She stood in front of him and gazed at him with a beady-eyed stare. He did not move, just looked at her in his usual pacific manner. She took a speculative look at his front paws, glanced back at him, then, quick as a striking snake, she pecked one of his toes. Two hundred kilos of indignant feline leaped into the air with a startled yowl. He retreated to a far corner and laid down. He made sure all four paws were tucked safely beneath him. The hens barely fluttered. They already knew this creature was no threat to them.

A defeated Malcolm Curry sprawled on the bench. "Sarah, how much does one of those hens weigh? About five kilos? Right?"

"Erm, maybe, if that."

"So, that two-hundred-kilogram lion just got beat up by a five-kilogram hen. Not just any hen, but an old hen. I can't stand it."

Tactful Sarah asked, "Speaking of the hens. Mal, what do we do now? Do we try to keep them in there? If we open Rollo's door, they will all likely go out and fly over the fence."

Malcolm said, "Well, it would be ideal if you could keep them in there a few days, maybe he'll decide to attack them at night. I suppose they will need food and water. Blast! I really didn't think we'd have to worry about this."

Obert got up and headed toward the truck. "No problem, I have a feeder and water container right here. Also, a bag of chicken feed and a tin can. All you have to do is rattle the feed in the can and they'll come running."

Sarah turned to Malcolm. "Mal, how about this? We put the

chicken feed at the far end, where Rollo's water is located, then entice the hens with food. We can release him and shut the door, he'll be outside all day, but that's fine. Let's try it now, my poor boy hasn't had breakfast. Besides, if we don't shift those murderous hens off his bed, he may stay there all day."

Malcolm stared at her. "By all means, let's not deprive the poor starving beast any longer."

Sarah's plan was simple, but it worked. The hens heard Michael rattling their food can and made beelines toward him, Sarah released Rollo and shut the door. The lion picked up his breakfast and stalked toward his favorite olive tree.

Sarah had a final question for the vet. "Malcolm, what do you think? Should we do this for three days and then just open the door and let them out. I'm sure they will fly out of the pasture, but so what. They will hopefully find their way back to the flock."

"Sure, do that, if he hasn't reacted to them by then, he probably won't ever react to them."

Michael mumbled under his breath. "Seems to me he reacted to them in a big way, just not what we wanted."

Bob, standing next to Michael, replied, "that's the problem with this big, goofy beast, he never does what we want or expect him to do."

Malcolm got up. "I'm going to see patients, but don't worry, there has got to be something that triggers his prey drive. I'm not giving up, just need to think of something else."

Sarah, Bob, Michael and Obert all looked at one another.

"Glory," Obert said, " I know I've said this before but I don't think I can survive too many more of these episodes."

Sarah smiled. "Oh shoot, people, look at it this way, what in the world did we all do for laughs before this animal came into our lives?"

✸ Rollo ✸
Chapter 10

The next morning, I awoke to find Bob and Sarah sitting on my bench. Not again, I thought. Where is my food? And what is that noise? Two trucks drove into the yard, Obert and Michael in one and Malcolm in the other. Some creature, or creatures, were making an incredible racket in Obert's bakkie. It was louder than Samantha. The three men placed a large cage at the far side of my den. I've decided this space is my den, a bit large, but a den, nonetheless.

Sarah pushed a tiny piece of meat through the wire. I ate it in one bite. Suddenly three squawking creatures flew into my space. They're hens, I heard the humans talking about them. The three are different colors, one dark, one white, and the third a reddish hue. They all settled and began scratching in the dirt. This was clever of them; they only have two legs. They must have excellent balance.

Nosey me, I began to walk toward them. I wanted to examine them. Hopping hippos! All three went crazy. I got halfway across the length of my den when they went flying into wire and walls. What a sight! They were flapping and screeching. I sat. One of them smacked into my side, another flew in my face and, the last straw, one pooped on my head. I went to my platform to observe them from a safer distance.

The black one decided that flying straight up was the way to escape. Watching her ascend, I wanted to tell her it was a bad idea. My den has a solid roof. I know this because the sun doesn't shine through it. I'm also sure, when it rains, I'll stay dry. Anyway, this hen flew until she hit the top. With a loud bang, she collided with the roof, then made a speedy and, in my opinion, very undignified return to earth. The poor bird crashed right in front of me. I thought she was dead. Her scaley, yellow feet were twitching, She was flat on her back. I felt sorry for her, having had a recent blow to my head. It was quite painful, but at least I wasn't dead. To my amazement, she opened her eyes and flopped to her side. I gave her a cautious sniff. She uttered a feeble squawk and pitched to her chest. The poor thing was dazed, much like I was after my accident. I could see she was having balance problems. She probably couldn't see well. That's what happened to me. I was encouraged to see her attempt to walk. It's a good thing she has those two side appendages. They help her balance. I found out later, they are called wings. Very handy, they also allow her to fly. I can't imagine how nice that would feel, unless, of course, you hit something solid.

She staggered to join her friends and, in no time, she was pecking the ground and chasing bugs. These creatures must have hard heads. Now that I think about it, my head must be quite sturdy. The white hen hopped onto my bed and the other two followed. They were tossing straw everywhere. Right in front of me! This is my sleeping place but they didn't care. They conversed in their odd language and threw stuff in all directions. I must admit, they were interesting to watch, I was intrigued by the three of them. How do they stay upright on two legs that resemble sticks?

The humans stared at us with such intensity, it seemed they were waiting for something to happen. As usual, I hadn't a clue what they expected. I was sure they had forgotten about my breakfast. Again! Sarah spoke to Malcolm about feeding me. I realized it was going to be one of those episodes where they went to and fro, opening this door and that door. While they were discussing how to best waste time, the black hen walked over to me and stared up into my face. That bird has beady, mean-looking, black eyes. She cocked her head and pecked one of my front toes. Startled, I leaped up, howled, and retreated. I laid down and tucked all four paws under my body. Sarah came to my rescue. She had Obert maneuver those three harridans to the far side of my den and released me to the outside. I was glad she shut the door. Those hens can stay indoors. They will destroy my bedding. But I can have my breakfast in peace. I hope they have been removed by this evening.

Chapter 11

A week later, Sarah trotted down the steps. Well, she thought, today's the day. Those hens are still alive. Rollo isn't going to eat them. I'll feed everybody and leave the door open. The old biddies will fly over the fence. Probably rejoin their friends by noon and be settled in their old coop by dusk. Sarah walked across the yard, fed everybody, and pulled the big door open. That's that, she thought and went into the house.

Rollo took his meal to his favorite spot under the olive tree, the hens wasted no time in following. They were delighted to find new dirt, plants, and bugs to demolish. They pecked, scratched, took little dust baths, and were quite content to stay in the paddock. Noon found Rollo napping. The hens, taking a break from their industrious digging, settled next to him. An hour later, the lion roused himself for his daily paddock patrol. He got to his feet, yawned, stretched, and began his inspection. He turned to find his feathered roomies marching along behind him. All four creatures took a turn round the yard. Rollo went into the den to await for his evening meal.

Sarah went to the outside kitchen. She selected a slab of beef, threw it in the little cart, and made her way across the driveway. As expected, Rollo was sitting in front of the tray, patiently awaiting dinner. What she didn't expect to see were the three hens, eating their own meal at the feeder. Holy newts, she thought, the girls are still here. She fed the lion and shut all four animals in for the night. That done, she strode to the house to report the chicken news to Bob.

"What the hell are we going to do now?" he wondered aloud.

"I don't know. Maybe follow this routine for a few days. Surely, those birds will figure out how to fly over the fence."

"Hmph," Bob replied. "Well, that seems a reasonable and easy thing to try. It scarcely matters, he isn't going to eat them."

"Oh no," Sarah agreed. "Not much chance of that. Okay, let's give it a few days. Who knows, maybe they will trigger his prey drive?"

Five days later, the hens were still alive and settled into their new routine. They spent the day outside, roosting in the trees, pottering about on the ground, and dozing in the sun. One morning, Sarah fed them and looked up from the feeder to see Obert arrive.

"Morning, Sarah, how are the troops?"

"Well, as you can see, they're just too robust for words. I'm going to leave Rollo's door open tonight. Before the hens arrived, we were allowing him out at night. Bob and I saw him doing late-night patrols. He seemed to enjoy that, besides, if the hens won't leave during the day, they surely won't leave at night. They're tucked in by dusk, right in the middle of Rollo's bed."

Obert turned to Sarah. "I've been thinking about these birds. We should name them."

Sarah exploded with laughter. "Malcolm will kill us! You know how he is dead-set against humanizing these animals."

"I know, I know, but it is too cumbersome. Where is the black hen? Is the white hen in the tree? Think about it, they're unique, living with Rollo. They need classy names. "Simple classy names? Okay, let's hear it. I can't think what a classy chicken name would be. I'm all ears."

"Well, that black hen is the boss. She can be Ebony, the red girl Ruby, and the white one can be Pearl."

Bob bellowed from the porch. "Woman! Where's my breakfast?"

Astonished, Obert turned to Sarah. "Is he talking to you?"

Sarah waggled her eyebrows. "I don't think he's talking to you."

Another shout from the porch, this time. showing concern, "Hey! Is everything okay over there? Is that big fur pile, okay? Are the girls–?"

Sarah waved her hands. "Oh yes, Obert was just explaining a new idea. About the hens."

Bob trotted across the yard, stared at Obert, and paled. "Not another crack-brained Malcolm-like scheme? Remember the last two episodes?"

"No, nothing like that, Obert thinks we should name the hens." She gave a brief synopsis of the classic name idea.

Bob blew out a breath. "Malcolm will kill us."

Sarah and Obert looked at one another, nodding their heads in agreement.

"Yes, we know," Sarah said, "but it does make sense, Ebony, Ruby, Pearl, much simpler, especially since they aren't going to leave."

Bob replied, "I can't argue with that. The other afternoon, Rollo was heading back here and those three birds were marching along behind him. He looked like a brigadier general with his troops."

"I know, I have seen the black hen, erm, Ebony, fly over the fence and an hour later she was back in the yard.

Obert said, "So they've figured out they can leave, they're coming and going, as they please."

"Yes," Sarah said, "they aren't so dumb, they're roosting at night with a big protector, not so dumb at all. Besides, with only three of them at the feeder, they're getting more chicken scratch than ever."

Obert laughed. "I'm going to wrestle that cranky windmill in the south pasture. I swear, I no sooner think I have it fixed and it breaks down again. I'm convinced it'll be my life's work."

Bob said, "I'll join you shortly, maybe the two of us can bring it to heel, just as soon as I get some food." He shot his wife a pitiful glance.

"All right, all right, let's go find something to eat." Sarah threw an arm round her husband's shoulder. "Can you make it into the house? Or shall I carry you?"

Bob
Chapter 12

Mid-afternoon found Bob and Obert sweating and swearing at the windmill from hell. Bob tossed his spanner down and turned to Obert. "I give up, let's call Michael, maybe he can think of something else to try. He knows more about these temperamental contraptions than you and I put together."

Obert, high on a ladder, replied: "Sounds good to me, let me call him. I'm not sure where he is today."

Bob wandered to the fence and looked into Rollo's yard. He leaned on the fence. There was a space between the two pastures that served as a road for farm vehicles, but Bob could easily see into the corner of the lion's private reserve. He heard brush moving, then, to his astonishment, saw the three hens gliding along, presumably, in mid-air.

"Obert!" Bob shouted. "Come over here! Look at this! Have those hens learned to levitate?"

A pair of amber eyes peered through the bushes, followed by a huge shaggy head, followed by a booming purr. The rest of Rollo appeared, with three chattering hens perched on his back.

Obert said, "Looks like they are riding on a magic carpet. I can't believe my eyes. Gotta take a video of this. If we don't, no one will believe us."

"Amen to that." Bob followed Obert's lead and both phones recorded the scene.

The lion and his entourage headed toward his shed: the hens showed no inclination to proceed under their own power. They were content to let the lion do all the walking.

Bob sent the video to Malcolm. That evening he and Sarah started evening chores. Bob took the chicken detail, while Sarah got meat for the lion.

Bob stared in amazement at Rollo. He was napping, the girls roosting on his back. When the hens shuffled their feet, the lion would purr and groan in pleasure. His lips vibrated gently against his gums. Bob thought it resembled someone getting a massage. What's next? Never a dull moment with this crew. Well, everybody seems happy if Rollo wants to bond with these chickens, that's up to him.

Sarah asked, "Where is he?"

"Come over here and take a look."

She deposited the meat in the tray and joined Bob. "Ach, another video is required. You're right about documenting this stuff. People will think we're daft if we describe it without proper backup." She recorded the scene, thought for a moment, and sent it to Malcolm, Obert and Michael.

Bob said, "I'm sure our big hairy boy is becoming a permanent resident. He can't leave. It would be like putting a toddler in the bush."

"Yep, I wish we could peer into his noggin and see what's amiss. If we had a clue, maybe the vet school could do something to treat him."

"I don't know, I don't want to see him poked and prodded. Other than his lost prey drive, he's fine. He has a great appetite, gets exercise, and sleeps most of the day. What the hell, if he wants to bond with three old hens, so be it."

"We've bonded with him as well. Don't you wonder how he feels about us? I think about that whenever I'm working with him. I suppose you're right about the vet exam. I don't want to see him stressed either. Bob, do you think we are in denial about what's best for him? I see his behavior through a lens that assures me he is perfectly fine with his life. I worry he is somehow unhappy or stressed in a way we can't see.

"I know what you mean. Are we exploiting him so we can keep him with us? Could we be trying harder to return him to his wild home? Maybe we should transport him to a sanctuary. Would he recognize lions? Would he remember how to act in a pride. I couldn't bear it if he was injured by other lions. He's safe with us."

Sarah frowned and gnawed on her lip. "Do you think we should try to integrate him? Is that what you want?"

"Hell, no, I love this big goofy beast. I want to care for him for the rest of his life. I don't know what to do."

"Nor do I, but I think we know enough about animal behavior to see he is content. We have Malcolm as a great resource. I vote for taking it one day at a time. If we see a change in his habits, we consult with Malcolm. He can talk to the specialists at the vet school."

"I'm easily talked into that plan. Let's go have dinner."

Chapter 13

On a Friday evening, two weeks later, Sarah turned to Bob and asked, "Can you spare an hour in the morning? I need assistance on a project."

"Sure, what're we doing?"

"We need to give Rollo's den a thorough cleaning. I know we're in there every day, but we need to remove the old bedding, replace it, and look between the back edge of his raised platform and the wall. Our boy may have a pile of old bones stashed. Also, I want to look at the boards that make up the back wall and partial sides of that enclosure. The chicken waterer is growing new life forms. We need to give it a good scrub. One last thing, let's install a few perches in the back corners. Maybe if the girls had a proper roosting area, they would stop using Rollo for a bed."

"Okay, that sounds fine. Tell you what, let me call Obert before it gets too late. We need a new bag of chicken feed; he can deliver it and help us. It'll take less time with three of us."

"Excellent! Done and done! We'll buzz through it in an hour."

The next morning, Sarah and Bob crossed the yard to the waiting animals. She fed Rollo and noticed only Ruby and Pearl in the paddock.

Sarah turned to Bob and said, "Where the heck is Ebony? That girl has been making herself scarce. Ha! Maybe she has a boyfriend, I wouldn't put it past the old bag."

Once Rollo and the hens went outside, she secured the sliding door. Obert delivered the feed and went to work on the waterer. Bob hauled in new bedding and tackled the sleeping area. Sarah inspected the right side of the den. She proceeded to the left side and, that done, looked at the space between the edge of the platform and the back side of the enclosure. The area was only a meter wide, but large enough for items to be hidden. Halfway down, she heard an ominous sound. BRAAAWK! "Good Lord!" she muttered. Another step, another warning squawk. In the dim light, she saw Ebony, puffed up and menacing.

"Bob! Obert! Ebony is back in the corner, sitting on eggs. Oh geez, no wonder she's been missing."

Both men approached. The hen greeted them with more chicken insults. She rose off the nest, with feathers fluffed and neck outstretched. *Don't come any closer!*

Bob rubbed his face and asked, "What do you think about Rollo? He must know she's here. What's he thinking about this?"

Obert replied, "Well, remember, Ebony put him in his place the first day she met him, he's likely ignoring the whole situation."

Sarah asked, "How long have these birds been here? And when did she start incubating those eggs? I wonder how many eggs are in that nest?"

Bob looked at her, grinned, and said, "Sarah, you just heard Ebony, I'm not going any closer."

Obert laughed. "Me? I would rather take my chances with Rollo than get any nearer to that hen. I guess we'll have to wait until they hatch."

Sarah frowned. "But when they hatch, Rollo may injure them. He's so big, we should move Ebony and her eggs to a safer location."

Both men answered as one. "How? Forget it, that lion won't hurt them unless he accidentally sits on one."

Sarah grumbled a reply. "Well, I suppose the move might cause

Ebony to abandon the eggs. We'll have to incubate them and—"

Another chorus of negatives from both men.

"Oh, all right, we'll have to monitor the nest closely. We may have to move them once they hatch."

Obert and Bob agreed with as much unenthusiasm as they could muster. Obert fled to do chores, and Bob was right behind him.

"Bye Sarah," Bob said, "see you for lunch."

"Just one moment, you two. Let's think about this. How long does it take for chicken eggs to hatch? If memory serves, it's three to four weeks. Does that sound accurate?"

Obert scratched his head and replied, "I think so, that sounds about right. Bob, what do you reckon?"

"It's twenty-one days, and don't ask me how I remembered that scrap of information."

"Okay," Sarah said, "so how can we figure out when the eggs will hatch? We all missed Ebony building her nest, laying her eggs, and sitting on them. But let's see, the hens have been in there, what, almost two months?"

Bob said, "Yes, boy, now we know what she was doing when she flew over the fence. She did have a paramour."

Obert shook his head. "But we don't have a clue how long she has been sitting. The old battle-axe fooled us. The eggs could hatch within a week or closer to a month. Glory! And I always thought chickens were dumb. Think about it, who is going to bother that nest with Rollo around?"

Sarah grumped. "We'll have to be hypervigilant. When the chicks hatch, we can move them to a safer place."

Both men looked at each other. Bob cleared his throat and said brightly. "Yes, well, let's see what happens. As Obert said, this could take a while."

✺ Rollo ✺
Chapter 14

Merciful meerkats! What a strange time this has been. That dratted Malcolm is determined to keep my life in an uproar. Those three hens! Well, I must admit, after that first wild day they settled into a routine. After a few days, Sarah released them to the yard. I heard her tell Bob they would fly over the fence and disappear. Bah! They flew over the fence, then they flew back and slept in my den. I'm surprised that I've gotten used to them. They stay close to me. One day, while on patrol, Pearl fluttered onto my back. I thought she was slow-witted. I was wrong, she's clever. Ebony and Ruby followed her. They perched on my spine as I walked round the paddock. Bob and Obert saw us and got excited. Who knows why? I'm big enough to carry three chickens. I hope they don't forget how to walk. Well, I didn't mind carrying them on patrol. Especially important, those patrols. I need to remain vigilant and won't tolerate intruders. I'm especially concerned about those loathsome hyenas. They're dreadful beasts, I hear them calling at night, but they haven't approached our den.

I got off my subject, I was talking about Pearl. On a warm afternoon, instead of sleeping in the straw, she hopped on my back. Almost asleep, I thought, this is the limit. The other two birds joined her. I turned my head to dump them in the straw when they started shifting around to get settled. My goodness! Their six feet were scrunching on my spine. It felt wonderful! I began to purr, then groaned and fell into a deep sleep. Since then, they've been roosting on my back every night.

My relatives would be aghast to hear me say this, but, in some weird way, those birds are pride members. Bah! Chickens and humans as pride members. Well, the humans, even Malcolm, are kind to me. They do stupid things, but I know they're trying to help me. I don't know what they expect me to accomplish. Never mind, I make allowances for their lack of intelligence. They mean well.

Back to the hens, there's something wrong with Ebony. She spent days gathering twigs, grass, and small bits of straw. She used that stuff to build a weird looking bowl. That creation is between the wall and my bed. I wish those girls would realize this is my space, but they've taken over my whole den. Finally, for reasons I can't fathom, Ebony started sitting on the bowl. She's so crabby. Never pleasant, she's now beyond short-tempered.

She leaves for food and water, then flies back to resume sitting on that thing. Is it a chicken den? Dens can be very important, and, while it doesn't look like mine, maybe it's her safe place. My resolve to avoid it failed, and as usual, my curiosity got the best of me. When she flew out to eat, I walked over to inspect. Leaping leopards! That thing was full of smooth, oval, stones. How the heck did they get in there? I know the bowl was empty right after she built it because I peeked.

Ebony caught me staring in astonishment and had a spectacular fit. She fluffed her feathers, screeched, and pecked my nose several times. Okay, I might have very gently touched one of those rocks with my paw, perhaps giving it the tiniest nudge. I just wanted to see if it was as smooth as it looked.

My eyes watered for an hour. Ebony squawked at me for the rest of the morning. I decided she can have that entire corner. Lesson learned! I refuse to go near her. I just hope those stones don't cause me any more trouble.

The Hatching
Chapter 15

Ebony shifted in her nest. Just past midnight, she knew the chicks would hatch tonight, she felt them moving inside their protective prisons. Rollo, with Ruby and Pearl, slept on the other side of the den. The hen heard the lion's soft, snorting breaths, she shifted again, re-arranged bits of straw, and settled to wait for her children to arrive.

The first egg cracked an hour later. Ebony clucked soft sounds of encouragement as the chick struggled to free itself. By the time the bedraggled scrap of feathers was dry, several more chicks began their journey into the world. All seven hatched before dawn. They were dry and resting beneath their mother. Perched on the nest for hours, Ebony was hungry and very thirsty. She hurried to replenish herself.

Bored with confinement, the seven chicks shuffled restlessly in their straw home. An intrepid soldier made several hops to reach the nest rim. After a huge effort, the hatchling reached the top and toppled into Rollo's bedding. All six siblings followed and were soon tottering about in the straw. The sun began to claim the day. The chicks could see shapes in the emerging light. A large shape in the far corner looked intriguing. Two travelers began the struggle through the deep straw. The remaining chicks fell in behind them. With mounting trepidation, amber eyes watched the teeny advancing creatures. Ruby and Pearl, disturbed and annoyed by the night's activities, left their warm perch for the yard. All seven chicks reached the lion's front paws and looked into his face. Peep? Peep? Eep?

Two hatchlings hopped onto his front paws, the rest followed.

New legs and wings were tested. Two chicks lost their balance and fell into the space between Rollo's face and front paws. The lion remained statue-like, chin on the ground. Only his amber eyes moved, tracking the miniature versions of Ebony. Nestled in the mane, the two chicks peeped approval of the new nest. The others joined them. Rollo began to purr. Tired from their long trek, the hatchlings were lulled into sleep by the warmth and booming vibration.

Refreshed, Ebony returned to find her nest full of broken shells and no chicks. Panicky, she began an ever-widening search through the straw, calling as she searched for her brood. A sleepy cheep answered from the lion's corner. Screeching, the outraged hen fluffed her feathers to four times normal size, and, in full battle mode, flew toward Rollo. Rollo shut his eyes. Beady eyes blazing, she called to her chicks. Soft peeps responded. Confused, she looked round the area, she could hear them, but couldn't see them. She called again, a black and yellow striped head made a brief appearance above the lion's paw, regarded his mother, and disappeared back into the mane. One's feathers smoothed, she stood, considering the matter. Rollo opened one eye, then the other. Chicken and lion stared at one another. Ebony gave a satisfied cluck and flew into the yard to join her sisters. The newcomers resettled in their warm, fluffy nest and went back to sleep.

Chapter 16

Sarah waved her toothbrush. "Ob wa bay id be pind da best?"

A disembodied voice rose from the bedroom. "Sarah, are you having a stroke? I can't understand a word you're saying. What time is it?"

Sarah rinsed her mouth and tried again. "The nest. What day did we find the nest? Was it Friday?"

The voice from the bed. "Nope, Saturday, because Obert helped us. Sarah, what time is it?"

"Ah, Saturday, too right! Well, I am going to pop over and inspect it. I can't imagine where those chicks are."

Again, the voice rose from the bed. "I'd bet they're still inside the eggs. Sarah, what time is it? I know we ranchers are early birds, up before sunrise, working dawn to dusk, but isn't it the middle of the night? Every day you're up earlier and earlier to check on those eggs. What time is it? It's still dark, isn't it?"

Sarah looked out the window. "Erm, well, it's dim out there, but I'm sure it will be pre-dawn in an hour."

"Hah! I knew it. Predawn in the future means it's still the middle of the night. Correct?"

"Oh bother, all right, already, it's pitch black. I'm so worried about those birdies. That old battle-ax fooled us. We don't know how long she's been perched on that nest. And I always thought chickens were stupid, she outfoxed us. They must be close to hatching, and I'm worried about Rollo's reaction to them. I'm afraid he'll eat them. I know Malcolm will be happy. The little chickens might jump-start Rollo's prey drive. Ach, I can't stand the thought of them being eaten. I know there's nothing we can do about it. I still don't want them to be lion snacks."

"Sarah, I'm pleading, can I have another hour of sleep, and you're right, if Rollo decides the hatchlings are breakfast, there's nothing we can do. Remember, we're trying to release him into the wild.

"Okay, I'll dash over for a quick look. I've the yard lights and my trusty headlamp. When I get back to the house, I can do some paperwork and then fix a decent breakfast."

"I look forward to food and sunrise."

Sarah strode through the kitchen, pushed the start button on the coffeemaker, grabbed her flashlight, and headed for the stoep. Careful not to let the screen door slam, she stepped outside and looked at the lion's enclosure. Well, she thought, I can see shapes, they're still in black and white, but color will soon flood the landscape. She switched on the floodlights and paused to savor the alyssum scented air. She took several breathes to inhale the scent. Still dark, the air was already balmy, a quiet breeze whispered through the stoep, promising another hot day. Africa, she thought, what a fierce and magical place. We're lucky to call it home. She took another look at her flowers, gave the violets an encouraging pat, and looked toward the approaching sunrise. I'd better stop waxing philosophical and get my fanny across the driveway.

Halfway to the den, she heard hens clucking. The girls had started their day. At the fence, she trained the headlamp on the nest. It was empty, no sign of Ebony. Sarah climbed on top of a box she'd found for better viewing. Broken eggshells were the only occupants of the nest.

Oh no, she thought, he's eaten Ebony and all her babies, she inspected the lion, he looked odd. Chin on the ground, he refused to raise his head, his eyebrows shot up and down at regular intervals. Well, Sarah thought, at least he's purring, but he looks rigid. Maybe he has indigestion from the feet and feathers. Ach! I'd better get Bob, our simba may need Malcolm.

Sarah sprinted to the house, tore through the stoep, and let the screen door bang. "Bob, get up, Rollo ate everybody and now he's sick. Get up!"

"Wha–? Ate who?" Bob hauled himself to the side of the bed. His frantic wife threw clothes at him.

"Here are your boots, let's go. We need to call Mal. Rollo won't lift his head."

"Are you asking me to believe that Rollo ate Ebony? You're daft, that hen terrifies him. Where are Ruby and Pearl? Or did he eat the whole lot of them? Gad, if he did, no wonder he's ill, those old birds must be as tougher than shoe leather."

Sarah paused before answering. "I did hear hen chatter in the yard, maybe Ruby and Pearl escaped, I wondered why they went out so early."

"How do you know Ebony isn't with them?"

"Why would she leave her babies? The poor old thing tried to defend them."

Bob, the voice of reason, said, "Sarah, I can't believe Rollo attacked Ebony, maybe her chicks are behind the nest." The sound of the screen door slamming told Bob he was talking to himself.

Sarah stood at the fence. She turned to see Bob walking across the yard with two cups of coffee.

"Humans can't live without caffeine; it separates us from beasts."

Frowning, she pointed to the lion. "Look, see how rigid he is, he won't lift his head, maybe, erm, he has their little feet stuck somewhere inside him."

Bob looked at Rollo and said, "I agree, he doesn't look right, but what the heck can Malcolm do? He can't tell the beast to take a shot of stomach acid reducer. I'm going to check on Ruby and Pearl." Bob put the mugs on the bench, wandered down the fence line and called to Sarah. "Sarah, Ebony is here, she's taking a dust bath with Ruby and Pearl. I knew that old biddy was okay."

Sarah joined Bob and looked through the fence. "Why would she abandon her chicks? She doesn't even look distressed or upset. She looks normal."

"Peep? Cheep? Eep, eep?"

Bob and Sarah looked at one another and hurried back to the den. The sound of chicks was louder but neither human could see them.

Sarah craned her neck, "Bob, the cheeping is coming from somewhere near Rollo, I wonder if the babies are still between the wall and the platform? Blast, we're going to have to shift him outside, I wish we could walk in there. We probably could, he's never shown any sign of aggres—"

"Well, we can't just walk in there, we'll lure him out with food, lock him in the yard and then inspect the entire area. You're likely right; they may be round the nest."

A tiny, feathered head appeared above the lion's front paw, disappeared, and then reappeared, along with the rest of the chick. It sat on Rollo's foot and regarded the new guests. Peep, eep, cheep. It relayed the news to its siblings. The chick disappeared into the new nest. Rollo belted out a little purr.

Sarah sat back on the bench. "Bob, he's babysitting the chicks. That dear animal is in charge of the babies."

Bob sputtered a mouthful of coffee. "Sarah, he's not babysitting. I don't know why he isn't reacting, or just ignoring them, but he's not babysitting. Has it ever occurred to you this animal is brain-damaged?"

"Is too babysitting."

Okay, fine, have it your way. He's babysitting birds. We can get him a job at the local school. He can be the playground monitor and help with afternoon snacks. Who knows, maybe he'll be promoted to driving the school bus."

"Bob Aimtree, you just stop making fun of our li--"

The sound of Obert's bakkie interrupted their conversation. Obert, moving at his usual warp speed, hopped out of the vehicle and grabbed a sack of chicken feed. "Hey, what're you two doing? Have the eggs hatched?" The foreman hurried to the fence and looked inside. "Where is Ebony? Where are the chicks? Why is our big simba looking so odd?"

Bob and Sarah knew better than to attempt conversation. They sat on the bench and sipped coffee.

Obert moved closer to the lion. Cheep? Peep? Peep? He frowned and looked at his friends.

"Where are they? I can hear them but can't see them. Where the heck is Ebony?"

Sarah waved her hand toward the yard. "Oh, she's outside, gadding about with her sisters."

Puzzled, Obert turned to Bob. "You're playing a trick on me, where the heck are the chicks? Glory! Did Rollo eat them? Like Jonah and the Whale, we can hear them peeping from somewhere inside him."

Rollo lifted his head, several chicks plopped onto the straw, the rest tottered from under his chin, and began shuffling through the bedding. Obert opened and closed his mouth several times but was incapable of speech.

Bob said to Sarah. "Get your phone and record this. It's a first. Obert is speechless."

Whirring wings announced the arrival of Ebony. She stood in front of Rollo and squawked several orders to her brood. They hurried towards her. She gave all seven babies a thorough inspection, issued another order, and marched outside. Her brood marched behind her.

"Glory!" Obert exclaimed. "I can't understand what I just saw. Why the heck did that big cat tolerate all that?"

Sarah threw back her head and laughed. "Because our boy is an excellent babysitter."

Chapter 17

A month later, Sarah stared at her big furry pet. She stood at the fence and watched One's children have their way with Rollo. Several were tormenting him by pulling his mane and tail hairs. When bored with this activity, they used him as a platform to practice flying. Another bird napped between his forepaws while the last made determined efforts to join the hens in the olive tree. The bird wasn't quite proficient with wings, but soon would be.

Sarah turned to Bob. "Ach, and to think I worried about Rollo having them for breakfast. Honestly, if I were him, I would have devoured them two weeks ago. They are so pesty."

Bob grinned. "Well, seven plump, young chickens, we could put them in the pot. Chicken soup? Fried chicken? Chicken salad? What do you say?"

"I'm not that fed up with them, but they have to go. We need to integrate them with the main flock. Even if they were obedient and quiet, it's too many chickens for us."

"Wife of mine, I'm going to solve your problem. You'll see tomorrow. Once they learn to fly, we'll never catch them."

"You're right about that. Okay, what's the plan? Happening soon, I hope."

"Yes, in the morning. It'll take four of us. Let's go sit on Rollo's bench and I'll tell you about it."

Once seated, Bob turned to Sarah. "Obert found some sturdy netting. It's two meters on each side. He and Michael fashioned pockets on all four sides. Four light-weight poles slip into the pockets and have little clips on them that attach to the netting so they won't slide out. You with me so far?"

"Bob, I lost you several sentences ago, how on earth is that going to trap birds?"

"Ha, let me finish. Tonight, we take their feeder out of the den, they'll be ravenous by morning. First thing, you feed Rollo outside and shut the door, the chickens will be trapped inside. You and I will slip inside with this net contraption and hold it against the wall. Obert and Michael will move the big cage inside and place it near the spot next to the feeder. One of them will put the feeder in the den and rattle the can of chicken feed. Those birds will go straight to the food. We'll pick up the net, one on each pole, place it over the feeder, drop it on the ground and kneel on the poles. Voila! Ten trapped chickens."

"Erm, then what, we'll have ten crazed birds with no way to get them out."

"Let me finish, Obert has fashioned a little door in the netting. It has a metal frame and clips to the pole. This part may be tricky." Bob broke four branches off the shade tree and knelt on the ground. He placed the twigs in a square. "Obert will catch the birds and toss them into the cage. Michael will work the door. When Obert grabs our old girls, he'll release them."

Sarah looked at Bob. "I can see one thousand things going wrong with this plan. That said, I've no better plan."

In his best American cowboy accent, Bob patted Sarah's shoulder and drawled. "Now don't you worry, little lady. Don't upset your purty head, just leave this to us menfolk."

"Well, it sounds just wacky enough to work. We're doing this in the morning?"

"Yep, Michael and Obert will bring the cage and net, we'll have a run-through after you feed Rollo and lock him outside. Piece of cake, you'll see."

Early the next morning Sarah filled the cart with Rollo's breakfast and approached the yard.

"Come on, big boy, you're dining outdoors this morning."

The lion affably strolled outside to greet Sarah. She dropped Rollo's meat to him when the three hens rocketed above him and landed in the olive tree.

Sarah laughed and said, "Ach! You wise old girls know something is afoot. Well, good, you're three fewer things to worry about."

She shut the door and joined Bob just as the two brothers drove into the yard. Bob rattled the chicken scratch can and all seven pullets clamored for their breakfast.

Bob turned to Sarah. "I see the girls figured out we were up to no good and escaped."

"Yes," answered his wife. "No flies on those birds. Thank heavens the young ones have no such instincts."

Michael and Obert spread the net out on the ground, then put the poles in place and clipped them so they wouldn't slide out. They gave a short demonstration of how the process would work.

Sarah said, "Okay, let's go before they all get suspicious. Right now, all they want is food, but those three old biddies figured something was rotten in Denmark before I fed Rollo."

Obert agreed. "Yep, let's go."

Michael grabbed the feeder, the other three maneuvered the net into the den. As soon as the feeder was on the ground, all seven chickens dove into their breakfast. They were oblivious to any danger. The four humans walked the net over the feeder and on Obert's signal, dropped it and knelt on the poles.

For a split second, the pullets froze, and then, predictably, lost their minds.

From her vantage point, Sarah decided the trapped birds resembled the contents of an activated blender. Obert removed the birds while Michael worked the door. Sarah was amazed the plan worked. The only problem occurred when three birds were left in the net. With more room, they evaded Obert's long grasp. Sarah scooted forward and bunched up the net, creating a smaller space. Obert easily transferred the last three pullets and the job was done.

The two brothers placed the cage in Obert's bakkie. Sarah and Bob partially dismantled the net by removing two poles on opposite sides. They rolled it into a manageable bundle and placed it next to the cage.

Obert turned to his brother. "Let's go, these birds are stressed, I don't want them sitting in the sun."

Michael nodded and stepped toward the vehicle. He glanced at Bob and grinned. "Bob, you have chicken poop on your forehead."

Bob muttered a string of oaths and reached for his handkerchief.

Sarah grabbed his hand. "Bob don't smear it on your face. Why don't you head for the shower? I'll be close behind you. None of us smell like roses."

Bob trotted to the house, and the birds left for the main flock. Sarah plopped on Rollo's bench. Ach, she thought, good riddance. You little gangsters can go terrorize some other hapless creatures.

✸ Rollo ✸
Chapter 18

Flapping flamingos! These past few weeks have tried my patience. It goes back to the round white stones in One's den. The first time I saw them, I knew they were trouble. I'd no idea how much grief they would generate. After my first encounter with the rocks, I avoided them. Ebony had been sitting in the bowl for days, only leaving for food and water. Why does a creature want to sit on a pile of rocks all day, and night? Bah! It was none of my business.

One night I settled for bed. Chickens are not like lions when it comes to darkness, the sun hasn't set, and those birds are asleep on my back. Well, I don't mind, their weird little feet feel good on my spine. There were only four feet, instead of six, but it was sufficient. So, the three of us went to sleep.

I didn't sleep for long. It was barely dark when Ebony began to fuss. She clucked and chattered in her weird language, and I could see—we lions have excellent night vision—that she was shuffling about in her den. Several hours passed, she was still vocal and restless. No sleep for me, not with all the racket, besides, I was curious. What was she doing over there? Ruby and Pearl woke up and, annoyed by the noise, left for the yard. I should have gone with them, but no, my curiosity got the best of me. What would happen next?

Shortly before dawn, something happened to Ebony's voice. At first, I thought she was losing it, no wonder, all that racket for hours. I was wrong. There was more than one squeaky voice.

Wonderful, I thought, this is what happens when you don't get enough sleep. I'm hearing things. What's next? I'll see a parade of hyenas pass through, likely doing somersaults. Ebony got up and flew toward her food and water. I considered inspecting her den but thought better of it. I could sense dawn fast approaching, A tiny body bobbed over the top of the bowl, it disappeared and reappeared several times. It was a tiny version of Ebony. More squeaks and there were several more of the creatures peering at me.

The whole mob climbed onto my platform and began a determined march through the deep straw. They were headed straight toward me. Again, I made a judgment error, I should have fled when I had the chance. Where did they come from? How did they get in there? At first, I thought there was nothing to worry about. They were staggering about in the straw, and I couldn't imagine how they would cross my den. I should have known better, they were Ebony's cubs and had teeny, little spines of steel. Seven! There were seven of them and while they repeatedly fell flat on their little faces, they continued to move forward.

Much to my horror, all seven reached my front paws. Head down, I watched them hop, fall, and flutter useless wings. Two of them scrambled onto my paw and toppled into the space between my chin and leg. I did what I always do in a strange situation. I purred. It's a calming sound. The two stuck in my mane cheeped the news of this new place to their siblings. In moments all seven were camped under my chin. They shuffled around for a few moments and fell asleep. Well, that was a huge distance they had traveled, and so young, it made sense they needed a nap.

Ebony returned to her den and went berserk when she saw that it was empty. She ran up and down in the back of my area and then began making widening circles. I can't describe the desperate noises she was making. I'd never seen her so frightened. One cub woke up, heard her calling, and responded. Cheep? Eep?

Cheep, cheep? Several others joined in. The frantic hen fluffed her feathers and, eyes blazing, in full attack mode, came straight for me. I couldn't get up. I would have squashed all the cubs. Doomed, I thought, and, resigned to my fate, shut both eyes, and waited to get pecked to death.

The babies responded to her frantic cries with contented peeps. Ebony stopped, and her feathers returned to normal. I opened an eye and saw she was staring at me. Head cocked, she asked questions and the little ones answered, although none of the seven were moving from their new nest. Ebony gave a final cluck and flew out to join her sisters. Well, that left me with the seven new birds in my hair. They went back to sleep, and I joined them. I woke to the sound of Sarah clattering across the lawn. She climbed onto her box and peered into the little bowl. Then she had a fit. What is wrong with these two females? first Ebony, now Sarah. She hurried to look at me and, with a cry of dismay, ran back to the house, calling for Bob. Now what? Let's hope somebody remembers my breakfast.

Poor Bob, Sarah hauled him out of bed. He was half asleep. Sarah told him I had eaten Ebony and her cubs. Where do these humans get such crazy ideas? Anyway, Bob found Ebony and Sarah calmed down. The babies announced themselves, Obert showed up, and Ebony returned to collect her family.

The first week wasn't too difficult. I had some anxious moments about stepping on the little bounders, but I needn't have worried. During the night, we got into a routine. They slept under my head. The trouble started in the morning. They showed no inclination to join their mum. I was afraid to get up, lest I injure one. They were so tiny! So, I decided to carefully pick them up and place them next to my leg. After all, my mum carried us all the time, she was very gentle. Having some experience in this matter, I picked one up and placed it next to my paw. Good, now the second one, and so on. Bah! By the time I got to the fourth one, the first cub was under my chin. After the first day, their mother was no help. She flew out with her sisters and left her children with me. My next strategy was to carefully stand up and shuffle. I thought if I keep my feet on the ground, I can't step on anybody. The humans thought this was amusing and had many a laugh at my expense.

All this worry was a waste of time. By the fourth day, they were running around like two-legged cheetahs. They were tiny, but they zipped about on stick legs. So, I went about my business, and they avoided my huge feet—after all— I'm a lion. We have enormous paws. Anyway, after our morning meal, all eleven of us started our day. Ebony took charge of them so Ruby, Pearl and I could do morning hyena patrol. The youngsters tried to keep up with us but they were too small to navigate through the yard obstacles. That was fine with us, it was peaceful without them. After patrol, they preferred my company to their mum's. Well, no surprise, she's quite rigid and a better disciplinarian than I. So, my napping wasn't restful, with the seven of them bumbling about in my mane.

By the end of the second week, I learned more about them by listening to the humans. Ebony's den is called a nest, and the seven babies were inside the stones. What an odd way to reproduce. I also learned that the babies are called chicks. They were still manageable but making determined efforts to fly and accompany us on patrol. They grew so fast. And so pesty! Like all cubs, the seven of them were always up to mischief.

When they were six weeks old, they were driving us mad. Even their mother wanted no part of them. She and her sisters would fly up into the trees to avoid them. All of them were making determined efforts to join the hens in the branches. I think the girls knew their days of peace were numbered. Well, we lions are skillful, athletic beasts, but we can't fly. Once the hens deserted me for the trees, those young chickens harassed me until bedtime. Even bedtime turned into a free-for-all. All seven wanted to be under my head, but they were too big to fit into the space. They would fight for their spots, until several gave up and climbed on my back. The hens didn't appreciate having to share their space and flew up to the roosts. They didn't like the perches, but they were safe from the children.

Hyena patrol resembled a parade, the seven kept up with me, they hopped and half-flew as I inspected our area. The hens got shoved off my back by the little brats, who used me as a practice platform for their developing wings. One afternoon, Bob and Sarah stood at the fence and watched the pullets harass me.

My two humans had a plan to capture all seven and return them to the big pride of chickens. It sounded precarious to me, but I was at the end of my rope, even a half-baked plan was welcome. The next morning, Sarah brought my breakfast and placed it outside. The feeder had been removed the night before and all ten birds were clamoring for food. I was halfway out the door when the hens rocketed above me to the yard. Those old biddies! They knew the humans were up to mischief. Boy, they were right. Sarah shut the door behind me, trapping the youngsters inside. I'm not sure what happened next, but a few minutes later, it sounded like all seven were being murdered. The humans were shouting, the birds were screeching. Then, silence, I could see dust billowing and heard Obert's vehicle depart. Gone, the little gangsters were taken to the large pride. The hens and I were back to our peaceful routines. Well, it was an experience, but I hope Ebony doesn't repeat it.

Chapter 19

Two months later, Sarah stared glumly at the paperwork piled on the table. She eyed her empty mug. "Ach! She thought. I need more coffee to finish this ranch business," but I'm too lazy to get it. The best plan is to wait until Bob comes out and have him fetch me a fresh cup." Bob came through the screen door with coffee and his stockman's magazine. Sarah waved her cup at him and looked pitiful. Bob sighed, put his mug down, and returned to the kitchen to get her a refill.

Settled in his favorite chair, he asked, "Sarah, do we have anything on for this weekend? Is our social calendar full?"

Sarah slapped her forehead and cried. "Oh Bob, I forgot to tell you. The President of the United States and the King of England will join us for lunch on Saturday."

"Very funny, so we could pencil something in, there's room on our dance card?"

"Pencil away! What do you have in mind?"

"Well, Obert and I want to talk to Brandon about his cross-bred calves. I know they don't impress you, but Obert and I think they have enormous potential. Brandon has his third calf crop on the ground. Obert and I want to know about reproductive difficulties, growth rate, and health issues. Brandon wants to talk to Michael about irrigation systems. One of his pastures either needs irrigation or requires updates. I thought the Von Bergs could visit, we'll have a short meeting, you and Filly are welcome to join us, and then lunch."

"No thanks to the talks about pipes and hybrids, but I'd love to see Filly. I can show her my new quilt project. This all sounds good, maybe a simple lunch, sandwiches, salad, and something decadent from the bakery. Erm, will Sam be with us?"

"Well, sure, she likes to come here, she'll bring toys, or coloring books, or whatever kids that age do to amuse themselves."

Sarah leaned back and stared at the ceiling. "So, by my calculation, there will be six adults. Am I correct?"

"Yes, why do you ask?"

"Remember Sam's high wire act with Rollo? I still have nightmares about it, but really, six adults should be able to monitor one small child."

"Nothing to worry about, last time Sam was right near the fence. This time, she'll either be with us or with you and her mother. Besides, she's older. What is she? Almost six? Honestly, Sarah, you worry too much. What could possibly go wrong with all of us supervising her?"

Saturday morning found Sarah puttering in the kitchen. She sliced the roast for sandwiches, made a simple salad, and whisked a vinaigrette dressing. She opened the refrigerator and took out a large cake box. "Bother!" She thought, "I gain weight looking at this thing. What did the lady call it? Chocolate caramel decadence? Well, it's a treat. Sam will love it and I won't say no to a piece either." She moved to the stoep to make sure everything was ready for lunch. Sarah smiled fondly at the small chair and table positioned near the door. She and Bob had purchased both items last year for Samantha. When the little girl came to visit, she used them to color or play with her toys. Her favorite activity at her table was to play restaurant. Filly and Sarah would be servers. They would take her order, fetch a drink, and serve the little girl. The entire experience delighted Sam.

Both the Von Bergs and the two brothers arrived at eleven. Sarah greeted the group and got them settled on the stoep. She heard Felicity speak to her daughter.

"Sam, do you want to join us? Sarah and I can take your table and chair to the sewing room."

Sam considered this and replied, "No, Mummy, I'm going to stay here and color."

She pulled crayons and a coloring book out of her backpack and began to search for a worthy subject. Felicity looked at Brandon and raised her eyebrows in a questioning gesture.

Brandon said, "Sure Filly, she can stay here." He scooted his chair six inches to the left. "Look, all I have to do is lift my head and I can see her."

"Carry on, Sarah and I are going to gossip."

Samantha
Chapter 20

Samantha, head bent over the coloring book, listened to the men.

Bob looked up from the table. "Well, boys, what's first? Pipes or cows?"

Brandon shrugged. "Either way is fine with me."

Obert interjected. "Nope! Let's talk about boring irrigation stuff first. I want to pepper Brandon with questions about his good-looking hybrids."

Michael pulled papers out of a folder and turned to Brandon. "Okay, Brandon, what do you want to learn?"

Twenty minutes later, Brandon had answers to all his questions. The topic turned to Beefmaster hybrid calves.

Sam stood up. "Daddy, I'm going to the bathroom."

"Ah, okay Sam. Can I show you the way? He began to rise from his chair.

Samantha, hands on hips, said, "Daddy, I can go by myself, I know where it is."

"Are you sure, Sam? I can go with you."

"I know where to go. Mummy and Aunt Sarah are in the sewing room. I'll find Mummy if I need help."

Brandon sat down. "Okay, go ahead, find Mummy if you need to."

Samantha entered the kitchen and stepped into the hallway. She knew the Aimtree house as well as she knew her own home.

Halfway down the hall, the guest bathroom was to the right. Just opposite, on the left side, was the door to the master bedroom. She stopped between the two doors and slipped into the master bedroom. Bob had built a small deck off the bedroom. It faced Rollo's yard and enclosure.

"I'm coming to see you Rollo. I can't let anyone see me. I know I'm not supposed to be in your yard. I'll be careful and no one will see me." She walked onto the deck and down the stairs. Knowing Sarah's stoep plant jungle blocked the view of Rollo's paddock, she hurried across the yard, entered the safety fence, and shut the door. Rollo's tray slid back and forth on a wooden base. It was pushed to the lion's side. Sam scrambled onto the wooden base, tugged it halfway to her, and scooted underneath to Rollo's side.

Samantha saw that Rollo's big door was open. He could be in the den or the paddock.

She walked to the den and looked inside. The lion and hens were napping on the platform. She trotted the few meters to the sleeping platform, scrambled on top of it, and approached the four creatures.

Finger against her lips, she whispered. "Shhhh, shhh, Rollo, you must be quiet. I'm not supposed to be here."

The hens, startled by the proximity of the small human, decamped to their high roosts in the corner of the shed. Rollo stared at Samantha and, with a startled snort, jerked to a sitting position. This was the first time a human was on his side of the wire. He began his signature sound. Giggling, Sam put both hands against his mouth.

"No, no, Rollo, you be quiet!"

The purr increased in volume: his lips fluttered against Sam's hands. She was transported into another giggling fit. She stood back and said, "Okay Rollo, you can purr." Then she did what she had been itching to do since the day she saw him.

She touched him, ran hands over his shoulder, feeling bone and muscle underneath the tawny hide. Sam leaned against his shoulder, patted his spine and flank. Crouching, she felt his tail, thick at the base, tapering to silky hair at the far end. Kneeling, she ran the tail hairs through her fingers. Now, the mane, Sam felt the thick hair, buried her face in it, and sniffed. She stepped in front of the enormous cat and carefully patted his nose. Rollo looked into her face and held her gaze. Sam knelt and looked at his feet. She examined the toes on each front paw.

"Boy, you have the biggest toes I've ever seen."

Her exam almost finished, Sam stood. Shouts drifted from the stoep. Her father called her name. She did what most children do in similar situations. She went deaf.

"Mummy says you have great big teeth. I want to see them. You hold still."

She carefully pulled on left upper lip and peered into his mouth, but the big lip oozed between her fingers and re-settled itself against massive canines. Sam tried the other side with the same result. She stood, pondering her next move, while the shouts from the stoep grew louder.

Sam, realizing she was in hot water past her eyeballs, decided to remain deaf. Perhaps, by some miracle, all these pesky adults would disappear, and she could finish her examination. Determined to inspect the lion's mouth, she stood in front of him, grabbed two handfuls of his whiskers, and hauled them straight up. All his formidable front teeth were now visible. She bent closer to his mouth for a better view.

"Mummy's right. Your teeth are really big."

Brandon
Chapter 21

Fifteen minutes later, Brandon realized his daughter's chair was empty. With mounting dread, he called Felicity and confirmed his suspicion. Sam had done a runner. He leaped out of the chair and bellowed his daughter's name. The other three men jumped up with him. They ran down the stairs. Brandon headed for the den. Bob and the two brothers looked round the yard. They heard Brandon, now at the fence, and knew the child was with Rollo. Years later, he still berated himself for not phoning Felicity to alert her that Sam was heading for the bathroom. But Brandon was focused on his beloved cattle. When his daughter disappeared into the house, she disappeared from his mind.

Brandon called to the brothers. "Get the rifle out of the truck."

Obert nodded, sprinted to the vehicle, unracked his rifle and joined Bob and Michael at the feeding station. All three slipped into the den. Brandon stood across from Sam and Rollo. He begged his daughter to walk toward the gate. He knew Sam was feigning deafness. She kept her back to him, it told him she was aware of being in big trouble. Horrified, he watched his daughter yank on Rollo's whiskers and bend to peer at the lion's teeth.

Brandon threw himself against the fence and shouted. "Sam, let go of him, please. Before he hurts you." Brandon watched as the big cat wrinkled his lips, opened his mouth, flattened his ears, and produced a sound between a growl and a rasping cough. He threw his head back and sneezed with such force, Samantha flew backward and landed on her fanny. Rollo produced four more enormous sneezes, shook his head, and gave Brandon a reproachful look.

"Sam, I know you can hear me, and I know you're ignoring me. I want you to look over your shoulder. You'll see Obert pointing a rifle at Rollo. You know what rifles can do. He'll shoot Rollo if you don't get up and walk toward the gate."

Unable to stop herself, Sam looked over her shoulder and saw her father was correct. On one knee, Obert was aiming his rifle at the lion. She leaped to her feet and shrieked, "NO, NO, DON'T SHOOT MY ROLLO!"

She ran to the animal's side, threw herself against him, and spread her arms to better protect him. Faced with the enormity of the situation, Sam's almost six-year-old brain went on 'pause'. Her father knew she couldn't respond to instructions or process information. Several tense seconds ticked by. Obert aimed the rifle.

Brandon called to the men. "Can you get a clear shot?"

Obert gritted his teeth and shook his head. "Yes, but she's too close to him, he could bite her in half by reflex action after he's hit. I can't chance it."

Using his no-nonsense voice, Brandon again called to Samantha, "Step away from him and walk toward the gate. We don't want to hurt him."

He knew his words were in vain. Sam hugged the lion even tighter and sobbed into his mane. Brandon watched Obert stand up, hand the rifle to his brother, and move toward the child. He crouched, swung Samantha behind him and whispered to Rollo in Maa. The two locked gazes, then Obert made a careful retreat. Once outside, he handed Sam to Bob.

Brandon started toward his daughter. Out of the corner of his eye, he saw Sarah and Felicity rushing across the yard. Halfway to the bench, Felicity went to her knees, then on all fours. Sarah crouched, grabbed her friend's shoulders to prevent her from collapsing onto her face. Brandon rushed to her side. He looked at Bob and asked, "Is Sam okay? Can I tell Filly she is unharmed?"

Exasperated, Bob answered, "Well, other than being covered in lion snot, she appears to be fine. We're going to the bench. She can sit for a moment."

Brandon cradled his wife against his chest and murmured to her. "She's okay, Filly. I swear she must have nine lives, well, eight now. I can't believe she did that to us."

Sarah stood and suggested. "Why don't you three sit here for a moment, catch your breath, and regroup. When you're ready, you can come to the house. I'm not sure anyone still wants lunch, but perhaps something cold to drink."

Sam crowed. "I'll have lunch, Aunt Sarah! I'm hungry!"

Brandon and Felicity exchanged a look over their daughter's head. Brandon rolled his eyes. Felicity gave him a wan smile and shrugged her shoulders.

"Okay, good," said Sarah. "Sam, you could do with a wash. Come over when you're ready."

The Von Bergs sat in silence for several moments.

Brandon turned to Sam. "You frightened us half to death. What were you thinking? You know he's a wild animal."

"I'm sorry, Daddy, I didn't mean to make Mummy sick. I wanted to touch him and be his friend. I love him. He's so pretty. Besides, Mummy said he had big teeth and I wanted to see them."

Felicity stood and walked to the fence. Rollo approached her. He peered at the three humans.

Brandon rose and said, "Filly, what are you doing? Are you sure you want to get close to him?" He clenched his fists as his wife approached the lion. He didn't know what either of them would do.

Felicity waved her husband back and approached the lion. She bent down, pushed her hands through the wire and stroked the sides of his face. "I'm not supposed to touch you, but I must pat your poor face. I'm sorry my little girl pulled your whiskers, I heard you sneezing from across the yard." Tears in her eyes, she reached up and scratched him between the eyes.

Brandon heaved a sigh of relief when Felicity returned to the bench. He glanced at his daughter.

Sam, already over her harrowing ordeal, tugged her mother's hand. She turned to her father and declared, "Daddy, big Rollo sneezed me right on my bottom!"

✳ Rollo ✳
Chapter 22

We had a long, trouble-free time. The hens and I, freed from Ebony's cubs, fell back into our old routines. We napped and went on patrol. The days drifted by peacefully. It's hot again and Sarah and Bob hosted a huge braai in celebration of a human holiday. These events are wonderful. I get so much attention! Like last time, the humans cubs clamored to come near my fence, I obliged by sitting on my knoll and purring loudly. When adults approached, they pointed the flat things at me. All the humans were less frightened of me, although Malcolm gave his usual stern orders to stay away from the fence. Bah! That Malcolm! He's always so serious. When little crowds gathered, I walked to the fence. My goodness, they all backed away. I just wanted to greet them, these humans are strange. I do have trouble understanding them.

Anyway, things were quiet, and the four of us were content. One morning, after hyena patrol, the hens and I went into my den for a little snooze. It's cooler there, any little breeze is a relief and, of course, it's shady. We were almost asleep when I heard cars approaching. First, the Von Bergs, followed by Obert and Michael. They all congregated on the stoep. I could hear the men talking. We lions have excellent hearing. Always interested in human affairs, I determined to follow the conversation. They began nattering on about water pipes and then switched the subject to cows. So boring, I put my head down to rest my eyes for a minute.

The next thing I heard was my food tray rattling. Confused, I looked round and couldn't believe it was already dinner time. How did I sleep through hyena patrol? I turned my head at the sound of pattering footsteps. Samantha was standing in the doorway. Shocked, I sat upright and watched as she trotted across the den, scrambled onto the platform, and stood in front of me. The hens, never thrilled by humans, flew to their roosts. Samantha was admonishing me to be quiet. Too upset to be quiet, I purred. A human has never been on my side of the fence. That's fine with me, I never know what the creatures will do, I'm safer with sturdy wire between us. The louder I purred, the more insistent this little cub told me to be silent. She put her paws on my mouth, but my big lips vibrated against them. Laughing, she patted my nose and told me I could make noise.

Bolting for the yard was the prudent thing to do. We all remembered Samantha's sprint and climb up the wire. I had visions of us galloping round the paddock. So, I sat still, besides, my blasted curiosity once again bested me. What did she want? What would she do? No human had ever touched me before, and I found the little pats pleasant. Well, Malcolm touched me after the accident, but I've no memory of that encounter. When the hens roost on my back, I do like the way their feet massage my spine, but these human pats were nicer.

Anyway, Sam examined me from head to tail. Her tiny paws felt my shoulder, spine, and flank. She patted my behind. My tail got careful scrutiny and then she stepped to the front of me. Enthralled with my mane, she buried her face in it and sniffed. She knelt in front of me, and I lay down to help satisfy her curiosity. She felt my front toes. I heard shouts from the stoep. Brandon called her name, ran down the steps, and flew across the yard. He stood at the wire, just opposite us, and demanded Samantha leave the area. Sam, like any cub, ignored him. Well, that's what my siblings and I would do when up to mischief. We went deaf and ignored our parents. Sam carefully felt my front toes, then announced she would inspect my teeth. Sam's behavior frightened her father. He shouted I would hurt her and begged her to walk to the door. By then, Bob, Michael and Obert were inside my den.

Sam pushed my lips up to see my dentition. She couldn't keep them up long enough to inspect my teeth. They, like my teeth, are large. They oozed through her fingers and slid back over my canines. As a last resort, she grabbed two handfuls of my whiskers and yanked upward. Ow! That was one way to see my teeth. I tried to contain myself but the pressure on my lips made me sneeze so hard I blew that cub backward. She landed on her rear end. Brandon again tried to reason with Samantha. Bob called to her and told her Obert was going to shoot me. Much to my horror, I saw this was a true statement. Obert, down on one knee, was pointing a long stick at me. Great, I thought, I'm going to join Uncle Sid in lion heaven.

Sam saw Obert, leaped to her feet, and tried to shield me. She threw her small body against my side, spread her arms, and sobbed into my mane. Good, I thought, Obert won't shoot Samantha, I'll be as quiet as possible. I was touched by her bravery, she'd been naughty to come in here, but she was frantic at the possibility of me being filled with holes. As was I. She was too frightened to obey orders. The poor cub hung onto my mane and sobbed. I could hear Bob and Obert discussing the best way to shoot me. Thankfully, they decided Sam was too close.

Obert stood, handed the weapon to his brother, and started toward us. I could see a transformation take place within him. He glided, rather than walked, and appeared to grow taller. He scooped Sam behind him, leaned toward me and whispered in Maa that I was a noble beast with the heart and soul of a true warrior. Of course, I understood him. Lions and Maasai have an ancient history together. We're totemic animals for the Maasai, they admire and worship us. However, that doesn't stop them from happily stabbing us with sharp spears. Bah! Just when I thought things couldn't get any worse, I find I'm living with two Maasai. I'd visions of my hide used for head adornments, robes, and who knows what else. Well, Obert, having said his piece, made a quick, dignified retreat to the gate.

The humans were back on their side of the fence. Bob sat Samantha on the bench and admonished her to stay there. Good luck with that, I thought. Felicity and Sarah were halfway across the yard when poor Felicity collapsed. Had it not been for Sarah, she would have fallen flat on her face. Brandon comforted her and had her sit next to Samantha. I heard Obert tell Bob he was glad I remained quiet. What a joke! Of course, I was quiet, the man was going to shoot me. What did they think I would do? Get up and dance the tarantella? If it were possible, I'd have turned myself to stone. I still wouldn't get up. Nope, not yet. Wise Sarah told the Von Berg family to catch their breath and, when ready, go to the stoep. I felt safe enough to walk to the front of the wire to better assess Felicity. She was so pale but seemed calmer with her cub and mate close by. After a few moments, she got up and came toward me. I considered running to the yard. What if Samantha got her speed and climbing ability from her mother? I'd nothing to worry about. She knelt and pushed her arms through the fence and gently patted my face. She also called me a splendid, beast, and then she scratched me between the eyes. Glory! As Obert would say. I have trouble reaching that spot. It felt wonderful to have another being give me a good scratch.

The Von Bergs disappeared into the house. Patrol was later than usual but I made sure the area was hyena-free before dinner.

Chapter 23

Sarah called down the hallway. "Bob, dinner's almost ready."

"Okay, be right there."

Halfway through the meal, Sarah looked up. "Geez, I heard Rollo sneezing today and thought about Sam's journey into his space."

"Don't remind me. It's hard to believe that was two years ago. I thought our hearts would stop in our chests when we realized she was with him. Some good things came out of that episode. It seemed to me Sam grew up overnight. She was so upset at the sight of her poor mother collapsed on the driveway. I can still see Obert when he walked into the den to grab Sam. He later told me he was channeling one of his Maasai ancestors. "

"Yes, I remember. Tell me again, what did he say to Rollo?"

"As best I remember, he told the animal he was a noble beast with a brave heart."

"I can't argue with that, it's a miracle Rollo didn't shred that little girl."

Bob nodded in agreement. "Well, what's that saying? All's well that ends well."

Sarah gestured to the stoep. "Let's take dessert outside. I've something to show you." When they were both seated, Sarah drew several round sticks from a carryall.

Bob said, "Sarah, why didn't you tell me you needed sticks? I could have brought you a truckload."

"Ah, but these aren't just sticks. Watch this."

She pressed a small button on the round, thirty cm stick, tugged on the other end, and telescoped it to half again its length. She activated a second button, which produced a small mechanical hand with flexed fingers.

Bob threw his head back and laughed. "Where on earth did you find that?"

"That new shop in town sells all sorts of stuff. Crafty stuff, kitchen stuff, and little gizmos like this. It's a telescoping back scratcher. I bought a dozen, they were cheap and will make great gag gifts."

"Can I have five right now? I want one, and I know Michael and Obert will also want one. Michael's kids will go nuts over these."

Sarah handed him five sticks. "My pleasure, I thought they were too good to pass up."

Bob activated his stick and gave it a test run on his back. "Ah, this works great, what a handy little device. I bet Brandon and Filly would love these things."

"They're on my list. I haven't heard from Filly in a while. She must be busy with Sam. She's got school now, I'm sure Filly is involved with field trips, meetings, and other school related projects. I'll call her tomorrow and see if she has a time to visit.

"Speaking of the Von Bergs, I ran into Malcolm yesterday. He told me Brandon has a two-month-old calf that isn't doing well. Mal says she's a pretty little heifer, but not thriving. Poor Mal, you know how wound up he gets about his patients. He's tried everything and can't turn this baby around. Brandon can't waste any more time or money on one animal. He may have to give up on her."

Sarah asked, "What's wrong with her?"

"Well, that's the question. Exam-wise Mal can't find anything wrong with her. He says she has the ADRs."

"ADRs? What in the world are the ADRs?"

Bob grinned, "Aint Doing Right, ADRs, get it?"

Sarah, not to be outdone, said, "Well, at least it's not the CTDs."

Her husband raised his eyebrows. "Okay, I'll bite. What're the CTDs?"

"Circling The Drain. CTDs are much worse than ADRs."

Bob groaned. "We're both ghouls. Back to your question, Mal is almost positive it isn't genetic, because the calf is a hybrid, she has many different genes. The dam is attentive, with plenty of milk."

Sarah nodded. "We know how that goes, we can only spend so many resources on one animal. I feel sorry for the Von Bergs and the calf. It's so hard to give up on an animal. And I'm sure Sam is in charge of this baby."

"You're so right. Sam has appointed herself as nurse. The calf has been handled so much she's a pet. Filly knows Sam will be devastated if they have to put the animal down."

"I'm sure she has a name."

"Oh sure, Sam's named her Arabella."

"I hope Mal can find a diagnosis."

"Yep, me too, it's very hard to know when to give up on an animal, especially a youngster like this."

Chapter 24

The next day, Sarah walked across the yard, shading her eyes from the midday sun. Rollo and the girls had returned from patrol. He napped while the hens murdered insects. Sarah paused and looked round. She did a mental count of everyone's location. Bob, Obert, and Malcolm were at the far end of the property, seeing to a lame Nguni bull. She knew Michael was busy with the windmill from hell. Good, she thought, I'm alone, because there'll be hell to pay if I get caught doing this. She approached the fence and pulled the telescoping back scratcher from underneath her shirt.

"Rollo, my boy, how are you today?"

Upon seeing his favorite human, the lion got up, ambled to the fence and purred a greeting.

"Rollo, this is our secret. You mustn't breathe a word to anyone." Sarah pushed the two buttons and carefully maneuvered the little hand through the wire. She gently scratched the lion's broad forehead. His eyebrows shot up, purring reached historic volumes.

"Isn't that wonderful? I know I'm not supposed to touch you. Well, technically speaking, I'm not touching you. Still, Mal will have a fit if he catches me."

Rollo sidled against the fence, looked over his shoulder, and peeped coyly at Sarah.

"Ha, you're so smart, I think you understand every word I'm saying. All righty, I'll go to work." Sarah started at the base of Rollo's mane, worked her way down the spine, and finished at the base of his tail. Explosive snorts of pleasure came from the animal. It was clear he enjoyed the contact.

"OK, done, for now, Rollo. We'll do this again. It's our secret."

Several weeks later, after dinner, the Aimtrees settled on the balcony with a bottle of wine. It was time for the African sunset show and they never tired of watching it. Sarah poured two glasses and settled herself in one of their Adirondack chairs. The retreating sun painted the sky shades of pink, lavender, and orange. Cotton candy clouds filled the sky.

Bob took a sip and asked, "Is this Rhino Tears? It's delicious, what a flavor."

"Yep, it's Rhino Tears, and I agree. It's a tasty white wine. Though, if it tasted like shoe polish, I would still buy it. It's for a good cause, a percentage of the price goes to Rhino conservation. It's a win-win situation for wine drinkers and rhinos."

"Shoe polish has never been on my beverage list, but I agree with you, if it did taste like shoe polish, perhaps we could buy it for our footwear."

Sarah took another sip and asked, "How's our lame bull? I hope Malcolm made a diagnosis. That young Nguni is one of the best specimens we've ever bred. I'd consider it a loss if we couldn't use him as a sire."

"Sarah, you won't believe this. That big, lame brute was hobbling on three legs. We got him into the chute, and Mal gave him a short-acting sedative. Obert and I tied a rope round his leg so Mal could examine him. The bull had a chunk of wood between the cloves of his hoof. Malcolm rummaged around in his truck and returned with the biggest pair of forceps I've ever seen. It took him five seconds to yank the wood out. It was funny, the bull hobbled out of the chute, put weight on his sore foot, and stopped. He realized the pain was gone and ran. Two seconds later, all we saw was his rear end, getting smaller and smaller as he galloped back to the pasture."

"Excellent! I take it there is no aftercare."

Bob laughed. "I doubt we could catch him. Mal said it was good we noticed it. That piece of wood would have caused an infection in the hoof. As it was, Mal puffed some antibiotic powder in the hoof and called it good. Um, Sarah, Mal had something else to discuss with us. You remember that sick calf the Von Bergs have been treating?"

"Yes, it was two months ago. Why? What's happened to her?"

Bob cleared his throat and shifted in the chair. "Ah, well, the calf isn't responding, it looks like they'll have to euthanize her. Brandon and Filly have spent too much time on her, um—" Bob's voice trailed off.

Sarah finished his sentence. "Malcolm wants to put the calf in with Rollo."

"Yes, Mal has never given up on the lost prey-drive theory. He thinks the calf will be more like real prey. You know, like an antelope. Perhaps Rollo never recognized the hens as prey. It's up to us, of course, we don't have to do this."

"Ach! A part of me doesn't want Rollo to be a normal lion, an apex predator. I enjoy having him here. I know that's selfish, we must keep trying to return him to the wild."

"I know that Sarah and I agree with both of your statements. We would like to see him free, although there are many times when I've thought he's comfortable here,"

"Yes, and I agree with that. Still, we must try. Have Mal bring the calf over and put her in his enclosure. I don't think I'll want to see it, hiding in the house seems a better option."

"What makes you think I won't be right behind you? Mal says this is a beautiful calf, but if our boy ignores her, Mal can put her down here. It'll be better because of Samantha. She doesn't need to see the calf euthanized."

"Okay, we have a plan. Call Mal in the morning and set it up soon before we change our minds."

Three mornings later, Sarah, Bob, and Obert stood in the yard. They were waiting for Malcolm. Rollo and the girls watched from the knoll. Sarah heard the hens talking to one another. Malcolm drove into the yard, called greetings to everyone, parked, and went round to the back of his truck. Bob and Obert hurried to help him. They lifted the small bovine out of the truck. Malcolm clipped a lead rope to her halter and led her closer to the fence. She plodded obediently along behind him. Bob and Obert stared at the calf. They looked at each other.

"Glory, Bob, she's beautiful! Look at those legs and topline."

"Boy, you said it. No wonder Brandon didn't want to give up on her. "

Both men dropped to their knees on opposite sides of Arabella. Obert began a thorough exam of her legs, while Bob felt her topline and chest. Sarah approached the calf and rubbed her curly forehead.

"Well, missy, I have to say, for a hybrid, you're gorgeous. Mal, she has almost perfect conformation. She has her sire's face. Look at those curls. I see what you mean, though, she's so listless."

Arabella looked up at Sarah with a weary expression, sniffed her pants leg, and stood quietly while the men continued their examination. Rollo wandered to the fence. He peered at the humans and newcomer. The lion looked at Sarah, jammed his forehead against the wire, and purred. A few moments later, he shifted his side along the wire. Sarah, red-faced to the roots of her hair, ignored him. Rollo turned his rump to the fence and, again, stared at Sarah.

Malcolm narrowed his eyes and demanded. "Sarah, have you

been petting him?"

"Absolutely not, I've not been petting him. Sometimes, he does strange stuff. Who knows what he's thinking?"

Bob turned to his wife. "Why are you all red? Are you blushing? Have you been in there? Lord, I wouldn't put it past you."

Unconvinced, Malcolm muttered. "He looks like an animal that's used to being petted."

"Nope, not true, Mal, I haven't touched him." Sarah thought, I haven't touched him with my hand, nobody's asked about a back scratcher. I'm not volunteering any more information.

Rollo gave Sarah a reproachful look, returned to the knoll and laid down. The hens scrambled onto his back, ready for patrol. The lion, head on front paws, watched the humans and calf.

Malcolm muttered. "Shoot, he's right here. How can you get her in there? That brute could close the distance in seconds. He could knock you down. He could take–"

Sarah sighed, took the lead rope, and turned to Bob. "Bob, open the gate. I'll take Arabella into the paddock, unsnap her lead, and step out. You close the gate behind me."

Malcolm continued to sputter warnings, but Sarah marched the calf inside, released her, and stepped out. It took less than thirty seconds. Rollo lifted his head but didn't get up. The hens, always suspicious of new things, kept a wary eye on the calf. Arabella sniffed the bucket clipped to the fence. A temporary water station for Rollo, it was replaced by a bigger receptacle a few meters away. Arabella took another look at the bucket, then shuffled along the fence. She looked at the group on the knoll, raised her head, and cut loose with a robust bawl. She charged the lion and butted all three hens off his back. The hens, howling protests, decamped to the olive tree.

Well pleased with herself, Arabella kinked her tail over her back and kicked both hind feet to the sky. She did a brisk hand gallop toward the tree, changed her mind, and ran back toward the lion. She butted him in the side and yanked out a mouthful of mane. Finding it unpalatable, she tried two more mouthfuls, spit it out, and approached the bucket with fresh interest. She snuffled into its depths, found it empty, and gave it a brisk whack with the side of her head.

Without taking his eyes off her, Malcolm asked, "Would you have any calf starter pellets here? I've never seen her this animated. If we could find—"

Bob and Obert made a run for the shed. The two men almost got stuck in the doorway. Loud crashing sounds followed.

"Is it over here–?"

"I know there is a half-sack of pellets in this shed!"

"Over here, Bob, I have it."

Another Laurel and Hardy exit and the two men returned with the feed.

Bob waved the bucket. "Should we fill the bucket?"

Malcolm replied, "Oh hell, just throw some in there. But what about the lion? He's still lying down. God knows why, after having hunks of his hair yanked out, but he could still attack."

Sarah grabbed the pellets and did a repeat of the calf entrance. Arabella dove into the bucket and ate.

Sarah turned to Malcolm. "Now what? What's next? Should we take her out of his yard? There's an empty enclosure next to this paddock. We can put her there, it would be easier to feed and examine her."

Malcolm wandered to the bench and flung himself down. "Hell if I know what to tell you. A lion and three old hens bested all my veterinary skills. I suppose it would be best to shift her to another yard. It would be easier and safer to feed her. I'm almost afraid to move her, but it would be better for you."

Rollo got up, stretched, and yawned, displaying his wicked-looking teeth. Then he started toward the corner of the paddock. The hens flew out of the tree and joined him. Sarah stepped toward the gate, lead rope in hand.

"Now's the time, Rollo will be gone awhile, I'll step in there, rattle the bucket, and lead her out when she approaches."

Malcolm rubbed his eyes and replied," Okay, that sounds good. You can also throw hay over the fence. She hasn't been interested in roughage, well, other than lion hair, but hay or grass will be beneficial to her rumen. It'll get some good bacteria growing in her gut."

Bob opened the gate and Sarah slipped inside. The calf looked at her and then Rollo. She took a step toward Sarah, produced another un-lady like bellow, and charged after the lion. This time, the hens remained unmolested. She fell in step behind them. The group disappeared into the bushes.

"Well," Obert said, "She's decided about her living quarters. We can supply hay. Mal, what do you think? Do you think our simba will attack her?"

Mal looked at Obert with haunted eyes. "Obert, I haven't got one thing right with this beast since he landed here. Never mind the calf. I haven't done her much good either. I doubt he's going to harm her. She can stay where she is, there's no competition for food. Besides, I don't think she wants to leave."

Sarah sat down next to Malcolm and patted his shoulder. "It's OK, Mal, it looks like a win-win to me. If we can help this calf, she can go back to the Von Bergs. Samantha will be delighted to have her patient return home."

Mal replied, "Nope, Brandon told me, if by some miracle, the calf survives, you can have her. You can always offer him one of her calves."

Bob grinned and looked at Obert. "Great! Obert and I can fight over who gets the first calf."

Bob
Chapter 25

Halfway through breakfast, Bob and Sarah heard Obert's bakkie in the driveway.

"Sarah, after our meal, I'm going to pop over and see if Obert brought hay."

She nodded. "Carry on, he's probably whispering sweet nothings into Ara's ear. Last week he was giving her a treatment with the scratcher."

Bob called from the stoep. "Hey, Obert, is everything okay? How's our beautiful Arabella? I see you're using the scratcher on her. Geez, Rollo's next to you. Is he waiting his turn?"

Obert gave a light laugh. "Ah, she's fine, and so is Rollo. I put more hay in the shed. Our girl looks wonderful. Living with our big simba for four months agrees with her. How much weight do you think she's gained?"

Bob came down the steps. "I don't know, but it's enough to make her look very robust, ha, that's a polite word for fat."

"Bob, when are we going to integrate her into the herd? I'm worried about tossing her in with adult cattle. I don't know if she'll relate to her own kind. She may think she's a lion or a human."

"Don't forget the hens, maybe she thinks she's a chicken. I've also been worrying about her introduction to the main herd. We need a plan."

Obert said, "Here's one, my small holding pen will accommodate three or four calves. I use it for my cattle when they need treatment. It also has a loading chute for transport. She can live with several calves and visit the herd through the fence.

"Splendid idea, Obert, I've seen Arabella looking across the access road at our cattle. One day, several cows returned her stare. Rollo wandered around the bushes and the cows ran for their lives."

"Glory! I bet they did. When Ara arrived, she was too young to be fearful of her hairy roommate, now, he's part of her world."

"Let's keep her here for three more months. She's eight months now, so she'd be close to a year when we move her."

"That sounds good. It'll allow me time to make changes to the pen and select a few calves. I'll have to feed them, but that's all right. They'll be released after a few weeks of confinement."

That night, Bob recounted Obert's plan to Sarah.

She laughed. "You realize this is a ploy for Obert to get his hands on Ara. You two are besotted by that girl. Good thing she's a cow or I'd be jealous. Kidding aside, it's a fine idea. I don't think we should toss her in with adult cattle, either. Let her live with calves until she figures out what she is."

Bob said, "Great, problem solved. Gad, Sarah, I'm so tired from checking fences, I barely made it through dinner. Parts of our game fence need repairs. We know where the weak spots are and how to fix them. But that's for tomorrow. I'm dragging myself to bed."

"Okay, I want to watch the news and do some paperwork. I'll take a look at my new quilt fabric. Then I'll join you."

At three in the morning, the full-throated roar of a lion jerked both Aimtrees awake. They lurched out of bed, fumbling for lights and clothes.

Bob, one boot on and looking for the second, shouted to Sarah.

"Oh my God, there's a wild lion out there. It sounds like he's right in the yard. Poor Rollo must be terrified."

"I know, where are my blasted shoes? I'll turn the floodlights on and grab the rifle. I'll drive, you're better with the gun than I am." Frantic about her big pet, Sarah ran down the hall, clad in pajamas and boots. She flew through the kitchen, raced down the stairs, and jumped into the truck. Bob joined her seconds later. Another booming roar from across the yard signaled the newcomer's presence.

Sarah drove the truck into the access road. Halfway down she could see dust swirling in the headlights. A pack of hyenas milled about at the end of the road.

Bob shoved the rifle barrel out the window and said to Sarah: "Stop here, let's see what those ugly brutes are doing."

Sarah nodded, stopped, and waited. A shrill, panicky bleating issued from the far corner of the paddock. The hyenas drifted toward the sound, chattering in their insane, whooping language. Another terrified cry. It was Arabella.

Sarah turned to Bob. "Arabella is trapped in the corner of the fence; I'm going to drive closer."

Another few meters and the Aimtrees could see one hyena digging under the fence. It had muzzle and forepaws on the inside of the wire. Strong rear legs braced; the animal was throwing showers of dirt behind it. The rest of the pack milled close by, muttering encouragement.

Another roar split the still night air. Startled, Bob whispered, "What the hell? That strange lion is behind us, in the paddock. How did it get in? God help Rollo, he won't stand a chance." From the corner of his eye, Bob saw a lion burst out of the bushes.

Roaring, mane flying, and teeth bared, the animal charged

toward the burrowing hyena. He grabbed the brute by the nose and tried to pull it into the paddock. The hyena was far too big and the hole far too small to allow that to happen. Squealing with pain, the animal backpedaled furiously and jerked out of the lion's grasp. Raising its bloodied muzzle, the animal galloped down the lane. The rest of the pack, whooping their displeasure at the lost meal, followed close behind.

Sarah looked at the lion. "Bob, that isn't a wild lion. It's Rollo! Poor Arabella, he may attack her. Talk about awakened prey drive. He was going to kill that hyena. Look at his eyes!"

Eyes blazing, Rollo roared again and pawed the hole, then turned, and looked at the Aimtrees. He swung round to see Arabella scramble to her feet and totter toward him. She lowered her head and leaned against his shoulder. Bob and Sarah could see her shaking. She butted him and pressed against his side. Rollo blinked at her and sat down. Bob opened the car door. Sarah shook her head and grabbed his hand.

"Don't get out of the truck. for once, I agree with Malcolm, we don't know what he'll do. I know you love that calf, but we can't stop an attack. Let's sit here and see what happens."

Rollo looked at Arabella, Bob could see confusion in the animal's expression. The lion gave her a careful sniff. He didn't seem to recognize her. Arabella, with the resilience of youth, had already forgotten the terrifying episode. She did something she hadn't done in two months. She grabbed a mouthful of mane, gave a brisk yank, snorted and did several hand gallops up and down the fence. For a finale, she sprinted into the den. The Aimtrees could hear her hooves clattering on Rollo's platform. The lion heaved himself to all fours and began his usual stately walk to the den.

Bob turned to Sarah. "Have you ever seen him move that fast?"

"Are you kidding? I've never seen him trot, let alone sprint."

"I saw him trot once. You weren't home, and I was a little late with dinner. He trotted the last few meters to the food tray. That's the only time I saw him break out of a walk. Let's drive to the end of our road. I think I know where those beasts got in. Obert and I saw a suspicious weak spot in the fence yesterday. We were going to repair it today. I want to see if that's where they got onto the property."

Sarah complied and Bob went out to inspect the fence.

"This spot had a couple of broken wires and a little sag. Now, look at it. There's a big hole underneath where the damn beasts pushed the wire up. Several strands are either bent or broken. Hyena hair is everywhere. It's scattered on the ground and stuck to the fence."

Sarah joined her husband and looked at the damage. "Ach, they did a proper job on it, they may be ungainly looking, ugly brutes, but they're smart. Thank God Rollo went into action. They'd have killed Arabella."

Bob started to respond, then stared at his wife. "Did you realize you're in pajamas? No wonder you beat me to the truck! Are you wearing shoes?"

"Yes, to shoes and no to clothes. I couldn't imagine how a second lion could be in the paddock. As for Arabella, I'm not sure she's home free. Not with the way our boy acted tonight. Let's see what they're doing.

Sarah positioned the truck so the headlights shone into the den. Arabella stood at the edge of the platform. She pawed the ground, dragging straw with her hoof. Rollo attempted to step onto his bed and got butted in the face. Sighing, he moved a few meters to the side and tried again. Arabella charged him.

Bob muttered to Sarah. "Looks like she's in the Plaza De Toros, somewhere in Spain, on a Sunday afternoon."

After the fourth face butt, Rollo sat down. Arabella ran out of steam and collapsed in the straw.

"Looks like she burned all her adrenaline," Sarah said.

"Well, she was likely awash in the stuff. Hell, I'm awash in it. Fortunately for her, Rollo's back to his old self."

The lion cautiously approached his bed, stepped up, and retreated to his favorite corner. With a sigh, he settled himself for sleep. Arabella hauled herself to her feet, walked to his side, and laid down beside him. She scooted closer and put her chin across his back. Rollo's purring put her to sleep in less than a minute.

Sarah said, "Let's leave them for the rest of the night. We've all had too much excitement."

"Yes, good idea, I'll call Obert after breakfast. He can get a crew together and we'll fix the fence. I doubt the hyenas will be back tonight."

"After dealing with Rollo, the wonder lion, they may never come back. We can't count on that. Those animals are voracious hunters. They don't just eat carrion. If the pack is large enough, they'll drive lions off a kill. They attack and kill old lions and cubs. Yikes! We had a tribe of the devils in our backyard. Ach! Let's go back to bed for an hour. We'll sort this out later."

❊ Rollo ❊
Chapter 26

Well, that dratted Malcolm did it again. He lives to keep my life in turmoil. The seasons changed. The hens and I followed our simple routines and we were content. One morning, I finished a skimpy breakfast when my nemesis drove into the yard. Bob and Obert assisted him as he removed an odd-looking creature from his vehicle.

What fresh hell is this? What is that odd-looking creature? It tottered after Malcolm and stood while Bob and Obert examined it. I needed to make a closer inspection. It resembled the large beasts across the road. But so small! Besides, Sarah might have that scratcher thing. I gave her several hints that a good scratching would be welcome, but she ignored me. I don't understand her reluctance to use the gizmo when other humans are present. She's not the only one doing this. Last week, Obert delivered ranch supplies. I walked to the fence and politely waited for him to notice me. He looked round to make sure he was alone and just like Sarah pulled out his device and gave me a satisfactory session. I startled him by standing on my hind legs so he could attend to my belly. He kept muttering about getting caught. Getting caught doing what? It made no sense to me. When Bob called from the stoep, Obert hastily pocketed the device.

Annoyed by Sarah's behavior, I retreated to the knoll. The hens, always suspicious of humans, kept a wary eye on the newcomer. Bah! They're smarter than I am. Surely, this little creature would join the pride across the road. I paid no attention as Malcolm led it across the yard. I heard him talking about the prey drive business and knew bad luck was on the horizon. The humans thought this beast was beautiful. Are they kidding? It's a scrawny little pipsqueak! During their conversation, I learned this beast is a calf, female, and has a name, Arabella. This cub is sick. Malcolm wants to put her in my enclosure. What the heck is the man thinking? Is he daft? What am I supposed to do with a sick calf?

Sarah, the traitor, released Arabella into my space. I ignored her, in hopes the humans would see their mistake and remove the beast. It was time for patrol, the hens settled on my back. We were leaving when that cub charged over and knocked them to the ground. Shrieking, they flew to the tree. Arabella bellowed and chased them for a few strides. I'm uncertain if the humans are correct about her being sick. She produced a tremendous sound and ran like an impala. She had no odor of sickness or death. She turned to me. Those hens are lucky, they can fly. I knew mischief was coming but was surprised at what happened next. That bratty beast yanked out several mouthfuls of mane. She rampaged along the fence, then butted a bucket.

I heard the humans talking and was relieved they would move Arabella. Halfway to the corner, that cub bawled again and chased us. Oh boy, I thought, the hens are, again, going to get clobbered. To my amazement, Arabella stayed behind me and behaved herself.

So, she moved in with us. Bob, Michael, and Obert thought she was gorgeous. Personally, I didn't think she was attractive. Like all cubs, she was clumsy. She also drooled. The men gave her plenty of food and that youngster ate like a starving elephant. In a few weeks, she gained weight and looked healthy. Bah! Another weird creature living here. At least she has four legs. Don't misunderstand, I'm fond of the hens, but how they zip about on their two sticks amazes me. The humans have two legs, but they don't look like sticks.

Arabella was a pest. After a month, she yanked out so much mane I resembled my mum. She licked the side of my head with her raspy tongue. She rubbed her large, slimy nose all over my face. I had calf drool on my body most of the time. It was a gesture of affection, but, gad, so unpleasant. She did everything we did. Her pride members would come to the fence opposite our paddock and stare at her. She looked at them, but her heart was with us.

When she was eight months old, I heard Bob and Obert discussing a move for her. The news surprised and saddened me, but she needed to be with her pride. She would stay for another few months, then move to Obert's property. A few nights later, a dreadful event happened.

We settled down for the night. Arabella slept close to me and enjoyed the vibration my purring produced. Lying next to me, she would be asleep in minutes. I awoke to utter darkness and heard the whooping cries of hyenas. They were close. Their disgusting odor filled my nostrils. Well, they do eat rotten meat. I leaped to my feet with a roar. The poor hens, frightened and disoriented, flopped off my back and fled to the space between the back wall and my sleeping platform. I roared again, amazed that I could produce such a sound. Arabella was not in the den. Had she gone for a drink? I took several steps toward our indoor water supply, but she was gone. The hyenas screamed again. I saw Bob and Sarah on the access road, driving toward the back of the yard. The intruders fell silent, and I heard Arabella crying. She was outside. I sprinted across the den and into the paddock. Roaring, I covered the distance in a few huge bounds. Once round the corner, I saw those devils on the road. One of them was tunneling under the fence. Arabella lay huddled in a corner.

Another sprint down the fence and I was on top of that digging monster. I braced both forepaws, grabbed its muzzle, and hauled back with all my strength. It wouldn't fit through the hole. I yanked a large piece of skin off the brute's face. It scrambled backward onto our access road. The pack fled into the night.

Arabella got to her feet and walked to me on unsteady legs. She's now taller than I am but leaned against my side. She was terrified. Well, I, too, was distressed. I sat down to catch my breath. Why did that silly cub venture out alone? She picked the wrong night for an adventure.

Bob and Sarah were also upset. They stayed in the truck and waited for whatever happened next. Well, that was the question. I wondered myself, not sure if the hyenas would return for another try at their meal. They would have to go through me. I would fight to the death for a pride member. Even if she is an obnoxious calf.

Arabella yanked out a hunk of my mane. Like all youngsters, she placed the terrifying ordeal behind her in minutes. Cubs! They're all like that. She didn't know she was almost breakfast for a pack of hyenas. She scampered up and down the fence, yanked out another clump of mane, and ran toward the den. Not me! No more galloping for me. I hauled myself to my feet and walked toward the enclosure.

Bob and Sarah pulled round to the den. They saw Arabella on the edge of the platform. She butted me in the face several times and wouldn't let me step onto my bed. Too weary to argue, I sat down and waited. A few moments passed. Arabella walked several strides and collapsed. Wonderful, we can go back to sleep. Settled in a deep pile of straw, I relaxed. Arabella joined me, she felt my sides vibrating, put her chin on my back, and slept. I saw six black, frightened eyes peering at me from the edge of the platform. The hens fluttered into the straw and cautiously settled on my spine. I scared the poor old girls half to death. My behavior also frightened me. My normal temperament was changed into something ferocious and terrifying. I didn't understand it.

Bob
Chapter 27

A week after the hyena night of terror, Bob met Obert in the driveway. "How can we get Ara out of the paddock without incurring Malcolm's wrath? We can't walk in there and lead her out. I agree with Mal. We don't know how Rollo will react His behavior with the hyenas was terrifying."

"He really showed his true lion colors. Sarah told me what he did. I had trouble believing it. We've never seen him behave aggressively. You're right, we have to be careful. Here's my idea. Ara loves watermelon. We know Rollo sleeps most of the day. We'll wait until he's passed out on the knoll, then rattle her bucket and stand near the gate. She'll be putty in our hands. You open the gate, I'll clip the lead on her halter and lead her out."

"Brilliant, Obert, let's try it. Sarah noticed Ara's halter is getting snug. We'll replace it with a larger one."

The men watched the animals return from patrol. Rollo settled for his afternoon nap. Ara saw her pals and came to the fence. A minute later, she was in the yard, chomping on watermelon slices.

Bob asked, "Can you lead her away from her hairy friend? Let's see if she stays calm. "

She did. Bob suggested the lawn and Ara was soon grazing on the fresh green grass. "Obert, this is great, she's so relaxed. Next time, bring the trailer. We'll practice walking her up the ramp. Do you think she'll do that?"

"Of course, she'll do it. Do you want to place a bet? This beautiful heifer will follow me into the trailer."

Bob gnawed on his lip in an effort not to laugh. "Obert, you act like she's your relative. I mean no offense, we both know it can be a battle to get these critters into a trailer. Remember that enormous Brahma bull that burst through the escape door? He took half the side of the trailer with him. Or that daft cow that did a back flip off the ramp? I'll shut up, I don't want to jinx us. Let's practice leading her away from the paddock for a week. You can bring the trailer when you think she's ready.

"Fair enough, I've got three heifer calves in my holding pen, waiting for our beautiful girl."

A week later, Obert rattled into the driveway with his stock trailer. Bob joined him.

"Okay, Obert, let's walk her around this contraption."

Arabella sniffed the ramp and peered at the hay net hanging inside the trailer. Obert stepped halfway up the ramp and offered a watermelon slice. Bob stood quietly and patted her back. Ara put her front foot on the ramp and snorted when it vibrated. Obert waved more melon and took another step up the ramp. Arabella flipped her ears and walked into the trailer. Bob quickly snapped the butt chain, pulled the ramp up and shut the door.

Both men beamed at the heifer. Obert slipped out the escape door and said, "Piece of cake. She loaded like a pro. Are you coming with us?"

"Yep, I can help if she panics."

"It won't happen, she'll ride like a veteran. Let's go."

After an uneventful ride, Obert led Arabella out of the trailer and slipped her into the pen. The four youngsters were soon chewing on each other.

"Obert, this is wonderful, she's fine."

"Yep, she's a star I'll leave them here for two weeks then shift them into the pasture."

Two months later, Bob clattered through the screen door. "Hey Sarah, where are you? Have I got time to run over to Obert's this morning? I want to see Arabella before he puts her in with the main herd."

"He hasn't done it yet. Isn't she adjusting to her own kind? Hasn't she been there for two months? You moved her shortly after the hyena debacle."

"Heck no, nothing's amiss. She lives with three calves that are her age. The adult cattle visit from their side of the fence. Obert is the problem. I'm waiting for him to tell me she's moved into the house. They could watch TV, have a meal, and so forth. He's nuts about her and delaying reentry into the herd." Bob poured himself a coffee and sat at the kitchen table. "Obert has to move her this week. We're going to the cattle auction in three days. He likes two groups of heifers. The newcomers, should he buy them, will go into that space. He'll keep the new cattle isolated for a week."

Sarah grinned. "Ah, the cattle auction, am I to understand these heifers are hybrids? Perhaps Nguni-Beefmaster crosses?"

"Well, yes, but haven't you changed your mind since you met Arabella? Even you admit she's beautiful."

"I admit she's impressive. I could tolerate a few like her, providing we breed them back to our young Nguni bull."

To curry Sarah's favor in this matter, Bob would have agreed to breed them to a warthog. "Sure, sure, that's fine, three-quarters Nguni and one-quarter Beefmaster is a good cross. We need to make sure they are quality animals. The catalogs make all the cattle look like show winners but, when you look at them in person, they don't match their descriptions. That's why we're leaving early, we want to get there and inspect the sale animals. Obert will pick me up, he's bringing the trailer. I am, for once, going to be sitting on the stoep, with my coffee and auction catalog in hand.

Every time we do this, I'm late. Obert sits in the yard, honking the horn. I have to listen to volumes of ridicule about not being able to get out of bed."

"Great! If you like, set a clock, set two clocks. I'll arise before you and pound on a pot with a rolling pin. You have a checkered history of being on time with Obert. I'm pleased to see you're proactive. I'm at your service if you need more help."

"Okay, thanks, but this time, I'll be waiting for him. I know it'll be a first and I can't wait to see his reaction. For now, I'm going to his house. We can talk about a potential suitor for Ara, it's too soon, but it never hurts to explore different possibilities. I suppose you have no objection if we use one of our bulls. Perhaps that black one you favor so much? That said, she'll be in Obert's herd, it'll be easier to use one of his sires for the first calf.

"Either way will work. We have months to decide. Now, just clear out and go visit your favorite cow. I'll see you for lunch."

Bob pulled into Obert's driveway and strode to the house and called. "Obert? Where are you?

"Back here, with the cattle."

It startled Bob to see both Obert and Arabella were soaking wet. Water dripped off Obert's hat and ran down Arabella's face.

"Why are you both wet? What're you doing to our lovely cow?"

Obert waved the hose. "Bathing her. Look at this stuff." Obert handed Bob a plastic container.

"It's labeled Eulalia's Cattle Shampoo. Where did you find this? Why are you giving Ara a bath?"

Obert grinned. "I want her to look nice when she goes out with the herd today. I don't know Eulalia, but she makes a fine product. Just look at the shine on Ara's coat."

Bob stared at Obert. "You don't really expect me to believe that? Do you?"

"Nope," Obert allowed. "I confess. She's going out today, but I've been working with her so we can compete in shows. Some of our fellow hybrid breeders are having informal competitions and I want Ara to look her best. I'm giving her baths, grooming her, and teaching her to stand quietly while tied. I put her in the trailer and we go for short rides. The other breeders will waste their time. Ara will win."

Bob groaned. "Taking her for little rides. Do you two stop for ice cream? Maybe a beer?"

Obert shook his head. "I tell you. If I had a herd like her, I could buy a fine wife!"

"Once a Maasai, always a Maasai. Well, she looks wonderful and I agree with you about Eulalia. Her bovine shampoo-making talents can't be rivaled."

Obert slipped the halter off Arabella and walked to the gate. swung it open and waited. He had thrown hay over the fence, and several cows were snacking. The three heifers trotted through the open gate, Arabella close behind them. The adult cows barely glanced at her.

"A non-event," Bob said, "your strategy worked, those big girls of yours have already gotten used to her."

"This was an excellent transition! I'll tidy this yard and leave it empty for our new hybrids."

"We best not come home with all of them, I'll be sleeping with Rollo. It'll be safer than being around my wife. Bob glanced at his watch. "Geez, I'm late for lunch. Congratulations on a perfect herd entry."

Chapter 28

The afternoon before the cattle auction, Sarah tended to her stoep plants. Her hair lifted in a gust of wind and she frowned. She glanced at the cloudless sky. Wind tonight, she thought, no rain, but strong winds. Another gust and something fluttered in Rollo's yard. She crossed the driveway and peered over the fence. The white object was several meters from the fence, it fluttered again in a fresh burst of wind.

She muttered aloud, "What is that? Probably plastic, but I don't want it blowing round." Rollo wasn't on the knoll or in his den. Sarah knew he was likely snoozing under the olive trees in the far corner of the yard.

"I shouldn't do this," she said to the wind, then slipped through the gate and retrieved a piece of white plastic. Halfway to the gate, she heard an approaching vehicle. Sprinting the last few meters, she slammed the gate closed.

"Hey, Sarah! What're you doing?" Bob called from the truck.

"Ach! A piece of plastic blew against the fence, I just picked it up." She had a brief conversation with herself about telling colossal lies, but decided she wasn't up to a lecture from her husband.

That night, a bemused Sarah watched her husband bustle about the house. He set up the coffeemaker, then went to the bedroom where he carefully arranged his clothes on a chair. He fiddled with the alarm clock, set it, and rechecked it three times.

"Bob, you look well prepared for tomorrow's adventure. Obert will be surprised to see you waiting on the stairs. You'll gloat all the way to the auction."

"Yes indeedy, I'm prepared. When the alarm sounds, I'll leap out of bed, turn on the coffee, and head for the bathroom. Then into my carefully arranged clothes. I'll grab my coffee and catalog. I won't turn on the lights so Obert will think he's won again. Ha! He'll see me in the headlights, sitting on the stairs, sipping coffee, and glancing at my watch."

The wind moaned round the side of the house. Sarah heard the chimes singing on the stoep. "That wind has picked up. Isn't it supposed to blow all night?"

"Yep, according to the forecast, it should diminish by morning. Speaking of morning, Obert and I must be at the auction yard at eight. That's when the gates open. We'll be parked, and ready to enter the grounds so we can inspect those heifers. We're going to stop for breakfast. There's a great café halfway to our destination. I'll tell Obert, if he buys, I will shut up about being on time."

"Wonderful, I can only assume we're making it an early night."

"I may throw myself into bed before dinner."

"Ach, well, let's eat early, I don't think you need to do that."

Sarah heard the alarm ring and watched Bob vault out of bed. She smiled and closed her eyes for another hour of sleep. As she drifted off, she heard her husband in the kitchen.

Moments later, a loud scream ripped through the house. Sarah jumped out of bed, shoved her slippers on, and ran out the door.

Halfway across the stoep, her left eye registered movement under the Boston fern, but her brain was too busy to receive the message. Her brain focused on the sight of Bob sprawled on the stairs. She was looking at the bottom of his boots.

She crouched beside him. "Bob, what happened? Did you trip on the stairs? Are you okay? Do you need a doctor?"

A feeble groan arose from the lawn. "I'm sure seventy-five

percent of my bones are broken."

Sarah tugged gently on her husband's shoulder. "Can you get your knees under you? Maybe get your face off the lawn. What did you trip over?"

"A large, squashy object at the top of the stairs. I caught both feet on it and fell."

Frowning, Sarah looked at the stoep. "Are you sure? I don't see anything. Do you mean an animal was there?"

"I don't know. Can I brace on you and see if I can get to my knees?"

"Of course, I suggest we move to the truck. You can sit for a moment and catch your breath. It's only a few steps."

Bob couldn't pull his knees under himself. Sarah grabbed his pant leg and carefully tugged first one knee, then the other, onto the step. With Sarah's help, he lurched to his feet and hobbled toward the truck.

She asked again, "What happened?"

"I got my auction catalog, poured coffee into the new commuter mug, and backed through the screen door. I didn't turn the lights on. It was still dark, but I could see shapes. Obert's sly, it would be just like him to be sitting in the dark. When I started down the stairs, my feet snagged on an object, and I went headfirst down the stairs."

"You certainly did, people may have heard you in Cape Town. I couldn't imagine what happened. I thought you spilled hot coffee on yourself."

Halfway to the vehicle, Sarah paused, a new sound registered in her overworked brain. Bang, thud! Bang, thud! Bang, thud!

She asked Bob. "What's that noise? It's coming from the paddock."

Bob tottered to the truck and eased into the seat. In the growing light, Sarah saw, to her horror, Rollo's gate banging back and forth in the wind.

"Bob, you fell over Rollo. He's on the stoep, I thought I saw movement under the fern but discounted it."

"How could that be? How could he have gotten out?"

"His gate is open, hear that banging? It's blowing back and forth in the wind."

"How could that be? We have escape-proof latches on all our gates."

Sarah grimaced and said, "No time to explain now. Where's Obert?"

A pair of headlights swinging off the main road into the drive answered Sarah's question. She raised her hands to alert him of trouble. Rifle in hand, he joined Sarah and Bob. She gave him a short version of what had transpired.

Obert asked, "You're sure Rollo is there? I know his gate is open, but he could be in the paddock. He may still be—"

A familiar sound drifted from the stoep. Rollo's huge shaggy head appeared at the top of the stairs. An anxious expression in his amber eyes. He purred.

"Glory! He's on the stoep. How can we get him in his paddock? He's never been loose before. Heaven only knows what he'll do. Bob, can you handle your rifle? We may have to use it."

Bob turned to Sarah. "Un-rack the gun and hand it to me, I can manage the rifle. I still can't fathom how that gate got open."

Sarah, in tears, gave the weapon to her husband. "This is my fault. I went into his paddock to retrieve a piece of plastic. You almost caught me when you came home. I ran out and thought the gate was latched behind me. It wasn't. I'm so sorry, Bob, I didn't want you raving about me going in there. Now our poor lion may have to pay for my stupidity with his life."

Obert glanced at Rollo. "Well, so far, he hasn't budged. How the hell are we going to shift him back to the yard?"

Sarah squared her shoulders and said, "I'm going to feed him breakfast. Don't argue, either of you. This is my fault, and I'll take responsibility for it. He'll hear the familiar sounds of the cart and sliding food tray. With any luck, he'll go through the gate to eat. You both have rifles, you'll have to use them if attacks. Please don't shoot me by accident."

Before either man could argue, Sarah walked across the yard, slipped into the kitchen, and loaded the cart. Once across the yard, she stepped into the safety fence and shut the door. Secure now, she called Rollo.

"Over here, big boy, go down the stairs and through the gate. We know you can do it." Again, she trilled to the lion. "Breakfast! Come on, Rollo," She gnawed on her lip and listened to the men.

Obert muttered. "Is he afraid to climb down? Maybe going up was easier."

Bob groaned. "Well, he can't stay on the stoep for the rest of his life. What the hell do we do now?"

Sarah tried a third time. "Rollo, breakfast!" She rattled the tray and banged the side of the cart."

The lion remained at the top of the steps. He shifted his front feet, looked down the stairs, and purred louder. He put his left forepaw on the first step, then his right. More purring and anxious looks at the men followed this action.

Sarah fretted and listened to Bob call encouragement.

"Atta boy, come down the steps. First one paw, then the other."

Rollo complied with his front feet. He negotiated steps two, three, four, and five with his front paws. His hind feet remained on the stoep floor.

Exasperated, Bob muttered. "The great bloody oaf acts like his back feet are nailed to the floor. What the hell is wrong with him? Rollo! You daft creature, put your back paws on the stairs and walk down."

Obert made a wise observation. "He tries for step six and gravity will take over."

Sadly, Obert was correct. Rollo stretched a forepaw toward the next step, lost his balance, and slid. Like Bob, he landed forepaws on the lawn with the rest of him on the stairs.

His expression radiating misery, he looked at the men.

Despite the gravity of the situation, Sarah smiled at the sight of Rollo on the stairs. He looked exactly like Bob. The men continued their conversation.

Obert asked, "Did you look like that? Sort of sprawled all over the stairs?"

Bob glared at Obert. "Yes, I did look like that, minus the hair. Please shut up about my mishap. I could be seriously injured."

"Well, if you slid down as slowly as Rollo, you're probably okay. Did you look as miserable?"

"Obert shut up."

"Just wondering, why isn't he getting up? He needs to get his back legs under him. Did you have trouble with your legs?"

"Yes, I did, Sarah had to tug on the front of my pant leg to help me."

Obert couldn't resist saying, "Should we go over and tug on his back paws? Maybe we could—"

"Obert, shut up! Let's just wait, he'll surely figure out what to do with his rear end."

Rollo got his front legs underneath himself and stood up. He was canted uphill, rear paws still stretched on the stairs. He pulled his back legs down the steps and stood on the lawn. He looked at the men. Both tensed and took a firmer grip on their rifles. Radiating misery, head and tail down, he slunk across the driveway and entered the paddock. Obert kept a prudent distance behind him. Rifle raised, he followed the animal and latched the gate when Rollo entered the yard. The lion took the chunk of meat and headed toward the rear of his paddock. He disappeared into the bushes.

Obert called to Sarah, "Okay, Sarah, we're safe and secure. Let's see to Bob."

"Obert, I am awash with guilt and embarrassment. How could I have been so careless? I could have lost both of them. Yes, let's see if Bob needs medical attention."

The two friends crossed the driveway and found Bob making slow laps round the lawn. He had retrieved the coffee mug and catalog. Waving the mug at Sarah, he declared. "Sarah, would you look at this? This travel mug flew down the stairs and bounced on the lawn. It still has coffee! No spillage! It's still hot." Bob took an appreciative sip. "We must buy more of these. What an excellent product!"

Sarah stared at her husband. "Why are you prattling on about the mug? You must have hit your head. You may have a concussion. Another reason for a medical exam. What about your broken bones? I should haul you to the doctor."

"Ahh, I'm downgrading my broken bone estimate. I got the wind knocked out of me when I landed on the lawn. Now, wife of mine, am I correct in assuming you feel terrible? I know you're brimming with shame and guilt."

Sarah grimaced. "Yes, I feel awful. It's not like me to be careless. Never mind me, what about your injuries? You need a medical examination."

Bob smiled and waved the auction catalog. "If I can buy a few hybrid heifers, you are forgiven."

Sarah, hands on hips, knew she had lost the battle. "Okay, you have me over a large barrel, please don't come home with a herd of hybrids."

A restored Bob whooped and scrambled into Obert's truck, "Obert, you heard the lady. Let's go buy some cows before Sarah changes her mind."

✸ Rollo ✸
Chapter 29

Wallowing warthogs! I'll never understand these daft humans. Once again, they have blindsided me. We recently celebrated that lovely human festival. Everyone admired me. Arabella moved to Obert's den. She would join her own pride from his home. I had mixed feelings about her leaving. I helped her mature and had a paw in her care. She arrived a scrawny youngster, and left a robust, healthy cub. Goodness, when she left, she was taller than I. There were certain things I wouldn't miss. Ara was a slob. She drooled and licked my head with her raspy tongue. I knew it was a gesture of affection. But so unpleasant. Like all cubs, she was clumsy. She tore through the den, and, on several occasions, tripped and nearly squashed the hens. Though I missed her. It was nice to return to our old routines. The hens and I appreciated the quiet days.

One night, I awoke to a strange noise. Using my nose I shoveled the sleeping girls off my back, then went outside to investigate. Bang thud! Bang thud! I couldn't determine the source of the noise, so I padded down the fence line, and saw, to my astonishment, an open gate blowing in the wind. What to do? I should have gone back to bed. Someone would have shut it in the morning. It's best when the humans stay on their side of the wire. But no, my blasted curiosity got the best of me. Intrigued by the area near my bench, I stepped through the gate to inspect it. The cool grass beneath the trees felt wonderful on my paws.

I looked toward the human den and knew it merited a closer look. They enter it using a little hill. I've seen them climb up and down countless times. The top was reached by climbing flat spaces. Again, I should have inspected it from the lawn and returned to bed. But, no, not me, I climbed to the stoep.

The flat spaces were troublesome. My rear paws needed to track my front paws when climbing. How do humans bound up and down with only two legs? After a few moments, I got all four paws moving and reached the top. Plants covered the area, in baskets, on stands, and in little trays. There were structures the humans sat upon. They looked well used, and, if you were human, comfortable. One side of the stoep contained an enormous plant in a tall stand. Its leaves touched the floor and it was so big I easily stepped round the back and peered through the foliage. This would be a wonderful resting place. I could hear what the humans were discussing. Bah! A fantasy since I'm never out of the paddock, but it was pleasant to imagine peeping through the greenery and hiding from everyone.

After the stoep inspection, I returned to the top of the hill. A brilliant thought struck me. This would be an excellent vantage point to watch for hyenas. If the brutes came round, I would have the advantage of elevation and surprise. I could bound down the hill and dispatch them before they could react. I laid down across the top of the stoep to test my theory. It was correct, an excellent viewing spot. I would watch for a few hours and return to the paddock before dawn. I remained vigilant, scanning the driveway, pastures, and my area. Time drifted by and I put my head down to rest my eyes for a moment. The next thing I knew, two hard objects struck me in the side. I heard a frightful yell that I recognized as Bob's voice and leaped to my feet in time to see him catapult down the hill on his forepaws. Sarah shouted from the den and I bolted under the huge leafy plant, I was trapped. Sarah flew across the stoep and rushed to assist him. I'd fallen asleep on hyena watch. Ashamed, I hoped to slip away when the humans returned to their den. Luck was against me. Bob was making pitiful sounds and I was doubly ashamed that I'd caused him an injury. When I thought things couldn't get worse, Obert arrived. Wonderful! Now there were three humans to evade. The wind picked up and my gate began banging against the posts.

Sarah made an extraordinary confession, she had entered my paddock, something that was forbidden by Malcolm, and retrieved a bit of debris. She hadn't properly latched the gate, and knew I was on the stoep. Well, she was correct. Shamefaced, I purred, slunk across the stoep, and looked round the corner. The humans were staring at me. Sarah wept about the unlatched gate. She told Bob she would feed me. I would hear the familiar sounds of the cart and go into the yard.

Indeed, I would. An excellent idea! Bob and Obert worried I might attack her as she crossed the yard. They readied their long sticks in case they had to shoot me. Shoot me! What is wrong with these creatures? Why would I attack the person who is going to feed me? It was the second time I worried about joining Uncle Sid in lion heaven.

I had to get down the hill. I suspected it would be harder than climbing. Flustered, and not thinking properly, I started down with my front paws, first one, then two steps. I was off balance but kept moving my front paws. That decision was faulty. My back feet remained on the stoep. Fearful of stumbling, I refused to move them. Bob and Obert were staring at me with such intensity it made me nervous. When I reached the sixth step, I lost my balance and skidded down the rest of the hill on my forepaws and belly. I landed on the lawn, front legs, and chin on the grass with my back legs stretched out behind me. That dratted Obert laughed and laughed. Mortified, it occurred to me that I looked exactly like Bob. I struggled to my feet. Head and tail dragging, I slunk across the yard into my area. Obert hurried behind me and shut the gate.

Shaken and upset, I decided to refuse breakfast, but upon reflection, thought it would do me no good to miss a nourishing meal. I took my food to the olive trees and sulked until dinnertime.

Chapter 30

Sarah leaned on the fence and observed her hairy friend. "Rollo, you've been here for three years. We just had our third Christmas braai together. I'm convinced you'll never re-capture your prey drive. Malcolm is still optimistic, but not me. When Bob fell over you, we couldn't imagine why you were on the stoep. I decided you were lonely. Arabella was gone, and you wanted to join us in the house. Bob doesn't agree with me. Today, I'll conduct an experiment that proves my theory."

She picked up a small bag and walked through the gate. With a snort of surprise, Rollo sat up and watched her approach. The hens, predictably, left. Sarah rummaged in the bag and took out a grooming mitt.

"Look, Rollo, this is for horses, but it'll work on you. Let's try it."

The mitt was designed to slip onto a person's hand. It had small rubberized raised areas over the surface. Made to remove oil and dirt from the coat, it also gave a pleasant massage. Sarah slipped it on and groomed Rollo's side. The animal produced his signature sound. After a few moments, he toppled over.

Delighted, Sarah laughed and continued grooming. "I knew you'd love it. Now if you could just roll over, I'll do your stomach."

Rollo complied, he balanced on his back, both forelegs flipped up and down, and his rear paws beat a soft tattoo on the ground. When his stomach was properly groomed, he flopped to his other side and allowed Sarah to finish the job.

"Excellent, I know you're lonely. You need special attention. Now, look at this." She pulled an equine mane and tail comb from her satchel, along with a detangling product. "These two items will be perfect for your mane. It's full of snarls and dead hair. I'll start with a small chunk. Let's see if you'll tolerate it."

Sarah spritzed detangler on Rollo's mane and went to work . Groans of pleasure erupted from the animal. He sat up and let Sarah spray and comb, until his entire mane was snarl-free and fluffy. He shook his head, and a cloud of hair billowed round his face. Sarah glanced at her watch, "I must go, Bob and Obert will soon return from the bovine reproductive seminar. Don't worry, my friend, I'll visit often. You look splendid!" She picked up the pile of hair and tossed it in the bushes. "I can't let Bob see this, he'll think it's a dead animal." She laughed and went to the house.

Bob entered the kitchen in time for dinner. Sarah was tending several pots on the stove and asked if he could feed the hens and Rollo.

"Sure," I'll do it now before I get settled. I've so much new information about pregnant cows. I know you'll be breathless with excitement."

Sarah waved a dismissive hand and kept stirring. "Can't wait to hear, dinner will be in ten minutes."

Bob wandered back into the house, a puzzled look on his face. "Rollo looks different. He looks like he stuck his paw in an electrical outlet. Why does he look like that?"

Sarah, careful to keep her back to Bob, answered. "Ah… perhaps it's the static electricity in the air. Can't that make one's hair frizzy?"

"Static electricity, what're you talking about? I never heard of that."

"Grab some plates, dinner's ready. Forget Rollo's hair, tell me about the pregnant cows."

Sarah spent time with the lion whenever she was alone. She walked patrol with the group. The hens accepted her and settled under her gentle hands. As they strolled the large paddock, she held Rollo's mane and chattered to the animals. She talked about Arabella, the weather, her neighbors, Samantha, and every odd bit of information that she could recall.

✱ Rollo ✱
Chapter 31

A week after the debacle on the stairs, I saw Bob and Obert leave early. I heard them talking about cows. Later that day, Sarah crossed the yard with a little satchel over her shoulder. Happy to see her, I hoped she would have the clever back scratcher. A brisk scratch through the fence was always welcome. To my horror, she barged through the gate and approached me. I sat up and wondered if I should run away, but she was my favorite person. I didn't want to hurt her feelings. She sat down beside me and nattered on about how she knew I was lonely. I came to the stoep to enter her den. Is she daft? No creature in their right mind would walk into a strange den. Lonely? I'm not lonely, the hens and I are back to our simple routines. I'll admit Arabella's leaving was a disruption, but she needed to be with her pride.

Sarah removed implements from the satchel and explained they were for horses, for use on their bodies, manes, and tails. Manes and tails? Horses? What are horses? Could they be distant relatives of lions? Few creatures have manes like us, and the thought of them intrigued me. Anyway, Sarah slipped a device on her hand and said it was used to clean their coats and give a massage. She rubbed it along my spine. It felt wonderful. I made a spectacle of myself. Collapsed on my side, then on my back, with all four paws in the air, I moaned with pleasure. My tongue hung out of my mouth. Sarah explained about the tools for my mane. She used a comb and equine detangler. First, she sprayed a small tuft, then gently combed through the hair. Unsure I would tolerate it, she started with tiny sections. I sat up. She went to work in earnest and soon my entire mane was fluffy and tangle-free. I shook my head, my mane flew about my face in a soft cloud. Wonderful, it felt wonderful! To Sarah's delight, I did several more head shakes. She hid the loose hair, in the brush and returned to the house. She promised to return. Bob fed me that evening. Pleased with my resplendent hair; I shook my head several times. He stared at me before walking to the house, a puzzled expression on his face.

And so it began with Sarah. She would visit when everyone else was away from the ranch. Before long she accompanied us on patrol. She would take a handful of my mane and pace along beside us. Over time, the fussy old hens trusted her. She could stroke their backs. I was impressed because those crabby old biddies don't like humans. Even Ebony, settled under her hands. We walked patrol, and Sarah chattered to us. I welcomed the visits. Perhaps I was lonely.

Chapter 32

One late summer day, Felicity drove into the Aimtree yard, towing a horse trailer. She greeted Sarah. The two were going for a ride on the river path. Sarah put her saddle down and called to her friend, "Okay, Filly, let's see these two new horses, I can tell you want to show them off."

Filly laughed. "Too right about that. Let me back them out."

Two horses came down the ramp and Sarah's jaw dropped. "Filly, what breed are they? They're gorgeous."

"They're Andalusians, both ten-year-old geldings. You can see, one is buckskin, Caramelo, and the other is palomino, Oro. Aren't they aptly named?"

"How on earth did you get them? Were they expensive?"

Filly went round the trailer and got her gear. "They can be pricey, but I'll tell you the quick version. Which one do you want to ride?"

"I want to ride Oro. Look at his mane! I've never seen such long, lush manes and tails."

"Oro it is. Here's his bridle. Let's saddle them and head for the river."

A booming sound rose from the fence. Rollo was peering at the two newcomers with such intensity it startled Sarah. Mesmerized by the horses, the lion had his head pressed against the wire.

Felicity smiled and said, "Maybe he thinks they're beautiful, just as we do. He's laser-focused on them."

"He is. He doesn't get that excited unless a hyena is in the area."

Caramelo arched his neck and took a few steps toward the fence. Oro followed him. The two women took firmer grips on the lead ropes.

Sarah said, "Filly, I don't think we should let them approach Rollo."

"I agree, why is he so excited about my horses?"

"I don't know what's prompting his interest. You're right, he appears to be mesmerized by them."

The horses arched their necks and whickered at the lion. He purred his response.

Sarah said, I suggest the river path for our ride. We'll have to cross the main road, but there's little traffic. Bob and I have hiked it and it's beautiful. We've seen evidence of several animals along the route."

"You mean there's poop everywhere? From different creatures?"

"Well, yes, poop and damaged trees. Elephants push over trees to reach the branches they can't reach. They use the river for a highway. At night, when the wind is blowing toward us, we occasionally hear them, and hyenas."

Astride and heading toward the river trail, Sarah turned and said, "Okay, my friend, tell me about these two. I can tell they are properly trained. Oro is on the bit and waiting for instructions."

Felicity laughed. "Oh yes, they are both upper-level dressage horses. Two months ago, we leased a Connemara pony for Sam. She wants to learn to jump. These two geldings were also available for lease. The owner thought he could sell them for a good price. He discovered they are both too flashy for the dressage ring. One prospective buyer told him they had the ability to compete at the highest level, but their color would handicap them. Brandon and I fell in love with them, and we offered to lease the three. The owner jumped at our offer. He gave us a generous deal."

Sarah asked, "Does Samantha take lessons at the facility? Is she like all kids? Mad to jump."

Felicity laughed. "Indeed, she is, we told her she must learn to ride first. She and Boswell, her pony, will join us for our next ride. Sam's still getting used to him. Brandon and I take lessons as well. We're decent riders but want to learn more about dressage."

The two women rode onto the path that paralleled the river. Recent rains had produced lush foliage. The river was full of clear, fast-moving water. Felicity pointed to a huge brown pile of elephant poop. "Lordy, that's impressive! How do sanctuary people manage to keep their yards tidy?"

"Erm, with very large shovels? Obert knows the man who heads our local sanctuary. They're sainted beings for working with orphans. According to Obert, many babies die because of injury and PTSD."

"Few people could do that job. I wouldn't last long, especially if I lost an orphan."

"Too right, we're ranchers and see all sorts of ugly stuff, but watching a baby elephant die would be horrible."

The pair meandered along the lush path, turned around, and headed home. When they reached the Aimtree yard, Rollo was waiting at the fence. His posture indicated he was agitated. Jamming his head against the wire, he burbled a greeting. Caramello and Oro answered with nickers.

Sarah helped groom the geldings. "When can we do this again? I can't wait to meet Sam's pony."

"That little equine is a serious creature. He's so careful with

Sam. They're already hopping over cross poles, but I want them to trail ride as well. Would next week suit you?"

"Perfect! This glorious weather may not last much longer. We may as well take advantage of it."

Felicity loaded her beauties in the trailer and waved goodbye. Sarah walked to the fence and rubbed the side of Rollo's face.

"What's the matter with you? Surely, you don't think those two are hyenas. Why are you so agitated? Rollo, they're horses."

The following week found Sarah sitting on the stoep, her saddle next to her. She heard a vehicle turn into the driveway and correctly guessed that Filly and crew were approaching. The truck had barely stopped when Samantha flew out, raced to Sarah, and hugged her.

"Aunt Sarah, "How are you? How is Rollo? And Uncle Bob?"

"Sam, we're all splendid. And you? I understand you have an incredible mount. Is he in the trailer?"

Sam's face glowed with pride. "Aunt Sarah, Boswell is the best. Wait till you see him. He's teaching me to jump."

"Spoken like a true horsewoman, giving all the credit to the horse."

"Before we unload the horses, can I say hello to Rollo? He's at the fence. Why is he looking at the trailer?"

Sarah shook her head. "I don't know. He's very interested in your mounts. And yes, you can greet him."

Samantha stood a respectful distance from the fence. "Hello Rollo, how are you today? I'm still so sorry for tugging on your whiskers. Please forgive me. I didn't know how dangerous it was to go into your home."

Sarah put her hand on Sam's shoulder. "Sam, you're so grown

up. And so tall. I'm sure our boy doesn't hold grudges. Unlike some of us, he's patient and forgiving. I'm proud of you. Now let's see this wonderful Boswell."

Felicity unloaded the horses and tied them to the trailer. She handed her daughter and Sarah grooming brushes.

Sarah patted Boswell. "Look at this little character. He's beautiful, and just the right size for you. I love his snowy white color. Sam, Can you manage tacking him up?"

Filly said, "I need to help a bit with the cinch, but Sam does everything else."

The three were soon mounted and heading for the river path. Boswell shook his head, snorted, and fell in with his two larger mates.

Sarah said, "Sam, he's lovely and so well trained. Is he ever naughty? Some ponies are mischievous."

Sam shook her head. "Nope, he's always obedient and friendly. I'll be sad when I outgrow him, but I know that will happen. He'll help someone else and I'll get a larger horse."

Filly nodded her agreement. "Well said, Sam, but we needn't worry about it for a few months. Just learn from him and enjoy the experience."

Halfway through their ride, a loud crash ahead prompted the three to stop and look toward the water. Another crash, closer this time. On the riverbank, an elephant strolled into view, carrying a huge tree branch. The animal stopped, eyed the strangers, and turned away. The branch caught on limbs and produced more noise.

Wide-eyed, Sam gasped, "Mummy, Aunt Sarah, are we safe?"

Sarah answered, "Erm, that's a good question, Let's turn around and head for the barn."

Filly said, "Excellent idea. Sam is Boswell, okay? Caramelo is on alert but still calm. Sarah, how is Oro reacting to our enormous trail mate?"

"The same as your horse, he's alert, but he's not gathering himself to run."

The group turned and left the ellie. At the house, the three talked about their encounter. Sam was over the moon at the elephant sighting. Rollo was at the fence, staring at the horses.

Filly said, "Why is he so excited? I don't think he's moved a paw since we left,

"I've no idea why he's acting like this."

After Sam and Felicity left, Sarah spoke to Rollo. "I swear you know more than any of us realize. I wish you could talk. Well, never mind the horses, shall we have a grooming session before patrol?"

✷ Rollo ✷
Chapter 33

Summer drifted towards fall. One day a truck came into our yard, towing a strange-looking conveyance. Sarah came out of her den carrying an odd flat device with dangling straps. Felicity stepped out of the truck and greeted her. Sarah asked about the horses and said she couldn't wait to see them. Horses? I went on high alert, a chance to see horses. Two long-limbed animals backed carefully down a ramp after Felicity opened the rear door.

They had manes and tails that put mine to shame. Their manes flowed to their shoulders and down their long faces. And tails! Unlike me, the tails started at their rump and almost reached the ground. The horses had tawny coats. Like me! One was golden brown with a black mane and tail. The other was a lighter, golden shade with a white mane and tail. Both beautiful, they had the same proud, regal bearing as lions. The darker one tossed its head and attempted to approach me. Felicity and Sarah laughed and tied them to the trailer. Both horses appeared to recognize me. They called in odd voices and stared at me. Could these creatures be distant kin?

With great interest, I watched the women use the same tools Sarah used on my coat. Once that was done, Sarah and Felicity put the flat objects on the horses' backs and secured them with tight straps. Bah! No self-respecting lion would allow that. Those straps looked uncomfortable, although the horses didn't seem to mind. They stood quietly while the women placed a metal bar in their mouths and fastened more straps round their faces. How could they be so patient? Then, to my amazement, the two women climbed onto the animals and they set off down the driveway.

The horses walked at a brisk pace. A lion would not allow that. Still, I carry the hens, could that mean a small similarity exists between horses and lions? I waited for their return. Their feet clattering on the driveway announced them. Their feet! I hadn't noticed their feet. The poor creatures had round, hard objects on the bottom of long skinny legs. They looked more unstable than chicken feet. Even humans with their strange feet were better off than the horses. Arabella has a foot that's in two parts. It splays a bit to give her balance. It was a better design than the hard knobs the horses used for feet. Now, we lions have paws that flex and grip the ground when we walk or run, not that I do much running. Our paws help us balance when we travel. How could horses with their long legs and large bodies stay upright? But they carried themselves very well. They were graceful and balanced when they walked. I wondered if they could go faster. Surely, they would trip and fall if they attempted to run.

I pondered the similarities and differences between lions and horses, but Felicity's next visit put an end to my problem. I hurried to the fence for additional observation. To my surprise, Samantha hopped out of the truck and approached me. I hadn't seen her in months and was amazed at how she had grown. Well, cubs are like that. They sprout up like weeds. Anyway, she stood a respectful distance from my fence and apologized for tugging on my whiskers. So grown up! So mature! She told me she loved me. Sarah was proud of her. As was I. Sarah knew about Sam's horse. His name was Boswell. Sam would ride today with her mum and Sarah.

Felicity backed the Oro and Caramelo down the ramp, then reentered the trailer. A small white horse stepped to the ground. Is this Boswell? He was half the size of the other two, with a fuzzy, short mane. A cub, I thought, this is a cub, he was small. Perhaps because Sam was young, this beast was also young. After a few moments of observation, I realized Boswell wasn't a cub. His no-nonsense air assured me he was an adult and the perfect size for Samantha. She needed a bit of help from her mum fastening the straps but did everything else herself. Boswell allowed her to put that odd piece of metal in his mouth. She climbed on that small creature and followed the two women. That tiny horse impressed me. He tossed his head and maintained a brisk pace to keep up with his larger relatives.

Now, there are white lions but no matter their color, half-size adult lions don't exist. The size difference put paid to my theory of being related to these creatures. So, these interesting animals can't be related to us, the differences outweigh the similarities.

Upon their return, Samantha groomed Boswell and came to the fence to tell me goodbye. She apologized again and told me about an elephant they had seen on the river path. Elephants! My mum always told us to avoid them. Even the cubs are enormous. I admit, I was curious about the beasts. Little did I know. my education about elephants would soon begin.

Chapter 34

Six months later, Sarah crossed the yard one morning to find Obert staring at Rollo. Hands in his pockets, he stepped closer to the fence and sniffed.

"Am I daft? Or does he smell like perfume?"

Sarah laughed. "Obert, don't be silly. I smell nothing. There's something wrong with your sniffer." God help me, she thought, that new detangler was scented.

"I saw Malcolm in town this morning. He'll be calling you shortly, poachers slaughtered a dozen elephants, there are too many orphans for the sanctuary and Malcolm knows you have an empty field near Rollo. That's all I know; he can fill you in. I'm so upset I can't even talk about this. There are stricken babies that have lost their mums and herd."

"We'll assist in any way we can. We know nothing about orphan ellies, but we'll do whatever we can to help. I'm going to tell Bob."

"A BABY ELEPHANT! We've never had an elephant. When is it arriving?"

Sarah rolled her eyes. "Bob, you sound like an eight-year-old child that has just been told he's getting a puppy. We have to wait for Malcolm and the sanctuary to contact us."

The morning after hearing Obert's appalling news, Bob and Sarah were dawdling over a second breakfast coffee. Sarah's phone chirped, and after a brief conversation, she pocketed the device and turned to Bob."

"Malcolm wants to inspect our empty field with Peter Otieno, he heads the sanctuary. They'll be here within an hour. Malcolm knows Peter has questions best answered by us."

Bob smiled. "I imagine they're about Rollo."

"Oh yes, Peter isn't thrilled about having our boy next to one of his babies. He also wants to see the shed and paddock. Speaking of the shed, we've been calling it an equipment shed for years, but it's a graveyard for useless junk."

"There's a tractor in the building."

"I know, but we've been tossing stuff in there for several years. We need to empty it.

"Okay with me, We've talked about a clear-out for years. Lord knows what's in there."

Sarah rose to her feet. "Should we call Michael and Obert? Both need to be here to get information from Peter. They'll be involved in caring for this orphan."

"Good idea, why don't you go to the shed, I'll join you after I speak to them."

Sarah pulled open the double doors and stared with dismay at the contents of the building. She pulled on a pair of gloves and stepped inside. A long row of tarped objects stood at one side of the building. She gave one corner of the tarp a brisk tug and was surprised to find bales of shavings and straw stacked against the wall.

Bob stepped into the shed and muttered. "Oh boy, what a mess. What is all this stuff? I don't even recognize it."

"Nor do I but look, I just uncovered all this bedding. It will be handy if we get this orphan. Did you find Obert and Michael?"

"I did, they'll be here shortly. Who put all this bedding in here?"

"I don't know. Let's hope it's suitable for a baby ellie."

Michael and Obert appeared in the doorway.

"Glory!" Obert said, "Is this all junk? What a fine mess it is."

Sarah stepped forward and prodded an unidentifiable object with her foot. "Yep, a mess, but I've got an idea. Among the four of us, we have three trucks. We can load all this trash and haul it away. It'll only take a few hours. With or without this orphan, it's high time to empty this building."

Michael said, "Great idea! Let's start after we talk to Peter and Malcolm."

"Isn't there a tractor in here?" asked Obert.

Bob replied, "Yep, the only genuine piece of equipment in the so-called equipment shed."

Obert thought for a moment. "I could put it in my lean-to at home. I've a few chores that require a tractor to complete. If you don't mind, I'll take it home, I can always bring it back if you need it."

"Excellent," Bob replied. "One less thing to worry about."

Obert turned to Sarah. "I want to say I've known Peter Otieno my entire life. He's worked with elephants for over twenty years. Don't be insulted if he's abrasive. He'll say what's on his mind, with no regard to how people respond to it."

"Okay, got it," replied Sarah, "I'll fault nobody who puts animals first. Bob and I have thick hides, but thanks for the warning."

Car doors slamming announced Malcolm and Peter Otieno. Sarah glanced out the shed doors and saw Malcolm halfway across the driveway. She also saw a tall African man unfold himself from the sanctuary van, and, radiating tension, stride into the field. Malcolm had barely made introductions when Peter began to speak.

"I know you keep a big cat here. I've heard the stories, the child that tugged his whiskers, the chickens, and the calf, are all tales that circulated through our community. I'm not calling you liars, but these stories get embellished as they travel from person to person. I can't bring myself to believe any of them. Where is this monster?"

Sarah drew a breath and replied. "He lives in the adjacent paddock."

"I don't like that, he shares a common fence with my fragile orphan. I don't like that at all." Peter took a few steps toward the fence. "He could paw my baby through these wire squares. He could injure my ellie. Where is he?"

Bob glanced at his watch. "They're on patrol and should be back shortly."

Peter scowled. "What're you talking about? Patrol for what?"

Sarah said, "Rollo and the hens walk the perimeter of his yard twice a day. We think Rollo is looking for hyenas."

Peter stared at her in disbelief. "Hyena patrol? How can you imagine such a thing? This is what I mean about stories."

The objects of this discussion appeared. Rollo padded the length of the den and peered at the newcomer. Ebony, Pearl, and Pearl regarded Peter impassively.

"By the Gods! He's enormous. Look at the size of him." Peter peered round Rollo's fluffy mane and saw the hens. "Those birds must have a death wish. Do they always ride on him?"

Sarah said, "Well, they go on patrol with him and sleep on his back. Isn't that clever? They couldn't be safer."

Peter took a few tentative steps closer to Rollo. The hens fluttered off his back and began to peck and scratch near his feet,

Rollo sat down and shook his head.

"Am I daft? Or does he smell like lavender? Why is his mane odd-looking? It looks like he's stepped out of a hair salon."

Wisely, Sarah did not respond, she gazed at the top of her shoes. Malcolm gave her a speculative look but also remained silent. Rollo greeted Peter in his usual fashion.

Startled, Peter leaped back and cried. "By the gods! He's growling at me. No, no, no, this won't work. I can't have my orphan next to this animal."

Sarah stepped forward and placed her hand on Peter's forearm. "Peter, look at him. Listen to him. We know this is a unique situation but give our boy a chance."

Peter frowned but took a few steps toward Rollo. "I see he has a calm demeanor. That sound he's making reminds me of elephants rumbling. They don't just trumpet, they have several ways to communicate, some are sub-sonic. They have a social and communications network that would likely rival ours. I've worked with elephants all my adult life, and every year I know less, not more, about them. Enough about the lion. Show me the shed and the rest of this paddock."

Bob pointed to the shed and spoke. "Peter, this shed is full of junk. We're going to bring our trucks and take this debris to a proper burial place for useless objects. We found bedding that I believe will work for your baby should you choose to bring him."

Peter stepped into the shed. "The bedding is fine; we use the same thing. The double doors are excellent. If the orphan needs to be isolated, the top doors can remain open for light and ventilation. The space is more than adequate for one animal. This shed is well maintained, it has a good roof. Let's see the size of the paddock and check what foliage grows here. If the plants are too foreign to the ellies, they won't eat them. We're only twenty minutes away, so I hope your plants are like ours." Peter walked outside and examined some of the grasses and bushes. "Excellent, the grass is the same and lush from winter rains. This field has been empty, I can tell by the plant growth."

Sarah said, "Yes, it's been unoccupied for several years. I'm glad it contains suitable forage."

"Yes, this baby is old enough to nibble grass, but his appetite is poor. That brings me to another point. He arrived ten days ago, more stressed than the other orphans. Two days ago he broke with diarrhea and is now dehydrated. If he shuts down much more, I doubt he'll survive. This may be a sad, unpleasant experience for you. Malcolm has prepared medication that goes into red-stickered formula bottles, but our baby won't take one-quarter of a bottle and he needs one full medicated bottle every twelve hours. He's not interested in his regular formula either. I don't think he'll survive. We don't have room or help to care for him properly. Elephants are social creatures. We have animals that help us by bonding with an orphan that needs to be isolated. We have dogs, goats, and sheep that we use. All our animal carers are busy, save one. Agnes, a sheep, will accompany him and stay with him until reintegration if he survives."

Sarah asked, "Does he have a name?"

"Oh yes, one of our caregivers named him Tumaini. It's a Kenyan word for hope. The carer thought he needed an inspirational name, and I agree with her."

Bob asked, "Peter, since we have the space, could you bring two babies? Could your carers come here?"

"I've considered that. One orphan is about the same age as Tumaini, but Freddie is more resilient. He's eating well and is already bonding with his fellow orphans. I don't want to move him. Better to lose one than two. I know that sounds cruel, but that's the reality of the situation."

"Freddie?" Obert asked, "How did he get the name Freddie?"

For the first time, Peter smiled. "We have two American sisters that are volunteering. They both say he reminds them of one of their uncles."

Obert sputtered. "They have an uncle that looks like an elephant?"

Peter waved a hand. "They're Americans and a bit daft. I can't imagine what this uncle resembles, maybe he has a huge nose. Anyway, the name stuck. The sisters have volunteered to come here. Am I correct in thinking you four can help initially until we see if Tumaini will survive?"

"Absolutely," Sarah said," we'll need instruction. The Americans can eat with us. We have a spare bedroom with an attached bathroom. They're welcome to that."

"Splendid, transporting them to and from the sanctuary would be difficult."

Michael wondered aloud. "How did you find them? Did they sign up?"

Peter shook his head and managed another smile. "They came on a tour bus the day these babies were arriving. Unbeknownst to me, they told the bus driver to arrange for their luggage and gear to be brought to the sanctuary. They told me they knew nothing about elephants but could shovel poop. I was too busy to argue with them, so I gave them two of our green coats and shovels. I remember thinking they wouldn't last an hour. Six hours later they found me again, announced they were staying and what else could they do to help. I threw a fit and said we had no place for them to sleep. They laughed and said they would sleep on the floor. I set them up with two cots in the office, arranged for them to take meals with us, and showed them the showers."

Obert grinned. "They sound like quite a pair. Did they continue to be useful?

"By the Gods! The second evening they were watching formula being made, the next day they were helping, the third day they were preparing it and helping feed the little ones, plus poop detail. They amazed me! Last week, I asked when they were returning home. Etta said they had put their husbands off until the end of the month. I have them for three more weeks. Aretha added that by then, the husbands would be tired of cooking for themselves. They have fallen in love with Tumaini and want to care for him until they leave."

Obert's brow wrinkled. "Etta? Aretha? Didn't two famous American singers have those first names?'

"Yes, yes, the sisters will tell you how they got their names. Trust me, you won't even have to ask."

More wrinkles appeared on Obert's brow. "Weren't those singers women of color? Are your helpers women of color?"

"No, no, they're two middle-aged white ladies with blue eyes and gray hair. Now, there's one last thing. That tractor, does it have a front loader?"

Bob answered. "Yes, it does. What do we need to do?"

Peter walked to a spot between the fence and the shed. "You need to build an earth ramp about a meter high, with a gentle slope. The truck bed is too high for the orphan to exit the vehicle. Agnes will travel with him and she knows what to do. When we open the door, she'll walk down the ramp. The sisters and I will help Tumaini if he balks. We'll coax him to the ground. He's so weak, I doubt he'll put up a fuss. Make sure you don't dig a big hole for my baby to fall into, take dirt from different spots,"

Obert said, "Consider it done, I'll start on it this afternoon."

Sarah stepped forward. "Peter, let me call you the moment we clear out the shed. We can finish the haul away and ramp in two days. Will that suit you?"

"That sounds fine, call me when you are ready. I want Malcolm here, can you alert him as well?"

Sarah nodded. "Of course, I'll be on the phone when we're ready. One last thing, we have a well-equipped outside kitchen."

Peter, already on the way to his van, called over his shoulder. "Excellent, I'll look at it when we bring Tumaini."

Peter and Malcolm left. Obert eyed the tractor and said, "Let's make sure that tractor starts, I can begin on the ramp now."

Bob and Sarah said their goodbyes and headed for the house; Sarah turned to her husband. "We best get a good night's sleep. We need to be full of energy tomorrow. I hope everything goes smoothly. I like the idea about a dirt ramp, it's a sensible way for animals to enter and exit trucks."

Bob smiled. "I'm looking forward to our new adventure."

✸ Rollo ✸
Chapter 35

Several months later, I awoke to the sound of Obert's truck in the yard. Curious about such an early visit, I greeted him at the fence. He, like Bob, Sarah, and Michael, carry the scratcher devices and I hoped he would give me a brisk massage, perhaps along my spine. He gives me a satisfying scratch, but never when another human is present. Today was no exception, Obert looked round the yard before massaging the base of my tail. Another of my favorite spots! Why are these silly creatures so secretive? They used them on Arabella and didn't care if others were present. It's a mystery. Anyway, I was having a delightful massage when the screen door slammed and Sarah come down the stairs. Obert hastily stowed the device in his pocket.

Obert was upset. He went to the bench, sat down, got up, sat down, and returned to the fence. He greeted Sarah with a wave. She gave me breakfast, and I settled in my den to eavesdrop. Nosey me, I wanted to know why he was agitated. He told an appalling story. Two weeks ago, poachers had slaughtered ten elephants. Several animals were mums with babies. Those babies are orphans. The sanctuary was overwhelmed. One orphan was very ill and needed more care than the sanctuary could provide. Worried about his patient, Malcolm wished to move the cub to our ranch. Obert explained that the head of the sanctuary wanted to meet Sarah, Bob, and me and inspect our property.

I've always wanted to learn more about the huge animals. This might be my chance. Perhaps I could help and be a source of comfort. I'm experienced with youngsters. I tolerated the crazy pullets. I saved Arabella's life and put up with her drooling and silly antics. Never mind that scamp, Samantha. How difficult could it be to care for a young elephant? Bah! I couldn't have been more naïve or ignorant. I know little about these gigantic animals because my mum always avoided them. Hearing about them triggered a memory. When I was a half-grown cub, the pride came upon two dead elephants. Their tusks were gone, and only two bloody holes remained in their faces. Three pride members had cubs old enough to accompany adults, but still vulnerable. Hyenas were feasting on the carcasses. Our pride was a modest one, there were seven adults plus the cubs. We were out-numbered by the carrion eaters. Hyenas and lions hate each other. The hyenas saw a chance to kill lion cubs, and they attacked us. Our mums protected us, but that meant they couldn't fight. My dad killed several, and the barren lionesses helped drive off the rest of the pack. I was terrified. My dad was wounded but survived. Several lionesses limped and bled from slashing wounds for weeks. Make no mistake about hyenas, they're ugly, foul-smelling creatures, but they're intelligent and fierce hunters. They can bite with astounding strength, their poop is white because they chew bones to powder. I hate them! Anyway, I was eager to meet the baby elephant. I was impatient to learn more about this creature.

    The next morning Malcolm arrived, along with the sanctuary fellow. We went to the fence to greet him after returning from patrol. Wishing to make a good first impression, I gave him my loudest, friendliest greeting. So much for being friendly, he shouted about my unsuitability. He called me a monster. I'm sure our neighbors heard him ranting. Sarah interceded on my behalf, but Peter…that's his name … was having none of it. Convinced I would harm the cub, he wanted no part of me or our farm. I smelled fear and anger on him. I saw he was worried about this orphan and respected him for his concern. Sarah pointed out my calm demeanor and past history with cubs. He would soon see I would be helpful.

After much discussion, Peter agreed to bring his orphan to our home after the shed was empty. I couldn't understand the need for a dirt ramp. Sometimes, the humans surprise me. It was a clever idea. The ellie and his companion…more about her later…needed it to reach the ground. Peter was unsure of me but, on reflection, I admit he was correct in not trusting me. I was a stranger, and he was fiercely protective of his ellie. Finally, we were ready. The baby would arrive tomorrow. He would live in the paddock next to mine. I worried hyenas would return and attack the orphan. How could I protect him? Bah! Little did I know that wouldn't be an issue.

Chapter 36

Four mornings later, Sarah sat on Rollo's bench. She called Peter and Malcolm, to tell them all was ready for Tumaini. They set the arrival time for noon. Peter wanted several daylight hours to observe the orphan in his new home. The large truck turned into the driveway. Peter drove into the paddock, jumped out to check the ramp, returned to the truck, and backed to the top of the dirt mound. Two robust women exited the cab and hurried to the back door of the vehicle. Both carried bottles of formula slung across their chests like bandoliers. Peter opened the door and Agnes appeared at the top of the ramp. She strutted down like a wooly brigadier general. At the bottom, she turned and waited for Tumaini. Weak bleats drifted from the truck as the three people offered words of encouragement. Tumaini saw Agnes, and, on unsteady legs, tottered to join her. Malcolm entered the paddock in time to see the orphan lift his tail and eject a stream of diarrhea.

"Oh no, that's not good, he needs to take the medicine. Dehydration in an animal his age can be fatal."

Etta slipped a red-stickered bottle out of her pack and offered it to the youngster. After two swigs, he turned his head away. He stood in the grass, a picture of misery and depression. Rollo, back from patrol, leaned against the fence and rumbled a greeting. Tumaini lifted his head, flared his ears, and made a determined march to the fence. The caregivers couldn't stop him. The baby poked his trunk through the fence and examined Rollo's face with his prehensile trunk tip. He stepped to the lion's mid-section, worked his trunk through the wire squares, and draped it against Roll's side. Etta offered the bottle a second time. Tumaini drank until the bottle was empty, then, tired from the truck ride, closed his eyes and dozed.

"Glory!" Obert said. It looks like he's using a stethoscope to listen to Rollo's heartbeat."

Peter attempted to move Tumaini away from the lion, but the orphan wouldn't budge. With his trunk wrapped around Rollo, the baby ignored repeated attempts to get him into the shed.

Sarah asked, "Peter, doesn't this little one hear elephant rumbles every day? He must know what they sound like. Why is he locked on Rollo's purring?"

"Dear lady! I'm wondering about that myself. He hears the real thing every day. I can't imagine why he's intrigued by your lion."

Aretha smiled and said, "Maybe it's not just the sound. Maybe Tumaini sees something in Rollo that we can't."

Bob said, "That's how it was with Arabella. She walked away from us to be with Rollo. We still don't understand it, but she thrived under his care."

Sarah asked Peter, "May I make a suggestion? Let's move Rollo down a few paces. He'll follow me and we can see Tumaini's reaction."

Etta asked her sister, "Do you think our boy will have a little fit?"

Aretha snorted. "Little fit? Hot toe mighty! He is going to pitch a wang-dang-doozy of a fit."

Obert muttered to his brother. "Wang what? Hot what? Wang, ding dong? What's she talking about?"

Michael shrugged. "Must be an American expression. You heard Peter, these folks are odd."

Obert walked away, mumbling to himself. Sarah went to the

gate and called Rollo. The lion ambled toward her. Tumaini did pitch a wang-dang doozy of a fit. He lost contact with Rollo and screamed. Pathetic sounds of terror and desperation rose from him. Etta and Aretha moved forward with words and soft pats. They guided the baby to Rollo. His trunk touched the lion, and he settled.

Peter paced in circles and tugged his springy hair. "By the Gods! What do we do now? No one goes in with the lion. Isn't that correct? Mal, isn't that one of your edicts?"

"Yes, no one goes in with him. It's too dangerous, should he decide he's a lion. All the episodes we tried to activate his prey drive failed. Never mind Samantha sneaking into his enclosure. Still, he's a huge, apex predator and he showed that wildness when the hyenas tried to attack Arabella."

Peter grimaced. "I agree with him on that point. I know those ugly brutes are Africa's garbage collectors. They serve a purpose by eating carrion. I still don't like them."

Sarah squared her shoulders, blew out a breath, and stepped forward. "Since Bob fell over him, I've been going into his paddock. I thought he was lonely and wanted to be near us. Malcolm, I know you're mad, but I felt sorry for him. I've been using horse grooming tools, and, yes, you're all correct. He smells like lavender because I mistakenly bought a scented equine de-tangler. I brush him and comb out his mane, that's why he looks like he stepped out of a salon. Peter, I can be a caregiver. Rollo is used to me."

"By the Gods! Dear lady, you can't be serious? It takes a village to raise an orphaned elephant. It's all well and good that Tumaini is bonding with your lion, but he and Agnes can't feed him. This baby needs around-the-clock care. We must offer him formula at least every three hours. We don't know what the lion will do if people invade his space."

Bob said, "I'll volunteer and I'm sure Michael and Obert will also help. Rollo has known them as long as he has known Sarah and me."

Michael answered for himself and Obert, "We're in, will four people be enough?"

Peter shook his head. "It will if you're willing to put this ranch and your lives on hold. You'll either be sleeping or with Tumaini."

Aretha said, "We'll go in there. We can shadow Sarah and can take turns being carers. Peter said we can stay here, so it'll be easy. We can do the night shift, make formula, and shovel poop. We're excellent at the latter task."

"Absolutely not! It's too risky. What do I tell your husbands if you get mauled by a lion?"

Aretha hooted. "They'll be upset the cooks are gone."

Peter paced in circles and tugged his hair. "Six people are the bare minimum! I can't believe I'm even entertaining this idea." He paced a few more laps, threw his hands in the air, looked heavenward, and shouted. "Lord! Please! Give me a sign."

Tumaini lifted his tail and broke impressive wind.

Sarah seized Bob's forearm and hissed. "Don't you dare make one of your smarty remarks."

"Nope, not me, not one word will pass my lips. Unlike Tumaini, my lips are sealed."

The rest of the group kept a deafening silence. Peter stared at the elephant. "What if the lion attacks when we open the gate? Lions are territorial. Malcolm, should you ready a tranquilizer dart? In case we need to subdue the beast."

"Peter, you know damn well the darts don't work that fast. Let me say this. Two years ago, I'd have agreed with you. We tried to get Rollo to attack other creatures, and except for hyenas, he's never shown aggression. Do I think this is a good idea? I do not. What other choice do you have? You said Tumaini is likely to die. You're overwhelmed at the sanctuary. One good thing, he just drank an entire bottle of medicated formula, something he refused to do at the orphanage."

Peter paced a few more laps, looked heavenward, and implored. "Lord! What should I do? Give me a sign!"

Tumaini opened his mouth and produced an elephant-sized burp.

Obert stepped forward and grabbed Peter's shoulder. "Don't ask the Lord for more guidance. He's already sent two messages. Ask again and this ellie will grow his ears bigger and fly round the shed like a cartoon character. The earth will shake and pieces of the sky will fall on our heads. Don't ask again."

Peter glared at Obert, then spoke to Sarah. "All right, open the gate. Malcolm is correct, we have no other choice."

Sarah nodded and unlatched the gate. She pushed it open and Tumaini lumbered through Agnes, right behind him. The sheep took one look at the lion, lowered her head and charged. She butted him so hard he groaned. Rollo gave her an affronted look and turned his attention to the orphan, who, using his flexible trunk tip, was happily tugging on Rollo's mane. Agnes stared at the two animals and visibly relaxed.

Sarah gestured to Bob. "Step in here. Stay close to the gate in case you need to make a speedy exit. Let's see what our simba does." Rollo turned and walked toward the yard.

Sarah asked Peter, "Do you think this baby is strong enough to manage a short walk?"

"By the Gods! I'm sure he can manage it; I hope he doesn't get eaten halfway through your stroll. Sarah, take a bottle of formula with you. I know he just ate but get used to carrying one whenever you are with him."

"Will I know if he's hungry?"

Aretha laughed. "He'll open his mouth and whack some part of your anatomy with his trunk. Trust me, you'll know when he wants a bottle."

Sarah gestured to Bob. "Walk next to me. I usually stay alongside Rollo and grab a handful of mane. He seems to enjoy it. Peter, while we're gone, are you going to move and arrange bedding?"

Peter nodded, relieved his baby had not been torn limb from limb. "Yes, let's get the bedding shifted, I'll show you how I want it stacked. There are two mattresses in the truck that we need to move. One is for Tumaini, the other for his carers Will someone remind me to look at the outside kitchen? I keep forgetting to do that. He turned to see Ebony, Ruby, and Pearl leave their roosts and land on Rollo's back with the precision of planes landing on an aircraft carrier. Tumaini gawped at the birds and gently examined their feet. Ebony eyed him with suspicion, knew he was a baby, and chose not to peck him to death. Rollo led the way, Bob and Sarah alongside. Tumaini seized the end of Rollo's tail and Agnes strode next to her patient. The odd procession headed outside.

Despite himself, Peter laughed. "Look at that lot! They're candidates for a circus or parade. No one would believe it if they didn't see it. By the Gods! I'm seeing it, and don't believe it. Now, let's move some bedding."

Sarah paused at the far side of the den. "Bob, let's stop, I want to be sure this baby is able to walk with us. She turned to see

Peter directing his crew and smiled at the two Americans who had taken charge of the bedding project and the two brothers. Their conversation drifted toward her.

Aretha grabbed a wheelbarrow. "Boys, if you don't mind, we'll take the bales of shavings, and you can wrestle the straw. We know they aren't that heavy, but they're awkward to handle."

She heard Obert and Michael insisting they move the bales and laughed when the sisters ignored the brothers.

Sarah and her crew returned, Bob and Tumaini were intact. She looked at the stacked bales and two air mattresses in the den. She called assurances to Peter. "Your baby stayed with us, he nibbled a bit of grass and asked for a bottle."

"Good, it's more than I hoped for, let's get him settled, he's ready for a nap. I'll let you do it, the rest of us will step out. I don't want to stress this lion."

Rollo stared at the changes to his home. He stepped onto the platform and eyed the mattress with suspicion. Tumaini was tired, It took him several tries to step onto the wooden sleeping area, but once successful, he flopped onto a mattress. The lion stared at his new roommate, bobbing gently up and down. Sarah sat on one edge of the second mattress and encouraged her boy to try it. Not convinced, Rollo put one forepaw on the undulating surface and quickly withdrew it. Two more tries and he had both forepaws on the squishy surface. He scooted his rear close to the edge and pitched onto his side. His eyes widened in surprise as he, like Tumaini, bobbed up and down.

Sarah patted him and said to Peter," You're too right about his appetite, he hit me on the head and opened his mouth.

Was your lion concerned about Bob being with you?"

"No, remember, Rollo knows Bob almost as well as he knows me."

Peter asked about the kitchen. "Let's check for equipment and storage space. Aretha and Etta know how to prepare formula." Low gargling noises emanated from the mattress. Startled, Peter exclaimed. "By the Gods! What's he doing now? He sounds like a big woodchipper."

"Pshaw." Etta answered, "he's snoring, sounds just like my husband. Rollo is sawing logs, just like Clyde."

"Ah, yes, well, let's see about the formula-making supplies. We'll bring your gear; you can get settled in. I see there's no use arguing with either of you. I pray you don't get injured, although I have to admit, this beast has extraordinary patience." The group met in the kitchen. "This will do nicely; you've all the equipment to make and store formula."

Aretha nodded. "Nothing to it. It's like baking a cake. You add a little of this, a little of that, stir it around…boom…elephant formula."

Sarah said, "Good, you can instruct the four of us. We will be experts in no time. Let me show you our house, and where you will sleep."

Peter turned to leave. "Let me get back to the sanctuary. I know I'm repeating myself, but I hope you both are in one piece when you leave for home."

Etta waved a dismissive hand. "Peter, that big, ole fluffball won't hurt us. Now, if it was our nephew, Jake, who resembles a hyena, there might be trouble."

Aretha socked her sister's arm. "Shame on you! Jake doesn't resemble a hyena. I would say he's closer in appearance to a badger."

Once again, many wrinkles appeared on Obert's forehead. He whispered to Bob, "I can't imagine the genetics behind this lot. I'd love to see a family portrait."

Sarah headed for the den. "I'm returning to our patient. "Bob, can you fix lunch for everyone?"

"Got it in one. Let's all head for the stoep, I'll assemble a gourmet meal."

Sarah groaned. "That means sandwiches and coffee."

Later that afternoon, the group met near Rollo's bench to discuss a schedule that would work for all of them.

Obert walked to the fence and asked Sarah, "Except for you, only Bob has been with Rollo. That will soon change. Can I join you? Let's see what our simba does. You tell me what to do."

"Good idea, join us. As you can see, the tribe is snoozing on the knoll. Rollo sees you and won't be alarmed. You know animals, keep your energy dialed low, your movements small." The lion raised his head to peer at another newcomer. Tumaini used his flexible nose to snuffle in Obert's face. Using that same appendage, he snatched Obert's cap, lurched to his feet, and lumbered away.

Obert sighed. "So much for low energy and quiet movement. We have an elephant charging round with my hat."

"He must be feeling better. Maybe we can trade your hat for his bottle. I hope he remains enthusiastic about food."

"He's certainly enthusiastic about my cap."

Rollo got up, stretched, yawned, and started on patrol.

Obert stared at the yawning lion. "Glory! Look at those teeth. Thank goodness he doesn't have a prey drive. With his size and canines, he would be a formidable opponent."

"Do I hear the Maasai talking?"

"Well, the beast is totemic to our culture, but no thank you. Not me. I wouldn't tangle with him. Can I touch him? Will he allow it?

"Sure, walk behind me and pat his back."

Halfway round the paddock, Obert carefully put his hand on Rollo's back and whispered a few words in Maa. The lion cocked his head and boomed a response.

"Glory! Does he understand us? Maybe that blow to his head did more than end his prey drive."

"I agree. He seems to have a good command of English, and, it would appear, Maasai. Wonderful, we have a bilingual lion. Obert, can we do this? Sometimes, I feel we have bitten off more than we can chew. It's not just the elephant. It's how our huge, fanged beast will react to all the new activity. We may be asking too much from him."

"He's been patient with everything except hyenas. I hear what you're saying about strangers. I think our simba will behave in a dignified fashion."

"He wasn't too dignified the morning Bob fell over him. I won't forget that if I live to be two million."

"Well, there are exceptions. Bob wasn't dignified either. Rollo didn't harm us. I thought the episode embarrassed him."

"You're right, no sense borrowing trouble. I'm going to have Etta stay with me tonight. She can instruct me about night care. I'm troubled by the idea of a stranger with us. If I see any sign of stress in Rollo, I'll have Etta step out. Lord knows how I will stay awake."

✵ Rollo ✵
Chapter 37

Blubbering baboons! What is that saying? Be careful what you wish for. Bah! I thought caring for an orphaned elephant would be a good idea. I could help raise the waif. I did a stellar job with the gangster pullets and Arabella. They were healthy, although there were times I wanted to send them downriver on a raft. Compared to them, Tumaini was in a class by himself.

Preparations for the orphan were finished. The girls and I went on patrol early. I didn't want to miss the arrival. We returned to the sight of a huge truck pulling into the field. It backed up to the little hill. Peter and two ladies opened the vehicle's back door. A small creature, perhaps half the size of a young zebra, strutted down the ramp. I'd never seen such a beast. Its coat was a mass of tight, tiny curls. It was light-colored, almost white, and I could see it had a powerful personality. It reminded me of Ebony. Anyway, the beast reached the ground, stamped a foot, and with an odd guttural baaing sound. called to the truck's other occupant. The people were coaxing a reluctant baby elephant down the ramp. The little one fretted and squeaked but tottered along on unsteady legs.

Baby or not, the beast was already bigger than me and sick. We lions have an excellent sense of smell, this creature stood in a fog of ghastly odors. I could smell death, that odd sickening sweetish odor that is so characteristic. The orphan's head and tail drooped. It looked miserable. Well, no wonder, having lost his mum and the rest of the pride. We lions are also close knit and I couldn't imagine such a loss for a baby.

Perhaps it would be better if this cub lived next door. I could visit through the fence and offer solace and comfort as needed. I prefer no disruption in my life. The hens and I have our routines. I went to the fence for a closer look and greeted Tumaini…that's his name…and, yes, he's a boy. The cub heard me and marched to the fence. Good! He likes me, this will be a positive experience for all concerned. Peter and the ladies couldn't stop the little fellow until he faced me.

I opened my throttles and let rip with the loudest purring I could muster. That little hose-nosed twerp stuck his flexible appendage through the fence and nearly sucked my face off. Then he gave my mane several brisk tugs.

I didn't know that organ of his could grasp things. It reminded me of a human sprouting a hand at the end of his nose. I sighed, stood still, and suffered through the examination. Next, he poked his trunk between the wire until it rested against my side, in the back of my front leg. He gave a happy bleat of contentment and relaxed. Out of the corner of my eye, I saw he was dozing. That impressed me. We lions are expert nappers, but we can't sleep standing up. It never occurred to me that something so large could doze while upright.

The caregiver, Etta, offered Tumaini a bottle. It was the biggest bottle I'd ever seen. Well, he is an elephant. Everyone talked about how weak he was. He was supposed to be too depressed and sick to eat. Bah! He slugged down that bottle of food in less than a minute. Malcolm smiled when he saw the empty bottle. There was medicine in that stuff and Tumaini guzzled all of it.

Peter and his helpers made a determined move to move the baby to the shed, but he wouldn't budge. Sarah had me step forward and Tumaini lost contact with me. He screamed disapproval. I worried about what might come next. Much discussion ensued about what to do. Sarah suggested the ellie should live with me. What? In my area? What was she thinking? I wanted no part of that prehensile nose. It would harass in countless ways. He could pluck my hair and whack me in the face. What else could he do with it? Besides, he was already large and destined to get much larger. I listened to discussions about the danger to Tumaini, should he enter my area. Danger to Tumaini? What about the danger to me? What's wrong with these people? Would that odd-looking creature with the curly coat accompany him? I didn't like the looks of that animal. It looked mean, and pig-headed, like Ebony.

Peter was against the idea. I cheered him on with loud purring. Atta boy, Peter, squash this idea. I was sure Malcolm would side with him, but that traitor suggested putting the orphan and Agnes in my yard. Agnes? That creature is a female? Sarah and Bob also agreed to a trial visit. I knew both the elephant and his friend would be permanent residents. I had little choice but to go along with the insane plan. I didn't know how complicated it would be.

Sarah opened the gate, and the two entered my den. Agnes got a close look at me, pawed the ground, and charged. Ooof! She smacked me in the side and squared up for another run. She saw Tumaini happily tugging my hair. And relaxed. She tried to shove herself between me and Tumaini, but he wouldn't move. Agnes is brave, I'm much bigger than her, but she was willing to die for the orphan. I admire that kind of courage.

It was patrol time, and I headed outside. The hens left their roosts and landed on my back. The elephant grabbed the end of my tail, and Agnes fell in alongside. Bob and Sarah completed the group, and we marched outside. I could hear Peter shouting in disbelief as he watched us. To my surprise, Tumaini was respectful, he didn't pull or stop. Save for a brief inspection of their feet, he left the girls alone. Perhaps he clung to his mum in the same way he held onto my tail. Could it be a source of comfort to him?

When we returned from patrol, I was shocked at the changes made to my den. Stacks of bales lined the wall, two strange looking objects were placed next to them. Tumaini nearly killed himself by stepping onto my sleeping platform but had no trouble flopping on one of the objects. He stretched out and was asleep in less than a minute. He was bobbing up and down. Sarah sat on the other one and invited me to join her. Suspicious, I put one forepaw on the surface. It was squashy, my foot sank into it. I'd never felt such a soft surface. At Sarah's urging, I got both front feet on it and scooted closer. The little pipsqueak wasn't frightened. I needed to uphold my reputation. With trepidation, I shut my eyes and flung myself onto the thing. Oh my! I'd never felt anything so comfortable. It was soft, squishy, and wonderful. After the stressful morning, I was due for a nap. Tumaini flopped his trunk over one of my paws and we both slept.

Chapter 38

Early that evening, Etta strolled across the yard and waited for Sarah to invite her into the den. Rollo, and his entourage were settling for sleep. Sarah had Etta slip through the gate. She waited until Rollo saw the stranger before gesturing to Etta to approach the bales. Etta had the night's supply of formula, one medicated bottle and the rest plain. Tumaini squeaked a greeting from the mattress. Etta knelt and rubbed his knobby head. Rollo peered at her from his new bed and looked at Sarah. She spoke softly to him in tones that she hoped were reassuring and confident. He sighed, lowered his head and went back to sleep.

Etta whispered, "He didn't look so huge on the other side of the wire. Lawsy! Look at the size of his paws. We had large animals on the farm, but they ate grass and hay. Some of our bulls were mean and we stayed away from them. We'd never enter their pens. I'm both thrilled and terrified to be this close to an African lion. My sister and I planned a one-day tour of an elephant orphanage and look what's happened. It's been the adventure of a lifetime. We'll leave in three weeks, we're at your service until departure day."

"Excellent! By then, we'll have our routines settled. If no one has been eaten in three weeks, we'll have brave volunteers from the sanctuary."

Etta said, "I'm not so sure about that. Everyone is waiting to see how we fare with your huge predator. The sanctuary staff considers us guinea pigs. They're okay with throwing two crazy Americans into the lion's den. I'm kidding, although, I don't see anyone signing up for Tumaini duty in the next day or two."

"I know Rollo won't harm you. Heaven only knows what's going through his mind. He's relaxed round all this commotion. Sometimes I think he understands more than we know. Now, what should we do? What are the nighttime rituals? Should one of us try to nap?"

Etta thought a moment. "I'm not an expert, but one of us stays close to the ellie. The bottles are kept in packs and we feed them either on-demand or every three hours. Many times there's only one carer per orphan. This is a special circumstance. I don't see why we both can't snooze. He'll let us know when he's hungry. The next feeding will be medicated. Let's hope he takes it. If it's okay with you, I'll opt for the bales. I'll drag my sleeping bag up there. I'd hate to accidentally bang into our furry roommate and startle him when he's asleep. There's no use tempting fate."

"Fair enough, I'll lie down with our patient. Let me unroll my bag and grab a corner of the mattress."

The night shift went better than expected. Tumaini woke at midnight and pummeled Sarah with his trunk. Etta slipped off her perch and offered a medicated bottle to the baby. Much to the joy of the women, he drank the entire amount. Rollo also woke and peered round his space. Sarah thought he looked bemused by the activity. She immediately chided herself for assigning human characteristics to the animal. The hens fussed and decamped to their roosts.

Bob and Obert took the day watch. Rollo tolerated them. Agnes and Tumaini were used to strangers in their midst. The hens continued to grumble. Within three days, the six people had routinesthat worked for them. Etta was correct in her observation that theorphan preferred Rollo's company to humans. He knew to approach his carers for food, but Rollo was his best pal. At night, he ensured his trunk touched Rollo. He was comforted by the lion's booming snores and purrs.

✻ Rollo ✻
Chapter 39

Early that evening, Sarah fed Tumaini and gave me a grooming. Delightful! It startled me to see Etta walk across the yard and enter the den. She and Sarah spoke softly for a few moments. They unrolled large bags and spoke of sleeping arrangements. What? Sleeping here? In my den? With us? All night? What madness is this? Etta opted for the top of the bales while Sarah settled on Tumaini's mattress…that's the name for the squashy things. I soon realized why the humans joined us. Our boy needed to eat several times a night. He woke up, bopped Sarah with his trunk, and made a tremendous fuss, until Etta descended from the bales and stuffed a bottle in his mouth. The hens suffered through the first feeding but fled to their perches after the second rude awakening. Agnes slept all night. She's used to this activity. I hope this little bounder will soon rejoin his pride, I'll never get used to all this commotion. We lions are nocturnal, but I'm used to a good night's sleep. By morning, exhaustion almost stopped me from eating breakfast. I looked forward to a much needed nap. Bah! I was delusional. Tumaini is a cub and eats constantly. And, of course, he needs humans for the bottle brigade. The people parade continued day and night. The hens abandoned me and spent the day in the olive tree. I didn't blame them.

Tumaini's human caregivers were my four pride members plus the ladies from the faraway place called America. I knew the ladies would leave in three weeks. I overheard Etta and Sarah talking about flight plans. Flight plans? The two sisters were going to fly. Like the hens? How is that possible? Neither have wings, besides, not to be mean-spirited, but they're both quite stout. They needed to cross an ocean to reach America. I don't know what that is, but it involves enormous amounts of water. It's much larger than any lake I've seen. I can't picture Etta and Aretha flying over an ocean.

Anyway, Tumaini made the pullets and Arabella look like saints. I know he's a baby and, like any cub, isn't responsible for his actions. However, to give an example, do you know how much young elephants poop? I can't imagine the volume adults produce. The humans were constantly cleaning up after him. Thank goodness! My den would have been a mess. Tumaini pooped day and night. It took two weeks for him to feel better and stop pooping so much. It was a lost cause, because as he grew stronger, he nibbled on bushes and hay. The humans were delighted the baby felt healthy enough to eat. Bah! Not me. All of that extra food increased the poop volume.

The six people split into three teams. Two were with us day and night. There were some bright spots. Sarah gave the sisters back scratchers. I had massages round the clock. The humans would sometimes give me a little scratch during night feeding. Sarah taught everyone how to use the grooming tools. Sprawled on my soft comfortable mattress, I felt like a king. Well, we are the kings in Africa. I know this sounds selfish, but I hoped Peter would leave the mattress when our cub returned to his pride.

In a week, Tumaini was feeling strong enough to be playful. Playful! Do you know how baby ellies play? They sit on each other, that's their idea of a fun time. Because he had no elephant playmates, he sat on me and the humans. Even a baby elephant is large enough to cause damage when they use you for a bed. We ran when he approached with a certain look in his eye. It was the 'I'm going to sit on you' look. He was agile and smart enough to trap us against the wall or fence. He would pitch over on his side, squeaking with joy, while we grasped for breath beneath him. We learned to sit on him. He would roll onto his side and pound us with his trunk. Thank goodness he never tried it with the hens. I reckoned he considered them too small to be furniture.

Peter visited several times a week to check on Tumaini's progress. He was still nervous about me, but his orphan's progress told him I was no threat. I knew he would accept me. He told Sarah that he was amazed at the bond between Tumaini and me. Well, as I've said, I'm experienced with cub rearing. I knew this baby would thrive. One day, I heard Peter tell Sarah he had selected replacements for Etta and Aretha. Two Kenyan women would replace the sisters. Bob said they knew women in Team Lioness. What is Team Lioness? I was eager to meet them. Perhaps they were knowledgeable about lions, and we might have things in common. I hoped someone gave them back scratchers.

Chapter 40

Three weeks flew by. Aretha and Etta were scheduled to depart in two days. They shed many tears at the prospect of leaving but were delighted that Tumaini was thriving. Peter visited often and was amazed to see Tumaini blossoming under the oddest group of caregivers imaginable. On their last day, Aretha paired with Obert while Etta packed their gear. The two carers walked with Rollo and his entourage. Tumaini charged through the bushes, chasing butterflies. He snorted and crashed about in the foliage

Obert laughed at the ellie's antics. "He's so much better than when he arrived. His diarrhea cleared up, and he's eating well. I swear I can see him growing."

"Yep, I agree, not the same bedraggled little twerp that landed here three weeks ago. My sister and I wouldn't have missed this for the world. We must go home but are sad to leave."

Obert replied, "You've helped us so much. None of us knew about elephant babies. We're all glad to have met you. Can I ask how you got your names?"

Aretha grinned and said, "Lawsy, we've been so busy we've forgotten to volunteer that information."

Dark-skinned Obert blushed to the roots of his hair. His face turned an interesting shade of mahogany. He asked, "How did you two get the names of internationally famous singers? Was it a coincidence?"

"Oh, Lawsy, no coincidence, our parents were corn-fed Iowans right down to their rubber boots and bib overalls, but they loved the music those two singers produced. I remember, as kids, Mom and Dad would dance in the kitchen to music from an old radio. When Etta and I approached our teen years, it mortified us to have our friends visit because our parents thought our teeny-bopper music was pure noise. They weren't shy about broadcasting that opinion. Our names could have been Big Mama and Koko. My folks loved them as well."

Obert asked, "Do they still listen to that music?"

"Well, my dad passed several years ago but Mom lives next door to me. That's the only music she enjoys."

"It seems odd to me that your folks would be so in love with that music."

"Obert, music is like lots of stuff in life, it can cross many lines, age, race, whatever, and thank goodness it does. It makes the world a better place."

"Do you and Etta listen to it?"

"Absolutely not, it's not for us. Gimme that good old rock and roll. My sister, the traitor, listens to Country and Western. Spare me!"

The next morning, Etta and Aretha took a last walk with their four-legged friends and said a tearful farewell to the two-legged ones. Two carers had tentatively agreed to take their places. Both women had done a walk with Rollo and Sarah. They would begin the following day.

Sarah and Bob watched the van roll down the driveway with Etta and Aretha. Sarah wiped her eyes and turned to her husband.

"We couldn't have done it without them. I'm going to miss their help and wacky sense of humor."

Bob, whose own eyes were none too dry, agreed. "I'll send them progress reports, they got us through the growing pains associated with orphaned elephants. Let's hope these two sanctuary caregivers aren't too terrified of Rollo."

"Yes, let's hope he doesn't yawn and display all those gleaming teeth. Even Obert was a bit shaken by those four canines."

"Well, you're convinced Rollo understands us, ask him not to yawn in front of the new people."

Sarah nodded. "Bob. What did you think of them?"

"They seem kind and knowledgeable. I'm not sure about how they'll do with Rollo. I think it helps that Aretha and Etta are still alive. The new carers are both Kenyan and Hawla has friends in Team Lioness. Remember, they remained calm when they walked with us on patrol. I agree they're nervous. Who, in their right mind, wouldn't be? Our two American friends were exceptional, and maybe not in their right minds."

"I know, they're experienced with ellies. Hawla will shadow me tonight. I can do the feedings and let her observe until she gets used to Rollo."

"Sarah, do you think there's even a tiny chance Rollo will harm them? I worry that he'll sense their fear and react to it."

"Sarah shook her head. "Rollo won't harm them. He'll sense their fear. He won't react. Don't ask me how I know this, but I know it in my bones."

"Fair enough, I believe you."

"I'm going to nap before Hawla arrives because I may be awake all night. See you at dinnertime."

✷ Rollo ✷
Chapter 41

Hawla paired with Sarah for her first night shift. We all settled in my den and prepared for sleep. I saw she was nervous. I didn't wish to frighten her. She and Faraja, the other new carer, had visited and walked with us. They are, of course, familiar with Tumaini and Agnes. I, on the other hand, am a different matter. Both ladies were Kenyan. I heard them speaking with Sarah about their homes and duties at the orphanage. It intrigued me to hear Hawla had a friend in Team Lioness. What is this pride? Is it all female? I vowed to eavesdrop every time they discussed the subject. The ladies hid behind Bob and Sarah when they entered my area. I was a model of decorum. I kept my mouth shut, minimal purring, and no yawning. Even Obert was goggle-eyed when I yawned in front of him. Honestly, can I help it if I have large canines? I'm a lion. I now realized that our new carers would be with us for months. Tumaini's health improved, but he was a baby in elephant years and would need human help for months. I heard Malcolm and Peter talking last week. Peter worried his orphan wasn't with other elephants. Malcolm felt Tumaini should stay with us because he was eating well and healthy. Of course, he was doing well. He had several humans, one sheep, and me waiting on him around the clock.

We settled for sleep. I could see Hawla was very nervous, she reeked of fear. Sarah explained that my purring relaxed Tumaini. Sometimes he wants to play. It's the middle of the night. The rest of us want to sleep. I purr to calm him, it makes him drowsy. Anyway, Hawla opted to sleep on the bales. Sarah climbed into her sleeping bag. As usual, she slept with Tumaini.

The midnight feeding went well. Hawla climbed from her perch and Tumaini drank his formula. She kept a wary eye on me. Sarah assured her I was used to this procedure. At three AM our baby woke up fussy and hungry. Hawla, now more confident, told Sarah to stay in her bag and that she would feed him. Wouldn't you know it? A bit of gristle was lodged in my back molar. I felt it after dinner but couldn't shift it. I ignored it in hope it would be gone by morning. Hawla was standing next to Tumaini, who was halfway through his bottle when that dratted object in my mouth began to irritate me. I rolled to my chest, opened my mouth, curled my lips, and made another attempt to remove it. It was terribly unfortunate that Hawla glanced up and saw my slitted eyes and canines in the glare of her headlamp. She shrieked, threw the bottle aside, trampled over Sarah, and shot up the bales. Her name, Hawla, means antelope, or speedy like an antelope, something like that, and she lived up to her name. Long-legged, she was on top of the bales in seconds.

Sarah struggled to get out of her bag, while Tumaini, deprived of his bottle, threw a little tantrum and sat on her. The poor woman was trapped. She couldn't free herself. Hawla, still yelling, was no help. I knew it was up to me. I got up, sat on our ellie, and purred. I'm so clever, he recognized the invitation to play, got off Sarah, and sat on me. Hawla, still in the rafters, giggled. Sarah staggered to her feet and found the lost bottle. She waved it at Tumaini, who finished his meal.

Hawla was alternating between giggles and explanations. She heard me wake and roll to my chest. Then, in the glare of her headlamp, saw my gleaming eyes and wide-open mouth. She was sure I would spring to my feet and attack her because she had disturbed me. More giggles from the ceiling. She was aghast about trampling Sarah, but felt she needed to flee for her life. Sarah convinced her I'd been yawning. Hawla descended, and we went back to sleep. I wasn't yawning, but never mind.

Over the next year, several more caregivers joined our team. Hawla and Faraja were now confident. Faraja loved to groom me. She spent hours brushing and combing my body. Newcomers always had the same reaction. Initially, they were terrified but we were soon friends. Back-scratcher episodes, grooming, and massages were available to me around the clock. It was wonderful!

Tumaini grew so fast that it was frightening. As the weeks passed. Peter supplied hay and foliage so the youngster could have a snack at night. The Von Bergs got involved in caregiving. Samantha was excited to be with me and a baby elephant. She had matured so much in the past year, I barely recognized her. Brandon couldn't relax in my presence, but Felicity and her daughter had no fear. They would arrive during the day to help feed and clean up after our orphan. Several times, Samantha stayed to help with night duties. She, her mum, and Sarah would be the carers. Staying awake all night was a treat for Sam.

Tumaini adored Samantha, and she felt the same toward him. maybe they recognized each other as cubs. One day Malcolm came to examine our baby. Peter was in attendance, as were Sam and Felicity. We waited for Malcolm to finish so we could walk. Malcolm, focused on his patient, was listening to Tumaini's heart and lungs. That little, long-nosed brat swiped Malcolm's hat and took off at a brisk trot. Sam chased after him and seized one of his ears. She led him back and made him give up the cap. It was funny, this small girl scolding this large animal for hat stealing. Tumaini would take a hat or bottle from humans and ignore all pleas of returning it. Samantha was the only one he would obey.

Malcolm felt our orphan should stay several more months before moving him to the sanctuary. Peter worried about Tumaini being away from his own pride. The tentative plan was to move him in the summer of the following year. Bah! We would have to endure his antics for another year. As he grew, he became more mischievous. Bob installed a huge water tank because my puny container wasn't adequate for an elephant. Obert dug a small depression near the tank. The overflow created a muddy area which I found disgusting, but Tumaini spent hours wallowing in the mess. He also learned to suction water into his trunk and squirt anybody that came near. It was a disgusting mix of water and elephant snot. He drenched the hens one day, and I thought Ebony would blind him. She flew at him and bopped him in the face with her wings. He never tried that again, but the rest of us were fair game.

We settled into Tumaini's routine, and the months drifted by. One day, Obert arrived to join Bob for the day shift. The man was so excited he could barely speak. Arabella had given birth the night before. The baby was gorgeous. Well, he's prejudiced about that cow. The cub was female and the image of her mother. Obert was alert to any sign of Arabella's health issues but, so far, the little one was robust. Thrilled to hear the news I, hoped the little one would thrive. Ara and her cub would stay at Obert's barn until next year, then return to us.

Tumaini had been with us for three months when Sarah decided to open the gate between my area and the adjacent field. She conferred with Peter and both agreed more space and foliage was a good idea for our growing boy. This new arrangement made me happy. It meant an expanded hyena patrol. It was summer and Sarah left the shed doors open so we could escape the afternoon heat. Fall approached, and we were content. I might have known it wouldn't last. Peter and Malcolm continued arguing about moving Tumaini. Peter was adamant. Malcolm wouldn't budge from his position. Finally, the men agreed to six more months with us. Peter declared the ellie needed to be with his own pride, he was getting bigger and the ride in the truck might be problematic.

Being so comfortable around me would be dangerous when he re-integrated into the wild. The move must be made by late winter or early spring. We had a reprieve of several months.

Chapter 42

Sarah leaned over the porch railing and turned her face to the spring sunshine. She watched silly Tumaini butt bomb into the mud wallow. Several moments later, he wandered to the water trough and hosed water into his trunk. He started toward Rollo. The lion was no fool. He moved out of firing range. Sarah spoke with Peter that morning and they finalized the decision to move Tumaini. Peter knew it would be harder to return the orphan to the sanctuary. The baby wasn't the sick, weak, terrified being he was two years ago. Peter would bring the truck, park it at the base of the ramp and place Tumaini's favorite food in the vehicle. Hopefully, he would get used to eating in the vehicle. He was too big to shove up the ramp, he had to learn to walk up and down the earthen platform and remain calm when the carers shut the door. Peter warned it might take days to habituate Tumaini to the vehicle. Agnes was an experienced traveler. She would trot up the ramp if her favorite sheep nuggets were available. Everyone hoped the elephant would follow his woolly friend.

Bob joined his wife on the porch. "What a project this has been. I don't know if I'm happy or sad that our orphan is leaving us. We've met wonderful people and learned so much these past eighteen months."

"I know, but he can't stay here. He needs reintegration into the orphan herd. Besides, his sheer size would prohibit him from being here much longer. He could walk through our fences should the mood strike him. I'm surprised Rollo's sleeping platform hasn't collapsed under his weight. Erm, he's as big as an elephant." She laughed at her own wit and pulled out her chirping phone. After a brief conversation, she turned to Bob. "Peter's in-route with the truck. He'll park it and put food in the back. It's a clever way to get our baby used to being in the truck. I hope it works."

Peter backed to the ramp, waved hello, and leaped out of the truck. He bounded up to Rollo and gave him a vigorous scratching behind both ears. Tumaini ambled over and draped his trunk around Peter's neck. He got his share of scratches and slyly reached for Peter's cap. The man, wise to his orphan, stuffed the cap into his pocket.

Peter laughed and rubbed the lion's forehead. "By the Gods! Do you remember I how greeted you at our first meeting? Look at me now, cavorting with an adult male lion. What a wonder life can be, all the twists and turns it takes. I trust you with my baby and myself. You're a strange and paradoxical creature. I'm glad you've helped us with this ellie, but it's time for him to return to his own kind. I'm saying this out loud because Sarah is convinced you understand us bumbling humans and I won't disagree with her." Peter turned to greet Sarah and Bob. "Today's the day, I have elephant food and sheep nuggets in the truck. Agnes will go in, she's not frightened of the truck. Let's hope Tumaini joins her."

Agnes trotted into the truck and dug into her treats. Tumaini stood on the ground and waved his trunk at Peter. Peter waved elephant treats in response, but Tumaini remained at the bottom of the ramp.

Sarah offered a suggestion. "Rollo, and I could walk into the truck. Perhaps Tumaini will follow, see the food, and eat."

"Good idea, let's see if my baby will follow his hairy, vocal roommate up the ramp."

Sarah tugged gently on Rollo's mane and spoke a few words to him. The two marched up the ramp. Tumaini followed them. Once in the truck, the ellie saw his food and began to eat.

Peter rubbed his hands together with satisfaction. "Excellent! you two slip out of the truck." Sarah did as instructed. Tumaini stopped eating and trundled along behind them. Lines of concern wrinkled Peter's brow. "Ah, that was a good first try. Let's do it again."

After the fourth try, it was obvious Tumaini would not remain in the truck without Rollo.

"Erm, Peter, do we have a problem?"

Peter tugged his hair. "By the Gods! Dear lady, we have a huge problem, it's clear that Tumaini won't stay in the vehicle without Rollo. We'll never be fast enough to shut the door, if we managed that, I fear my baby would panic. I'm not sure what to do. Perhaps if we feed him in the truck for a week or two, he'll be more comfortable."

A week passed, Tumaini wouldn't stay in the truck without Rollo. Malcolm and Bob were in attendance one morning watching Sarah and Rollo march up and down the ramp with Tumaini tagging along behind them.

Malcolm groaned. "Oh boy, I see what you mean. Have you tried closing the door halfway and then shutting it when Sarah and Rollo exit?"

Sarah responded. "We did, Tumaini bulled his way out. Peter and I felt if a closed door would make him panic,"

Peter threw his hands in the air. "We're at a loss. I'm sure my boy would ride safely if Rollo accompanied him, but what happens when we get there? Am I correct in saying Rollo has never been loose? Except for the porch incident when Bob did a flying Wallenda act down the stairs?"

Sarah nodded. "Correct, Rollo follows me round the paddocks, but he's never been allowed to roam free. I think he'll ride well in the truck, but I can't control him at the sanctuary. And how do we get Tumaini to join his herd?

Peter turned to Malcolm. "What about a tranquilizer? Could you sedate Tumaini here? In the truck?"

Malcolm shook his head. "I don't like that idea. Funny things can happen with animal sedation. We have no choice if the animal is sick, injured or has to be transported. This is a unique situation. I'd hate to see a drug reaction I can't reverse."

Peter said, "I never thought I'd hear myself say this, but I'm confident Rollo will stay with Sarah. My bigger worry is the reaction the elephants might have when they see and smell this big predator. My herd may panic and frighten Tumaini. I suppose he could see his tribe and scamper through the gate without a backward glance, but I don't think he'll do that. If he's frightened, I believe he'll stick to Rollo like a piece of tape. I fear Rollo and Sarah will have to enter the elephant area with Tumaini. I'm worried about the safety of everyone. Rollo is a gentleman, but even he might panic if the elephants threaten him. By the Gods! I don't know what to do! I'm most worried about our two older female orphans. They are the mini-matriarchs of the herd. Both have assumed their roles as leaders and protectors of the younger ellies. They are between four and six years old. If they, or a herd member is threatened, they'll attack. They could kill us. I've no way to control them. We must hope for the best. I'd be happy if they were off on some elephant adventure when we arrive."

Bob said, "People, we agree this animal has to be moved. We all know there are problems connected with it. I think we'll have to take a leap of faith. We put Rollo, Tumaini, and Agnes in the truck and shut the door. Sarah and I will follow in our vehicle. If we hear a commotion, we can phone you to stop the truck. If we make it to the sanctuary, we open the door and let our orphan follow Rollo to wherever he needs to be. Sarah and Rollo may have to enter your field with the herd."

Malcolm nodded. "Bob's right. We can second guess this situation forever and still not know the outcome. While you were talking, I had an idea. Peter, could you build a small fence around your main gate? It could resemble the safety fence round Rollo's food tray. Maybe Tumaini, Sarah, and Rollo could stay there while your ellies got accustomed to Rollo. Plus, Tumaini could safely see other elephants. He might walk through the gate to join them. Freddie will be in that field. Correct?"

Peter scrubbed his face with both hands. "I like the idea of the safety fence. We'll build one and hope Bob's theory is correct. We have to take action. I hope Freddie recognizes Tumaini."

"And vice versa," Sarah said. "Let's hope our boy recognizes his old pal."

Peter, already striding toward his van, said, "I'm going to start on the fence, and will let you know when it's complete. In the meantime, keep feeding Tumaini in the truck, I know Rollo will be with him but that's fine. He'll get more comfortable in there."

It took five days to build the fence. Tumaini, Rollo and Sarah had many practice sessions in the truck. On their walks, she tugged on Rollo's mane to turn him. He did what she asked. Sarah thought he looked bored, but he stayed with her. She fretted she couldn't control Rollo at the sanctuary. He would be free, and a gentle tug on his mane wouldn't stop him should he panic or decide to attack.

Peter called to let Sarah know he was ready. The next day he drove to the Aimtree's, accompanied by Hawla and Faraja. Sarah walked Rollo up the ramp, Tumaini and Agnes beside her. Once the animals were loaded, she hurried down the ramp. Bob closed the door and Peter jumped into the truck.

"We must get moving immediately don't give them a chance to think about it. Sometimes the motion will keep them quieter."

Sarah, already in their vehicle, turned to Bob, "I'm glad the top of the truck is partially open. It's too high for Rollo to leap out and it's light in the back. Maybe that will keep them calm."

"Everybody but Agnes, that old battle-axe is worse than Ebony, she's probably asleep and we aren't even to the main road."

The twenty-minute ride was uneventful, Peter backed against the ramp and joined Sarah at the top. Bob opened the door and Agnes bounded down the ramp. Sarah spoke to Rollo, took a handful of mane, and started down, Tumaini seized Rollo's tail and followed. Peter directed the three into the holding area and shut the gate.

Ominous rumbling came from the field. The two matriarchs, Njeri and Gasira, were on full alert at the arrival of the newcomers. Heads, tails, and trunks up, they flared their ears and shifted uneasily back and forth.

"By the Gods!" groaned Peter. "Just what I didn't want. The two guardians are by the gate. Wait until they get a whiff of Rollo."

That wait wasn't long. Seconds after Peter spoke, Njeri screamed a warning and strode closer to the gate. Gasira mirrored her actions. Tumaini, terrified, huddled against Rollo. He wrapped his trunk around Rollo's neck and pressed his forehead into the lion's mane.

Freddie barged over and attempted to reach Tumaini with his trunk. Like most youngsters, he ignored his elders when they didn't agree with his plan. Tumaini peeked at him through Rollo's mane but wouldn't leave the lion's side.

Peter mopped his sweating brow. "Let's give them a minute. Perhaps my big girls will calm themselves. Thank heavens your lion is calm. I hope he doesn't purr. I don't think my girls will like that."

Rollo remained silent. Njeri saw Tumaini cuddled against Rollo and stepped back. Confused, she clearly didn't know how to respond to the situation. Freddie blared another greeting and leaned against the fence. Tumaini lifted his head and looked at his friend but wouldn't approach him. Several moments ticked by. Sarah stepped toward the gate, taking Rollo and Tumaini with her.

She said, "We'll stand here all day, I'm moving closer to the gate. Maybe Tumaini will sniff Freddie through the fence. I hope so because I don't want to be in the pasture with those two enormous girls. I know they're only doing their job, but they frighten me."

"By the Gods! They're frightening me. At least Tumaini and Freddie are visiting through the fence and that's wonderful. Let's give them more time, perhaps Tumaini will go through the gate."

Ten minutes later, the Aimtree orphan showed no interest in joining Freddie. Sarah swallowed a huge lump of fear and said, "Peter, open up. Rollo and I will go in there. Let's hope we don't get trampled to death. We'll slip inside and stay right near the gate."

Once Rollo was inside the yard, Tumaini bounced in behind him and began to play with Freddie. Njeri and Gasiri came forward and gave Tumaini a thorough exam. The little orphan turned and clutched Rollo's mane while the two older elephants sniffed him. Satisfied, they turned their attention to Sarah and Rollo. Sarah, teeth chattering with fright, allowed them to inspect her hair, face, and arms. Next, Rollo got a detailed exam. Gasira prodded the top of his head, Njeri sniffed the length of his body. Then, to everyone's amazement, they positioned themselves alongside Rollo and Sarah and watched the youngsters frolic.

"Whew! By the Gods! Sarah, you two did everything right and my two girls accepted you. They see Rollo is a comfort to Tumaini. Excellent, while those young ones are away from the gate, you two slip out. I'll drive your big boy home and our job is done."

Sarah and Rollo were halfway through the gate when Tumaini screamed, hurried up the hill and trotted through the open gate. Sarah, Peter, and Bob offered words of comfort, but Tumaini wouldn't leave Rollo.

"Ah well," Peter said, "we made some progress. We'll try again the day after tomorrow. Tumaini needs time to bond with the herd. At least Gasiri and Njeri will be receptive. They won't forget you and what you mean to Tumaini."

The second and third trips to the sanctuary were as Peter predicted. Tumaini happily played with Freddie until Rollo stood to leave. Then, he scampered up the hill and followed his friend into the truck.

On the way home after the third trip, Sarah said, "I don't know about you, but I'm discouraged. Tumaini can't let go of Rollo. I'm wondering how much longer Peter will try to get our ellie to stay with his tribe."

"Well, I can't see any difference in behavior, but Peter sees signs that Tumaini is bonding with his herd. He's the expert. We need to follow his instructions. We'll be back in two days. Maybe the fourth time is the charm."

The fourth trip was like the first three. An uneventful truck ride and another romp with the two youngsters. Gasiri and Njeri ambled over to say hello and watched the orphans play. After twenty minutes, Peter gestured to Sarah and opened the gate. She and Rollo were two paces from the fence when Tumaini hurried up the hill. He went to Sarah, wrapped his trunk round her waist, and leaned into her side. He then turned to Rollo and tugged on his mane. With his trunk round the lion's neck, he leaned down and rumbled quietly. He stepped back, raised his head, and trumpeted to both human and lion. He slowly turned and followed Freddie into the trees at the bottom of the hill. The two mini-matriarchs stepped forward and gently touched Sarah and Rollo, then followed the two youngsters.

Sarah, mopping tears from her face, said, "Oh Peter, he said goodbye to us. You were so right. I don't know whether to cry or shout with joy."

Peter nodded. "I was thinking we would be dragging him back and forth for another six months."

Bob took out a hanky and wiped his own streaming eyes. "Not a dry eye in the house. I wonder what Rollo thinks. At least he's done with the truck rides, save this last one to get him home."

"Erm," Sarah said, "I've an idea, I know you two won't like it. I want Rollo to ride in the Landy with us. I've put the seat back and will try to coax him in."

Both men looked at her in horror.

Peter declared. "What if he panics in there? He could hurt himself. Or you! Or cause an accident. What if he escapes and gets hit by a car? This is a truly insane idea. I can have him safely home in twenty minutes."

Bob knew his wife. "Okay, Sarah, let's see if he'll fit in there. I want you to promise if he looks the least bit stressed, we'll have Peter drive him home."

"Done and done."

✼ Rollo ✼
Chapter 43

Creeping crocodiles! It's been an exciting month. The weather warmed and Tumaini grew like all cubs do, in leaps and bounds. One morning, Peter drove into the yard with his big truck. Nosey me. I ambled over to observe. To my amazement, the humans had a sound idea. Tumaini was too big to force up the ramp. He had to walk into the vehicle. A food reward would habituate him to the vehicle. Peter leaped out of the truck and greeted me with enthusiasm. I returned the greeting. That man has changed for the better. I remember our first meeting. He was terrified I would injure him and his orphan. Bah! So silly! Now, he rushed over and gave me a vigorous and satisfactory ear scratch. He worked his fingers behind my ears and dug in. He made my lips vibrate. It felt wonderful.

He set up a routine to load Tumaini. Sarah, Bob, and I watched the procedure. Peter put sheep nuggets for Agnes in the truck. She flew up the ramp. She loves those things. One day I tried one, I thought they might be a handy snack for me. Those pellets are dry and crunchy. They reminded me of straw, compressed into little balls. Well, she and Tumaini don't like my food, either.

Peter had a large bunch of fresh-cut grass, Tumaini's favorite. Hawla had a bottle. They stood at the top of the ramp, waving their offerings. Using his trunk, Tumaini waved back but wouldn't set foot on the ramp. Peter walked halfway down, waving the grass, He spoke to the ellie in a soft, coaxing voice. Tumaini refused to move.

Sarah suggested she and I walk into the truck. Tumaini followed us and tucked into the grass. Peter smiled. Not so fast, I thought. Wait until Sarah and I start down the ramp. The vehicle fascinated me. It had solid wooden sides and no roof so I could see the sky. It was too high to leap to the outside. I had no desire to leap out. The humans often travel in these conveyances, and I wanted to experience the motion. I rode in Malcolm's truck, after my accident, but I was unconscious. Peter quietly ushered us to the door, and we started down the ramp. Tumaini left his food and followed. No surprise to me! Peter tried again, and we marched up and down several times. Our ellie wouldn't stay in the truck without me. Wonderful! I would ride with Tumaini to the sanctuary. I knew it would take time for the slow-witted humans to understand they needed me.

They wasted a week on this useless activity. One morning, Malcolm and Peter arrived to meet with Sarah and Bob. They discussed my truck ride. What would happen when we got there? Would I run away or attack something? Oh, too bloody right, I'm going to attack an elephant. How did these two-legged creatures evolve? How did they transmit their genes before being killed by predators? Anyway, Bob solved the problem. We would go to the sanctuary and I would stay with Sarah. Peter would direct us, and with luck, Tumaini would remember his pride and leave us. I wasn't sure about the last part, but the plan was moving forward. I was eager for the truck ride. Sarah spent the next week marching me around in our fenced areas. We would go right or left when she tugged on my mane. What nonsense, but I tolerated it because of the truck ride. Peter would build a fence at the sanctuary. I ignored that conversation, but let me tell you, I was glad the fence was built. More about that later.

The big morning arrived. Tumaini, Agnes, and I rode in the truck. Sarah and Bob followed in their vehicle. I could feel the truck's vibrations through my paws and the wind blowing through my mane. Looking up, I saw the sky, clouds and treetops passing overhead. The truck sides were solid wood, so I couldn't see the countryside. Once there, we went down the ramp. Agnes scampered off to join her friends. She knew her job was done. I could feel Sarah's nervousness. Tumaini stared at the elephants. Peter guided the three of us into this little fence by a large gate.

The rot set in minutes after Peter closed us into the small space. Two half-grown elephants approached and sounded an alarm. Suspicious of me, they alerted the other ellies that a threat was present. They terrified Tumaini, and he wrapped his trunk round my neck and hid his face in my mane. Sarah tightened her grip on my back and I knew she was also frightened. She wasn't alone. Those animals were huge. I heard Peter call them mini-matriarchs because they assumed roles as leaders for the orphans. There was nothing 'mini' about those girls. Orphans themselves, they were still formidable. We stood inside our little enclosure while Peter tried to talk sense into Njeri and Gasira. What names! Gasira meant the brave one, and Njeri meant the daughter of a warrior. I would hate to meet Njeri's father; she was a chip off the old block.

Several tense moments passed. Peter said their body language indicated confusion about Tumaini plastered against my body. A young elephant, Freddie, tried to touch Tumaini through the fence, but our cub was too frightened to respond. The big girls wanted to see Tumaini. They stomped, blew, and trumpeted at me. Liquid streamed down their faces. Peter told us that was a sign of stress in ellies. Freddie wanted to play, but Tumaini wasn't interested. Several more moments slipped by. Sarah offered to take us inside the fence. What? Inside the fence? With those two large, angry elephants? How could she have a worse idea? Peter and Bob agreed with me, but we all know Sarah and she started toward the gate. Peter had a fit, he sputtered and yanked his hair.

Sarah told him to let us out if the matriarchs attacked.

So, we went in, I sent a mental message to my uncle Sid. This is it, Sid, I'm about to get stomped into lion jelly. I'll see you in a few minutes. I know you don't like humans, but I may bring one with me. She's nice and shouldn't be much trouble. There is an outside possibility we'll also bring a young elephant. I hope you have enough room.

Sarah held my mane in a death grip. Freddie squealed with delight, and invited Tumaini to play, our baby greeted the other youngster but wouldn't leave us. Gasira and Njeri rumbled and flared their ears, then approached and examined Tumaini. They sniffed him from trunk to tail and stepped back. Our baby squeaked with surprise. He tentatively returned their greetings. I thought they looked confused, but Peter whispered to Sarah that their body language had changed, they were no longer on high alert. Tumaini found Freddie's overtures irresistible, and the two moved a short distance away and gamboled about the paddock. The mini-matriarchs came up to us and cautiously inspected us. They gave Sarah a quick sniff but were more interested in me. I could smell fear and anger emanating from their huge bodies. Sarah's teeth were chattering and she was drenched in a toxic-smelling sweat. I sat still and kept my mouth shut. No purring. To our relief, Gasira and Njeri moved away and watched the youngsters romp.

Peter was delighted, he mopped his sweating brow and proclaimed a successful reintegration. Sarah and I were through the gate when Tumaini came screaming up the hill. Sounds of terror and desperation rose from him. Peter had no choice but to open the gate and allow Tumaini to join us. Bah! So much for the reintegration. We went home and I looked forward to another ride. The second and third trips to visit the sanctuary were identical. Tumaini went into the field and played with Freddie. Gasira and

Njeri would stand alongside Sarah and me. The four of us would watch the youngsters romp. They sat on each other, played tag, and lumbered round the paddock. The trouble started when Sarah and I headed for the gate. Tumaini would leave Freddie and come huffing up the hill to join us.

Bob and Sarah expressed disappointment after a visit, but Peter said Tumaini was bonding with his pride. We couldn't see any change. Bob knew Peter was right in his expert assessment of the situation, we needed to be patient. The fourth trip started like the previous visits. Tumaini went to the gate and joined Freddie. The humans, matriarchs, and I watched the play session for half an hour. Peter opened the gate and Sarah and I moved toward it.

Tumaini saw us, I swear he had one eye on us the entire time. Halfway up the hill he gave a credible elephant-size trumpet, raised his trunk, and went to Sarah, wrapped his long nose round her neck, and stood close to her. He approached me and wrapped his trunk round my neck and carefully leaned against my body. I purred. He rumbled like the older elephants and stepped away from us, raised his head, and trumpeted again. The four elephants paced down the hill and disappeared into the trees.

Well, everyone but I was weeping. These humans are so emotional. Our cub had said goodbye in true elephant fashion. I was both sad and happy. We lions don't weep, but my eyes got moist from all the dust. I'm sure it was the dust. Peter started toward the truck to prepare for the drive home, but Sarah stopped him. Bless that woman! She had a wonderful idea. The men hated it. Fortunately, she's stubborn and got her way.

Chapter 44

Sarah walked to their vehicle. "I'll open both doors and have him step in on my side. If he's anxious, I can reach over the seat to soothe him."

Bob grumbled. "Yes, well, let's see if he'll fit in there."

Sarah led Rollo to the passenger side. "Okay, Rollo, can you step up with your front paws and follow with the rear ones? It's only one step. Keep your front paws on the floor and slide your rear end on the seat. Can you do that?"

Rollo carefully stepped into the vehicle and sat. Booming purrs of approval floated from the vehicle.

Sarah said, "Bob, shut the door, don't close it on his tail. He can walk out if he's uncomfortable.

Bob carefully shut the door. Rollo looked round the vehicle. He showed no inclination to leave.

Peter squatted next to him and took the lion's face in his hands. "Rollo, my boy, I want you to know you're safe, don't be afraid. I'm going to follow you. If you get nervous, we can transfer you to my larger vehicle."

Sarah knelt on the car seat and patted Rollo. He gave her an exasperated look that appeared to say, 'Let's get on with this.' Doors closed, Bob crept down the driveway. He reached the main road and sped up to five kph.

Sarah stared at him. "Bob, at this rate, it'll take all day to get home. Drive at a normal speed. Rollo's calm, he's looking round and purring.

Peter behind them, they accessed the main road and picked up speed. Rollo bashed his head into the window.

Sarah said, "Put the window down, he wants the wind in his face. He's fine, he won't jump out."

Bob grudgingly did as asked. Rollo's purring reached epic volumes. He shoved his head out the window and turned his face into the wind. This resulted in two things: his mane flew straight up from his body, which made his head look five times its normal size. The second unfortunate consequence of the wind was to blow his lips open, exposing his lethal-looking canines. The first car coming from the opposite direction swerved at the sight of him and pulled onto the verge. Three more motorists caught sight of the hair and teeth. They also landed on the verge. The fifth vehicle to pass them was a police car, which promptly made a U-turn and gave chase with lights on and siren blaring. Bob stopped on the verge with the police car behind him.

Bob muttered, "I told you this was a bad idea. Now, what're we going to do?"

"Oh, bother, we'll explain why Rollo is here. Peter will help us."

The officer, a tall African man, approached with his hand on his sidearm. Keeping a prudent distance from Rollo, he asked, "Sir, why do you have a lion in your backseat?"

Bob squirmed and babbled. "Ah, we were on our way home from the elephant sanctuary."

"I see. On your way home from the sanctuary. Were you visiting the elephants?"

"Umm, well no, we've been caring for an orphaned ellie. He lived with our lion, ah, he bonded with him. He was supposed to bond with Agnes, but he preferred our lion. We think it's because he purrs."

The officer frowned. "And who is Agnes? The lion's aunt? Or perhaps the elephant's sister?"

Bob continued to babble. "Ah, no, Agnes is a sheep that came with Tumaini…that's the elephant…but he liked our simba better. He's lived with us for over two years. It was time for him to rejoin his herd but he wouldn't leave our lion, so we've been driving back and forth. Today, he said goodbye to us and stayed at the sanctuary."

The policeman's frown deepened. "How did you transport the elephant? Did you strap him to the roof of your car? Sir, have you been drinking? You aren't making sense."

Peter hurried to the rescue. "Officer, I heard Bob's explanation. I know it sounds daft, but it's all true. I'm Peter Otieno and am in charge of the sanctuary."

"Peter Otieno! I've friends in the park ranger service. One of my cousins is a member of Team Lioness. They all speak highly of you and your work."

Peter nodded. "Those men and women save many animals. They risk their lives every time they go to work."

Peter gave a condensed version of Tumaini's life with the Aimtrees. Bob, red-faced, offered an apology for not realizing how Rollo might look to passing motorists. Sarah said it was her idea to put this large beast in the Landy and also apologized. Rollo greeted the man in his usual fashion. Startled, the man tightened his grip on the gun and stepped back.

"Don't be alarmed," Peter said. "Rollo always makes that sound. He purrs."

"Rollo? His name is Rollo. My kids are always banging on about a lion named Rollo. I've discounted the crazy stories. Should I re-think them?"

Bob smiled. "All the crazy stories are true. We've lived with this beast for several years. It's been one adventure after another."

The officer stepped closer to the car. "Do you think he would allow me to touch him?"

Sarah said, "Of course, come to the window and pat him. Don't be surprised if he ups his volume. He's startled many people with that sound he makes."

The man approached Rollo and touched his broad forehead. He spoke a few words in Maa and stepped back.

Peter looked at the man's badge and exclaimed. "Ntagusa! Dennis Ntagusa! You are Maasai. This animal is special to you and your culture."

Officer Ntagusa nodded. "Yes, this interaction means the world to me. Our old ways, the ritual killing of a lion, are obsolete. We're now involved in the conservation of this magnificent beast. Am I imagining that he smells like flowers?"

Sarah said, "No, some of his grooming products are scented. This one is lavender."

"Grooming products! He allows you to groom him. So that's why his mane blew out to such astonishing proportions." Officer Ntagusa threw his head back and laughed. "Would you allow me to take a photograph? My kids will be so jealous when I tell them I touched the super lion."

Once the photo-op was complete, the policeman said, "I know you meant no harm, but this bruiser is a visual hazard to oncoming motorists. I suppose your neighbors will get used to seeing him in the car. For now, take him home. I would suggest short rides until folks get used to him. I will say he looked like he was having the time of his life. I would hate to spoil that for him. Just use discretion with his road trips."

Once home, Bob and Sarah sprawled on the stoep with cold beers

Bob groaned. "All I could think of was Rollo's prey drive awakening when officer Ntagusa was patting his head. We would have all been in jail. I'm glad Peter was there. He saved our hides."

Sarah took a healthy swig of beer. "Ach! That would have been frightful. Rollo taking a chunk out of an officer of the law. Bob, I'm already upset about our fuzzy boy being lonely. He's had companions for months."

"He may be glad they're gone. Rollo might like his old, routine, just him and the girls."

"I don't know, maybe I'll follow the officer's advice and take him on little rides. He loved having the wind in his face."

"I suppose it's a waste of breath to tell you to let sleeping lions lie?"

"Yep, I'll put him in the Landy, drive for twenty minutes, and return home. What a day! Let's have a decent meal and watch the sunset."

✸ Rollo ✸
Chapter 45

Sarah wanted me to ride in the Aimtree vehicle. Unlike Peter's truck, the top half of it was open so humans could see the road. I wasn't exactly correct about the open part, there were clear panels that were controlled by the driver or passenger. It was a terrific idea, I never thought the panels existed, I assumed the wind blew through the entire vehicle when it was in motion. Anyway, Sarah and Bob had a long discussion about getting me in the backseat. It was even longer because Peter kept interrupting. I sighed and waited for somebody to open the door. Sarah had a point about my size, it would be a tight squeeze. She opened both rear doors I entered the vehicle. She suggested I put my rear end on the seat and keep my front paws on the floor. It was a splendid idea. I hopped into the back seat. Sarah worried aloud about trapping my tail in the door. Peter insisted on following with his van in case I got upset and went wild in the backseat. I thought this was a dumb idea, but changed my mind, as you will soon learn. Bob crept down the driveway at such a slow pace I could've walked faster. Sarah insisted he drive faster. When he turned onto the main road, we were zipping along at a brisk pace.

I discovered the top half of the vehicle wasn't open. When I put my head out, I nearly brained myself on a clear barrier. Windows, they're called windows, because I heard Sarah tell Bob to roll the window down on my side. I must admit, these humans surprise me, what a clever idea to control the amount of air coming into the interior.

Bob grumbled about lowering the window, but he did. I pushed my head out, and the wind blew my mane straight up from my head. It felt glorious. I shoved my head out further and turned my face into the wind. All that fast-moving air caught my lips and blew them away from my teeth, both upper and lower lips flapped in the breeze. That same breeze put my canines on display. Bah! My dratted teeth were, once again, going to get me into trouble. We were sailing along when I saw another lion peering at me from the front of the car. I realized this was another vehicle device to enable motorists to see behind them. I was looking at myself in a reflective gizmo. Even I was startled at the sight of my blowing hair and gleaming teeth

Sadly, I wasn't the only one startled. Several oncoming motorists looked at me and swerved to the side of the road. I could see their amazed expressions as they passed by. A group of poor souls walking on the verge nearly got run over. The last car had odd markings. It passed, turned, and followed us. I saw it in the reflective device. To my astonishment, the vehicle howled. I didn't know these conveyances were alive. Could that be possible? It also displayed a series of lights that flashed. Bob pulled over and stopped. I thought he was going to offer help to the ailing car. It was making a dreadful noise, that sounded like a dying animal The howling stopped and a stern-looking man exited the sick vehicle and approached us. He demanded to know about me. Why was I in the car? What did Bob think he was doing? Red faced and flustered, Bob wasn't giving satisfactory answers.

Thank goodness Peter hurried to our car and took over explanations. He spoke of Tumaini, Agnes, the carers, and, of course, me. This man has authority over people driving. Laws must be followed. Apparently, I'm considered a visual hazard to other motorists. Well, I can't argue with that assessment. I got a look at myself in the mirror...the reflective devices are called mirrors... and I admit, I looked formidable

The man is a police officer and maintains order on the roads.

He's Maasai, wouldn't you know? He said his tribe no longer practice the manhood ritual of killing lions. Thank the gods for that! The Maasai are now involved in lion conservation. I rarely miss the ability to speak, but this time I wanted to ask about Team Lioness. Are they female humans? Do they monitor us? Anyway, everyone calmed down. The policeman patted me and took photos. I was delighted when he said Sarah could take me for short drives. We went home. It was a stressful, wonderful day. Would we see Tumaini again? Perhaps Sarah and I could visit the sanctuary. I didn't have to worry about seeing Tumaini. More on that at a later time.

Chapter 46

Sarah hurried down the stairs. Car keys in hand, she looked across the driveway. Rollo stood near the fence, he gently tapped the gate with a forepaw. Delighted, Sarah called to him. "Just one moment, my big, beautiful boy. I'll start the car and open the gate for you."

The animal purred a response. Sarah moved her vehicle closer to the paddock and then opened the doors to the back seat. She released the gate latch and watched as Rollo carefully entered the car. He arranged his back end on the seat, shuffled about with his front paws, and looked at Sarah.

"All righty, you look splendid. We're off to town. We have three quick stops today, the post office, bakery, and gas for our hard-working Landy, I don't want you sitting in the car for too long. Our neighbors know you, but this is tourist season. We don't want to frighten a group of visitors." On the outskirts of town, Sarah pointed to the sign 'Snowtown, South Africa.' "Aha! Look at that, Rollo. A group of tourists, taking photos in front of our sign."

The name Snowtown gave its residents many opportunities for groans and eye-rolls. Europeans came to the area in the 1850s and created a settlement. One of the founding fathers was a man called Erich Snowton. He contributed time, money, and energy to the developing town. It grew from a small village to a proper town. In appreciation, the residents gave the town his name. By the early 1900s, Snowton was a hub for commerce. It produced goods for the local farmers, feed for their animals, and had a rail line to ship and receive products from other areas. During the second world war, a fire destroyed the town's written records. When re-documentation began, somehow, a 'w' had been incorporated into Snowton. It became Snowtown. No one could remember if this was a simple mistake or if one of the town's humorists had done it deliberately.

The residents voted to keep the new name. Two large signs were erected on both ends of the town. They proclaimed the reader was, indeed, in Snowtown, South Africa. Because of the signs, the town enjoyed modest popularity. Tour buses stopped and visitors came to photograph each other in front of them. Everyone who lived there patiently explained the name had nothing to do with the cool, white stuff that fell from the sky.

As promised, Sarah zipped in and out of the post office and bakery. When she pulled into the gas station, she saw a tour bus refueling. The bus's occupants saw Rollo and spoke in a foreign language. The bus driver, no stranger to the Aimtree pet, greeted both Sarah and Rollo. He asked if the tourists could photograph the lion. Japanese, they were amazed to see an enormous lion in the Landy.

"Certainly, they can snap all the photos they want. Rollo is patient. He knows he's a celebrity." Sarah said.

Mr. O Malley gestured to his bus occupants and approached Rollo. He rubbed the animal's massive forehead and scratched behind his ears. The Japanese tourists came closer and began taking pictures. Mr. O Malley pantomimed to one of the photographers that she should come closer. For a few seconds, no one moved. Then, the young woman stepped forward. She reached out and gently touched Rollo. He responded with a booming purr, which sent her scurrying away. The bus driver gestured for the girl to return after putting his face against the purring lion. She did. She placed both hands on Rollo's face and spoke to him. Her companions, realizing a photo op, took pictures. Within five minutes, the occupants of the bus were posing for selfies with Rollo.

Driving home Sarah said, "Rollo, we need to charge for these photo sessions. You can earn your keep. What do you think?"

There was no response from the back seat. "Ah well, it was just a thought." She laughed at her own silliness. "I've been thinking, we've been motoring about the countryside for several months. I know you return to the paddock. Would you like to try the stairs? I know you had difficulty with them but you would love snoozing under the fern. I'm confident you won't wander."

Again, no response from the rear. Sarah parked close to the stoep and opened the door. The lion stepped out of the Landy and looked at the stairs.

"Take your time, there's no pressure. I'll help you. I swear you can understand me. You're going to give it a go. One step at a time, I'll coach you when to lift your back feet."

Rollo carefully put both front feet on the first step. He made his way to the stoep without incident. Sarah was delighted, and she led him to the fern. He settled beneath it, sighed, and looked the picture of contentment.

"Excellent, I'm going to call Bob and alert him. He'll be amazed to see you here."

Sarah called her husband and told him the news. He, Michael, and Obert were repairing fences in the west pasture. He said they were dropping their tools and heading for the house. It was close to lunchtime. Sarah began meal preparation and thought about Rollo's last experience with the stairs.

The men arrived and hurried to greet the lion.

"Look at you!" exclaimed Obert.

Bob rubbed the lion's face. "Congratulations! We knew you could do it. Not to invite bad luck, but let's hope you arrive on the lawn in one piece."

"I wonder if he'll do patrol, he may stay here until feeding time," Michael said.

Sarah glanced at her watch. "We'll soon know. It's almost time for his afternoon stroll. Have you noticed the hens? They're perched on the fence, waiting for him."

Rollo sat up, yawned, got to his feet, and stretched. He leaned forward, then back, elongating his spine in true feline fashion. He walked to the stairs and started down. Everyone held their breath.

Sarah whispered. "Let's not talk, don't distract him."

Unlike the stoep debacle that sent Bob flying down the stairs, Rollo remembered to use his back paws and walked to the lawn without incident. From there, he ambled to the paddock, and the hens joined him.

"Well, what do you think about that?" Michael said.

Obert grinned. "Our simba's a rock star. He learned the stairs in just one go."

Sarah sighed with relief. She rose and said, "I'm going to close the gate. This was wonderful. He can join me after a ride. Now that I think about it, why can't he join us every day?"

"Why not, indeed?" Bob said.

Michael stood and said, "I'm going to walk patrol with them. I haven't done it since Tumaini left. Obert, would you like to join me?"

"I would, let's follow the big simba round the paddock."

The two brothers left, speaking in Maa.

Bob said, "Sarah, do you think Rollo understands Maa and English?"

"I wouldn't be surprised. Lions and Maasai have known each

other for a long time."

"Michael mentioned Tumaini. Have you heard from Peter? How is our bouncing baby boy?"

"Peter called yesterday, Our ellie has settled in. He and Freddie are pals. Tumaini also interacts with the rest of the orphan herd. Those two mini-matriarchs have taken him under their…er…trunks. They make sure he is safe and well-supervised."

"So, our boy is growing? Thriving? All the above?"

"He is, Peter said he and Freddie will soon begin to wander. They'll spend longer times in the wild, eventually, they won't return to the sanctuary. It might take years. Peter said that elephants integrating into their original homes do come back for visits."

"That's interesting, I'm glad we took him and cared for him. We did a good job."

"Yes, although we couldn't have done it without Rollo. He saved the day."

Michael called from the paddock. "Do you want me to shut the gate?"

Sarah answered, "Yes, please, lock him in the paddock. I'll feed him and the girls in a few hours."

Bob stood up. "We men-folk are returning to the fence. Lord, I hate working on fences. Well, you had a great day with Rollo. If he could talk, I know he would agree."

Several months passed. Rollo accompanied Sarah on short rides. He spent part of every day on the stoep. Bob found a huge dog bed and placed it under the fern. One afternoon in late fall Sarah heard chicken chatter in the yard. Curious, she went to the stoep and saw the hens at the bottom of the stairs.

"What're you lot up to? You never join Rollo for his naps. Is today the day you join him? Lord, I don't like that. You'll poop on my stoep."

Pearl eyed the first step. She fluttered up and Ruby joined her. Ebony, suspicious of everything, remained on the lawn. Her sisters reached the stoep and began an examination of the plants. That done, they joined Rollo on his dog bed. Ebony unfurled her wings and flew to the railing. Like Ruby and Pearl, she couldn't resist looking at the plants. She murdered a few hapless insects and settled in the back of the fern.

A week after the hens conquered the stoep, Sarah looked out her kitchen window and saw Obert towing his stock trailer into the access road that fronted the cattle pasture. She called to Rollo as she hurried down the stairs. "Rollo, come with me. Look who's here."

Obert opened the trailer door and dropped the ramp. Arabella pranced out like a beauty queen. Rollo boomed his loudest greeting and met her in the yard. The happy bovine shoved her slimy nose in his face and licked the side of his head with her raspy tongue. Rollo scrunched his eyes shut and stood patiently until Arabella finished her greetings.

"Just like old times," Obert said.

Sarah rubbed the cow's head. "Obert, she looks beautiful. When did you wean her calf?"

"A month ago, I reckoned I'd better return her, you can arrange her next date."

"Yep, we will use our young Nguni bull. That bull is coal black. The calf may be an interesting color. Let her settle into the herd, we've plenty of time before her next baby."

Three days later, Sarah, Bob, Malcolm, Michael, and Obert sat on the stoep, slaking their thirst after a hard, hot, afternoon of moving cattle.

"Since when have the hens colonized the stoep?" Malcolm asked.

Sarah answered, "Umm, a few weeks ago. One day when Rollo was up here, they appeared on the lawn. It took them two minutes to master the steps. They now accompany Rollo every day."

"How old are those birds?" Malcolm wondered.

"Hah!" Bob said, "That's the question. Michael? You're the chicken pro. How old are they?"

"I can't even guess. I do know my kids picked the three oldest hens to put in Rollo's den."

Obert shifted in his chair. "They aren't hens."

"Eh?" Sarah asked, "Say again?"

Malcolm frowned. "Obert, what are you talking about? Of course, they are hens."

"Nope, they aren't hens. How long have they been here? By my reckoning, they arrived shortly after Rollo. What a day that was! I can still see them zooming around the den. So…that was about seven years ago. Malcolm, don't you agree they should be dead by now? They're beyond ancient."

"Of course, they should be dead, they should have died from old age several years ago."

"Aha! My point exactly, see this is what happened. The biddies were here a month when aliens transported them to the mother ship. They were changed into robots to spy on us. They have been collecting data on human behavior."

Dead silence followed Obert's remarks. Several seconds ticked by. Bob made a valiant attempt not to laugh. He failed. Great, braying whoops erupted from him. He grabbed a napkin and wiped his streaming eyes. "Oh my Lord, the aliens must think they're observing normal earthling behavior." He collapsed in another fit of hysteria.

In an other-worldly voice, Sarah intoned, "Yes, commander,

there is a large four-legged carnivore that is instrumental in calf and elephant rearing. The two-legged creatures spend time catering to this huge, fanged beast. With our superior mental abilities, we can read the carnivore's mind. We remain confused as to why he puts up with the silly earthlings. We will continue to observe their behavior. If nothing else, it is very amusing."

Malcolm rubbed his face. "Obert, you may have something with your theory. God help the aliens if they think any of us are normal."

✸ Rollo ✸
Chapter 47

Rampaging rhinos! The hens and I returned to our peaceful life. Tumaini left several months ago. We missed him when he joined his pride but we were joyous knowing he was reunited with elephants. It was so quiet around the farm. The carers were, of course, gone and it was just the girls and me. Peter…bless that man…left a mattress. He knew how much I enjoyed sleeping on it. Sarah took a leap of faith and invited me to accompany her while she drove the vehicle. I believe it's called a Land Rover. I don't know if those contraptions are alive. I did hear one howl. Also, Sarah would stop at a feeding station and use a tube to nourish the conveyance! The fluid in the tube smelled terrible. How could that stuff be food? It made my eyes water. The process reminded me of bottle-feeding Tumaini, although the vehicle can go much longer between feedings. The Land Rover displays no sign of life when it's not moving. Its status mystifies me. Is it alive?

One day, we traveled into town and stopped to feed the car. A huge vehicle was at the food station. That vehicle held many passengers. Our friend, Mr. O Malley, was the driver. He usually drove the human cubs to their school. He's driven them to our farm. Sarah and Obert talk to the youngsters about lions. I, of course, am the star of that show. On this occasion, he drove people that didn't live here. I believe they're called tourists. Sarah told me this group came from a faraway place called Japan. They traveled over an enormous lake to visit us. Was it the same body of water that Etta and Aretha crossed? Anyway, they were milling round the bus…that's what this big vehicle is called…when Mr. O Malley invited them to come over and meet me. I'm used to humans and I knew this group was afraid of me. I kept my mouth shut. No yawning or purring. The rot set in when this nice young lady held my face in her hands. It felt so comforting, I purred. Glory! As Obert says. She was so startled, she leaped away from me with a cry of terror. I'll never learn to stay quiet. The fearful humans think I'm growling.

Mr. O Malley saved the day. He gave me some splendid ear scratches and leaned his forehead against mine. Within minutes, the whole group of Japanese humans was snapping pictures of me. I enjoyed the interaction. Anyway, on the way home Sarah was nattering about photos and heaven knows what else. I dozed and didn't hear her. When we arrived home, she stopped the vehicle near the stoep, rather than drive into my paddock. I realized I had missed part of her conversation. She opened the doors and talked about the stairs.

The stairs. Doesn't she remember what happened to me the last time I tried to conquer the stairs? Well, it served me right, for not paying attention to her conversation. She wanted me to go up the stairs. Was she daft? I can't refuse Sarah, she wanted me to go up the steps, so, up I went. Honestly, I had no trouble. The key was taking my time. Sarah helped by tapping my back legs to remind me to step with them. Once on the stoep, I recalled what a splendid view it offered. I went up the first time to watch for hyenas. I settled under Sarah's huge plant. It's called a fern and takes up one end of the stoep. Bob, Obert, and Michael came home for lunch. They were thrilled that I had successfully mastered the stairs, but worried about my descent. I took my time and reached the lawn without a mishap.

I spend afternoons on the stoep. It was delightful. Bob found a huge fluffy bed for large dogs. I'm not sure what a dog is, but they come in different sizes. Some are tiny, and some are quite tall and robust. Bob got the largest one he could find, it was perfect. I could stretch on my side and snooze all afternoon. It was especially nice on hot days because it was cool under the plant.

Any breeze was a welcome respite from our blazing afternoons. Life was good. I went for short rides with Sarah and dozed under the fern. Several months drifted by and the girls showed no inclination to join me. Suspicious of humans, they would wait on the fence for patrol. They grew more tolerant because of Tumaini. Humans were always with us Still, they refused to join me on the stoep. One day, Obert drove into our yard with a cart hooked onto his truck. It resembled the cart Felicity used when she brought her magnificent horses. Well, there was no horse in Obert's cart. He parked on the access road between my paddock and the cattle pasture, sprang out of the truck, and released the back gate. He turned to me and said he had a huge surprise. To my astonishment, Arabella came down the ramp. She approached, slobbered all over me, and chewed on my mane. Yes, no doubt, this is Arabella. I was glad to see her. She was sleek and beautiful. Obert allowed us to visit and then released her into the cattle area.

One morning I settled on the stoep when I heard the hens chattering. They were on the lawn. Sarah noted their presence as well. Moments later, Ruby and Pearl were pottering around the stoep. The plant jungle intrigued them. Ebony, finally joined them, and couldn't resist the foliage. I fear many insects lost their lives before the three girls settled behind the ferns. I was pleased they joined me. We've been together for years. They're part of my pride.

One day, shortly before our huge, annual braai, the humans were seated on the stoep. Obert was explaining why the hens weren't really hens. Malcolm and Sarah questioned him but considered his theory. According to Obert, the hens had been transformed into creatures that weren't alive. I wondered if they were like the vehicles we rode in. While animated, they didn't seem to be alive. Not like me, or Tumaini, or the humans. Still, the hens seemed alive to me. They slept, drank, ate, and pooped, just like me. How could they not be alive? Obert talked about aliens. What are aliens? From the conversation, I reckoned they came from a place even farther away than the big lake that separates us from Aretha and Etta's home.

Chapter 48

Sarah stepped onto the stoep into the punishing heat. "Ach! If this spring weather is a harbinger of summer, God help us." She glanced at Rollo and the girls. They were asleep under the fern. On his side, Rollo gently snored, while the hens sat panting, with wings spread to dissipate heat. "You lot look more comfortable than I am. Why didn't I do this shopping trip early this morning? Rollo, you're staying home today. It's too hot to sit in the car. Gad! It's not even noon."

Rollo raised his head and flipped his ears at Sarah. He looked at her car keys, shook himself, and flopped back on the dog bed. "Atta boy, you know it's too hot. I'll be back in a couple of hours." Halfway down the stairs, Sarah stopped and returned to the house. She had a large pan of water. "How do you like this? Cool, fresh water, right under your nose and beaks. Wait! I can make it better." She went into the kitchen and returned with a bag of ice cubes. "Now, you have a pan of cold water. No use trudging through this heat to your water trough. Okay, I'm off, I'd suggest none of you move until it's time for your walk." Rollo shifted his front feet and purred in agreement.

The sun was past its zenith when Sarah swung into the driveway. A glance at her watch told her it was two o'clock. Halfway to the house, she saw Rollo sitting next to what resembled a heap of trash. Concerned, she accelerated until she was next to her pet. He was purring and gently prodding the lump.

"Rollo! What're you doing? You never venture this close to the main road. Oh my Lord, that's another lion! Rollo, is that poor creature alive?" She grabbed her phone and called Malcolm.

"Mal, you won't believe this. There's a lion collapsed on our road. Rollo is sitting next to him. I'm going to move the car to shade them."

"Geez, how the hell did another lion get in your driveway? Is it male? Or female? Does it look like it's been fighting with Rollo?"

"I don't think so. Rollo is purring and patting the other animal. The stranger looks emaciated. I hope he isn't rabid. That would put our boy at risk. He's maned, a male."

"You read my mind. Well, Samantha is accompanying me on patient calls. We'll be there shortly."

"Okay, I'll call the troops for more help. Should we do anything until you arrive?"

"Can you pour water on him? He may have succumbed to this terrible heat."

"Okay, I'll tell Bob to bring buckets of water."

"Be careful, stand in the truck bed when you dump water on him."

Sarah called Bob and set Malcolm's instructions in motion. She leaned out the window to better observe the prostrate lion. A tiny breeze stirred the dust. Sarah caught a whiff of a terrible odor rising from the lion. "Whew! Rollo, what's that smell? What's wrong with this poor lad?"

Bob drove toward her. Michael and Obert followed in Michael's bakkie. Bob peered at the lion in disbelief. "How in the world…?"

Sarah looked at Michael's truck and saw several containers of water. "Good, can we get water on him? Malcolm said he might be suffering from the heat. I don't know when he showed up, but I've been gone almost three hours."

Obert mopped his brow. "Shoot, that's too long to sit in this heat. What's that smell?"

Sarah turned to see Malcolm's truck approaching. "I don't know, but I fear something is far wrong with this animal."

Malcolm and Samantha arrived and hurried toward Sarah. "Is he still alive?" Malcolm asked.

Michael leaned over the side of his bakkie. "His sides are barely moving, but he's alive."

"Okay, can we get a pan under his head and put water into it? I need to see him drink. If he can, it will put paid to a rabies diagnosis. Well, at least a symptomatic rabies diagnosis."

"We have a dishpan on the stoep for Rollo and the girls. It's perfect for this," Sarah said.

" Mal, what about some ice?" Bob asked.

"Perfect, let's do that, meanwhile let's soak him. Michael, can you dump water on him?"

Michael complied. The lion stirred as the cool water cascaded down his back and sides. He made an odd cooing noise.

Bob said, "Obert, let's get that pan and ice."

Samantha asked, "Dr. Malcolm, what's that noise he's making?"

"Well, it's going to sound daft, but sometimes a mother lion will call her cubs with an odd cooing noise. The sound this boy is making reminds me of that call. Why he's doing it, is a mystery."

Sarah looked up to see Bob and Obert returning. Bob carried ice and two brooms. Obert had the pan. She stood by, ready to help if needed. Amazed by Samantha's calm demeanor and adult behavior, Sarah remained in the background and let her young friend shine.

Bob waved the brooms. "Mal, let's put the pan in front of him at a prudent distance. Since Michael is safe in the truck, he can use the broom stick to scoot the pan near the lion's head. I can push with the other stick. Let's dump ice into it before we get started."

"Brilliant! Let's do it."

Bob placed the pan behind the truck. Michael used his broom to slide the pan toward the lion's head. Bob pushed from behind the rear wheels. When the pan was next to the stranger's face, Obert jumped into the truck and dumped more water onto the animal. The animal snorted and raised his head. It was enough to slide the pan under his chin. The group waited in silence. Rollo purred even louder. The sick lion felt the cold water on his chin and drank.

"Boy, he's tanking up," Sarah said.

Malcolm agreed. "Good. Dump more water into the pan. We'll cool him inside and out."

Sam wrinkled her nose. "What's that awful smell? It's coming from his head, isn't it?"

Sarah smiled. She knew Malcolm recognized a teaching moment.

He asked Samantha, "What can you guess about the odor? What do you think is causing it?

Without hesitation, Samantha responded. "A porcupine struck him in the face. There might be broken quills in his mouth."

"Very good, anything else?"

"A bad tooth, maybe a broken tooth or one that's infected."

"Excellent, Sam, those are my two top picks for a source of the odor. My third guess is a necrotizing oral tumor. Now, what can we do next?"

"We sedate him and examine his mouth."

"Absolutely correct, before the exam, we'll take his vital signs. I'll bet his temperature is very high. Now, you stand with Sarah while I tranquilize this boy."

"Dr. Malcolm, can I see the drug you are preparing? I'll stand near the truck."

"Fair enough, Samantha, I'll show you what we'll need, based on our tentative diagnoses."

Malcolm prepared the sedative and asked the brothers, "Can you move the truck so the rear wheels are just behind this lion's butt? I'll crouch behind them to inject him."

Obert moved the truck. Malcolm knelt, reached round the wheel and injected the sedative into the animal's scrawny backside. He then stood and jumped into the truck bed. The lion never stopped drinking.

"Ach! Did he even feel that jab?" asked Sarah.

Malcolm said, "I don't think he was aware of it. Let's give him a few minutes. I'm going to prepare what I need."

Sam stood at the back of Malcolm's truck. Sarah joined her and said, "Sam, you're amazing. I see you already have some items in that tray. You're already thinking like a veterinarian."

Sam beamed. "Aunt Sarah, you know it's all I've ever wanted to do. I want to help sick animals."

"I'd say you have a running start on it. It's nice of Mal to let you ride with him."

"Yes, I'm very grateful, Mummy and Dad are pleased as well. I have to wait two years before I get my learner's permit to drive, but that's okay. I'll learn many things, shadowing Dr. Malcolm."

Malcolm glanced at his watch, he took Bob's broomstick and

gently prodded his patient. The lion never moved. Chin in the water pan, he looked asleep.

"Okay, I think our boy is in the arms of Morpheus. Let's examine him."

Sarah and Samantha approached the sleeping lion. "Sarah said, "He looks and smells awful. Mal, how can we help you?"

"Let me get his vitals, then I'll prop his mouth open. Someone can hold a light, so I can see inside his mouth. Someone else can hold his head back."

Malcolm began his examination. He started with the thermometer. While it was reading the animal's temperature, Malcolm listened to the heart and lungs. "His lungs are clear and I'm amazed to say, his heart is chugging along at a decent rhythm. His temperature is four degrees above normal. I expected that because of the heat and infection. Okay, let's examine his mouth." He placed a device in the animal's mouth to hold it open. Then, he ran his hand round the animal's lips and gums, peered under his tongue, and examined the teeth. Sarah held the torch and tried not to breathe.

"One of his back teeth on the upper left side of his jaw is so loose I'd wager I could yank it out with my fingers. It's likely infected and the source of the odor. Sam, can you grab the forceps for me?"

Sarah asked, "Mal, is that a molar?"

"Yes, I'm going to remove it and load this fellow up with antibiotics."

"Dr. Malcolm, I also brought saline solution and cotton wool. Is that okay?"

Sarah smiled at Samantha. "Malcolm, I think you have a terrific assistant. She's anticipating what you might need."

"Sam, that's exactly what I would have put on the tray. Now, if someone can steady his head, I'm going to yank this rotten tooth."

One brisk tug was enough to pull the molar. A torrent of bloody, foul-smelling pus gushed from the cavity. Malcolm grabbed a wad of cotton wool. He used it to sop up the drainage. When the flow lessened, he rinsed the area and asked Sarah to re-position the light.

"Whew, I don't know how this animal is still alive. He couldn't hunt, I doubt he could eat carrion. That infected tooth had to be incredibly painful. The tissue around the tooth is degraded from chronic infection. I'm not sure it's going to heal. The antibiotics should help, but this boy is very sick." Malcolm sat back on his heels. "Never mind the tooth, I'm still wondering how he got here. If he ran into hyenas or even other lions, they would've killed him."

Bob mumbled under his breath. "Maybe the aliens dumped him here."

Sarah shook her head and grinned. "Maybe so, but I think it was just a random chance he staggered into our driveway. Now, what do we do with him?"

Bob said, "Why don't we put him in the paddock next to Rollo's area? We prepared it up for Tumaini. Remember, the shed has double doors front and back. We can confine him and leave the upper doors open. I doubt he can jump out. I know he walked here, but he may not be able to walk now."

Sarah looked at Malcolm. "What do you think?"

"It's perfect. I'll get my sling. We'll drag him into the shed."

They deposited the sleeping animal in a thick bed of straw. Michael closed the lower back door. Malcolm gave the lion a shot to help wake him. Moments later, the old, gray-faced lion opened his eyes. His head wobbled.

Bob said, "He looks like Clancy at the bar on Saturday night

The animal blinked and peered up at Bob.

"Good Lord! Malcolm, look at his eyes."

Malcolm saw the animal's eyes were cloudy. "Good Lord is right. He must be almost blind. He may see light and dark, but I doubt he can objects."

Samantha said, "Uncle Bob, you named him. I'm the one who usually names animals, but you beat me to it. Clancy, his name is Clancy. The poor old fellow. A bad tooth and he's almost blind. It's a miracle he found us."

Michael took off his cap and wiped his sweaty face. "I think Bob had it right. Not a miracle, the aliens dumped him in the driveway."

Malcolm grinned. "We're getting tons of mileage out of the alien story. Can we get pans for food and water in this shed?"

Sarah said, "I've been thinking about that. We'll get another pan like this one. We'll punch two holes in the rim, drill two holes in the shed wall, then run wire thru the holes to anchor the pan close to the shed doors. We'll feed and water him by leaning over the door."

"Genius!" Bob said, "Obert, let's go get tools and another pan. It won't take fifteen minutes to do this. He looks half dead now, but he may surprise us tomorrow."

Malcolm added. "Exactly right, Bob, let's fasten his food and water containers to the wall."

Sarah asked, "What can we feed this boy? He just had a tooth pulled. His mouth will be sore. Can we try meatballs? He can swallow them without chewing."

"Sure, that would be great. We don't know if he'll eat. He's very sick."

Sam said, "Aunt Sarah, I can help you with the meat. I'll call Mummy to pick me up when we're done. I know Dr. Malcolm needs to see other patients."

"Great! Can you run to the outside kitchen? There's ground beef in the frig."

Clancy began making determined efforts to rise. He got to a sitting position and toppled. He tried again, and again. After several attempts, he stood and wobbled to the door of the shed. He looked at the men and made his odd cooing noise. Rollo stood on his hind legs, propped his front paws on top of the shed door, and looked at the newcomer. He purred. Clancy cooed a response.

Malcolm shook his head. "These two lions take the cake. They make the oddest noises. Has Rollo ever made real lion sounds?"

Sarah said, "Oh yes, remember, he roared the night the hyenas were tunneling under the fence. Arabella was on their breakfast menu. It's the only time we've heard him sound or act like a wild lion."

Michael beckoned to the returning Obert and Bob. "Hurry, I think this simba is looking for water."

In moments, they secured the pans to the side of the shed. Michael shut the door, grabbed a bucket, and poured water for the lion. Clancy snuffled in the pan and then drank until the pan was nearly dry. Michael provided a refill.

Sam hurried from the kitchen with a plastic bag full of ground meat. "Aunt Sarah, is this enough?"

"It'll do for a start. Let's make a few meatballs."

Once finished, she handed the bag to Malcolm. He leaned over the door and dumped the meat into the second pan. Clancy's nose twitched. He tottered over and inhaled a meatball. The rest disappeared in seconds. The animal peered up at the humans. He seemed to ask, 'Is there more'?

Sarah handed Michael several more meatballs. Clancy ate them.

"Excellent, Malcolm said, let him rest. This shed is perfect for him. Let's see how he does overnight."

Rollo settled himself in front of the shed door. He put his head on his paws and looked at Sarah.

She tugged his mane. "Are you the guard lion? I see you're going to stay with Clancy. That's fine, Lord help any hyenas that might venture near."

✸ Rollo ✸
Chapter 49

I awoke to a familiar sound. When my littermates and I were tiny, my mum would hide us from enemies. Hyenas were number one on her list. The beasts loved to kill lion cubs. Upon returning from her hunt, she would call us with a soft cooing sound. We'd creep out of the bushes and examine the food she had found. Anyway, the hens and I were on the stoep. It was late morning, but already beastly hot. Sarah had left for a shopping trip. It was too hot for me to join her. She left us a large pan of water. She's so thoughtful! It had small, white objects floating in it. My curiosity got the best of me after she left. I tried to grab one of those odd-looking things. They were so slippery, they squirted out of the sides of my mouth. I finally did snag one…my goodness…I've never felt anything that cold. I crunched a few and rejoined the girls. The poor hens perched behind the fern. They had their wings spread to help them stay cool. I don't think it helped.

I listened to the sound. Was another lion in our yard? Could a lioness have lost her cubs? I rose and walked across the stoep to determine the source of the cooing. I saw nothing on the lawn or near the cattle pasture. Again, the sound drifted to my ears. I went down the stairs into the crushing heat and listened. It was coming from the driveway. I don't approach the main road because I fear cars. One hit me. I don't want to repeat the experience.

Bah! One day, my curiosity is going to get me killed. I looked down the driveway after crossing the lawn. There was a motionless lump lying on the verge. I had a brief argument with myself. The lump was nearer to the house than the main road. Surely, it would be safe to venture closer for an inspection. So, that's what

I did. To my amazement, the lump was cooing. It was another lion, a male, collapsed in the dirt. The creature was thin and a terrible smell came from his head. It smelled like something dead. I carefully prodded the lion with my forepaw. No reaction. I tried several more times, then nudged the beast with my nose. He was too weak to lift his head but acknowledged me with more cooing. Where was Sarah? I sat next to the beast and waited. Sarah would know what to do. This poor creature was sick. My human pride members would help him.

I sat in that awful heat for what seemed hours. Eventually, I heard Sarah's vehicle swing into the driveway. She took one look at us and moved her truck to provide shade. Then she got help. Things moved quickly after the calls. Malcolm, Samantha, then Bob, Obert, and Michael arrived. Samantha's so mature. She's assisting Malcolm when her schooling permits. I remember her as a cub. Her incredible antics terrified us on two occasions. Not any longer! She's going to be a wonderful veterinarian. It made me proud to see her helping Malcolm. She knew what he needed before he did. Once everyone arrived, I wasn't needed but watched everything the humans did. Excited about another lion living here. I hoped he would survive. He could join our pride.

Malcolm went to work. First, he offered water and that poor old lion drank and drank and drank. He sedated the beast, and the humans moved him to the shed that was reserved for Tumaini. What a joke! That baby elephant couldn't be alone, so the hens and I cared for him for almost two years. Anyway, Malcolm's examination discovered an infected tooth. it was the source of the terrible smell. He removed it and was cautiously optimistic about a full recovery. Samantha was a brilliant assistant. We're so proud of her. She's poised on the edge of adulthood.

Our patient woke up, lifted his head, and peered at Bob. More bad news, both his eyes were cloudy. Malcolm was sure he was almost blind. Bob made a remark about someone named Clancy having too much to drink. I've never met Clancy, but all agreed that Bob had named our new lion.

Sometimes my two-legged pride members surprise me. Sarah had a brilliant idea to provide food and water to Clancy. She asked Bob and Obert to help. They fastened two pans to the wall. It was clever, they could lean over the half-door and re-fill the pans as needed. Sarah suggested meatballs as a meal. Clancy wouldn't have to chew, he could just swallow them. What are meatballs? Sarah and Samantha prepared them. We were hoping our poor old patient would rally, but Michael was especially concerned, he immediately bonded with the old fellow.

The ladies…yes, Samantha is now a lady…gave the meatballs to Malcolm. All of Malcolm's instructions about how to behave around me have been ignored. He didn't want people touching me. He became semi-hysterical when he discovered Sarah was driving me round the countryside. When I was allowed on the stoep, he gave up. The one rule everyone agreed to respect was no one hand feed me. My choppers were too big. I might bite someone by accident. Absurd! Samantha saw me eyeing the pan. She gave it to Michael but kept one meatball behind her back. That minx! Bless her heart. She backed up to me and opened her hand. I gently took her offering. No bones! Nothing to chew! I'd never experienced such a delightful treat. I know this sounds awful, but I hoped if Clancy had no appetite, I would eat the leftovers. No such luck. Malcolm dumped them into a pan. Clancy ate all of them.

Our patient settled on a bed of deep straw. He looked exhausted. My human pride members left, except for Michael. He was concerned about Clancy. I stood on my hind legs, peered over the door, and purred. Clancy raised his head and cooed. Michael laughed and sat outside the shed. I joined him. Together, we would protect our patient. He would be easy prey for the dratted hyenas. Not on our watch! He could rest and heal. I knew Michael would leave, but I would stay. After all, Clancy was the first lion in my motley pride. I would guard him.

Chapter 50

A week after Clancy's arrival found Sarah on the stoep, waiting for Malcolm. He would examine the animal to see if the infection had subsided. Michael appointed himself as Clancy's primary caregiver. Every morning Sarah saw his bakkie parked next to the paddock. She knew Michael fed Clancy and released him into the enclosure. Rollo would meet Michael and the three would take a slow walk round the paddock. Clancy would step outside the shed and put his nose against Rollo's flank. Michael would walk alongside Clancy. He kept one hand on the elderly animal's back. Gad, Sarah mused, we have a bilingual, seeing-eye lion. Malcolm's truck turned into the driveway and broke her train of thought. She went to the paddock and greeted the vet.

"How's our boy today? I see Michael and Rollo are on the job."

"Yes, Michael has bonded with this animal. Rollo's just doing what he always does with sick critters."

"I'd love to see a scan of his brain. I wonder if we could see any changes from normal lions."

Sarah laughed. "I take exception to that remark. Saying our boy isn't normal. I'm kidding, Mal. Rollo is anything but normal. The brain scan, it's possible to do?"

"Sure, he'd have to be transported to the vet school. That won't be a problem. He loves car rides. Do you want me to inquire about it? I can ask a professor."

"Ach! Let me talk to Bob. Rollo would need sedation. I'm not sure we want to risk it."

"Okay, it's entirely up to you. It'd be useful information"

"Let's discuss Rollo's head another time. What should we do with our geriatric patient?"

"I'm glad to see he is getting a bit of exercise. How's his appetite?"

"He has eaten God alone knows how many meatballs. He does this little walk after breakfast and goes back to bed. We leave the door open but shut the gate between his enclosure and Rollo's den. I don't want him wandering without Rollo. Michael and Rollo go about their day. Clancy will totter outside in the afternoon to relieve himself, sometimes he sleeps in the sun. He stays close to the shed. We lock him in at night and Rollo sleeps in front of the door. Heaven help any hyenas that think an easy meal is on offer.

Malcolm laughed. "Now, that's one time when Rollo behaved like a wild lion. He hates hyenas. I'll never forget your description of his behavior when those ugly beasts tried to eat Arabella."

"That was some experience. Bob and I couldn't believe our sappy lion could move so fast. And roar! We thought it was another animal. Not to change the subject, but speaking of Arabella, she's enormous. I think she'll deliver any day. We bred her to our black Nguni bull, and she's either pregnant or growing a huge tumor."

"I'd bet on pregnancy, are Bob and Obert over the moon about this calf?"

"Ach! Honestly, to listen to them, you would think this unborn bovine was a human child."

"Do you have any thoughts about her due date? I know your cattle are pasture bred, but owners have a general idea of the date of conception."

"Bob and Obert reckon it will be in the next two weeks. I don't argue with them. That poor cow is waddling, she's so big."

"Does she still visit with Rollo?"

"Yep, she comes to the fence and moos. Rollo walks down the access road and lets her slobber all over him."

"Sarah, if Arabella is that big, she could be carrying twins. It's rare in cattle, but it can happen. Are you planning on isolating her before she delivers? Should I look at her?

"Are you kidding? My husband and Obert are already watching her. As you know, we rarely isolate our pregnant cows, but Arabella has a maternity suite. Bob, Obert, and Michael built a small corral near the house. Half of it's covered. God forbid a drop of rain should fall on Ara's curly head."

"Can you confine her if she has twins? She may not have enough milk for both calves. Sometimes a cow will bond with one calf and forget the second one. She will wander off and desert one baby."

"No worries there. Arabella will have plenty of support. Examine her now and tell us your opinion. She's such a pet, she'll come right to her little corral when we call her."

"Okay, let's see about Clancy first."

Clancy, Michael, and Rollo finished their walk. Clancy settled in the shed, ready for a nap.

Malcolm looked at him and said, "I don't think I'll sedate him. He's gained weight and, all things considered, looks fine. Sedating him just to listen to his heart and lungs, and to check the healing in his mouth, isn't worth it. If he were failing, and not eating, we wouldn't have a choice. Let's leave him alone, I doubt he'll live much longer."

"Okay, Mal, I agree, he's on borrowed time. Let's not upset him any more than we have to. Let's go find Arabella."

Sarah found Bob and Obert tinkering with Arabella's new home. The two were installing a hay rack and water trough when she, Malcolm and Michael approached the fence.

Obert volunteered to get the bovine. He stood at the gate and yelled, "Ara, Arabella! Hup girl, come on in."

In seconds, an answering bellow came from the pasture. Bob said, "This may take a few minutes, she isn't moving fast."

Arabella plodded into view. Malcolm took one look and exclaimed. "Holy cow! No pun intended. You weren't kidding, she's huge. I'd start confining her now. If that's one calf, it's a whopper and she may need a c-section. We don't want to be doing that in the middle of your pasture. I'm suspicious she has twins. Ideally, we could do an ultra-sound, but since we're in the field, a rectal palpation will have to be sufficient. Let's get a lead rope on her. She's so gentle I can do it here."

Obert clipped the lead onto Arabella's halter and moved her against the fence. Malcolm did her vitals and then proceeded with the rectal exam. "I feel a calf in each uterine horn. If both calves are in one horn, it's harder to diagnose twins. This is straightforward. It's good she has this little pen close to the house. She may have trouble with their delivery. I assume you will watch her."

Sarah burst out laughing. "Are you kidding? Bob and Obert may as well be the expectant father. One or both of them will camp here until she delivers."

Malcolm patted Arabella's bulging side. "I don't think they'll be waiting long. This girl is going to pop soon." He turned to Rollo, who had wandered over to join them. "Well, big guy, you're going to have your paws full, caring for poor, old, doddering Clancy and two new calves."

Sarah said, "I wonder how Ara will react to him being around her babies. We'll have to make sure he doesn't get trampled by their protective mother."

Obert scoffed. "Are you kidding? She'll be fine, remember, he raised her. He also saved her from being hyena chow. She's so smart, she'll remember that experience."

Three days drifted by, then five, Obert and Bob took turns on maternity watch. A bemused Sarah watched the men fret and fuss over their favorite cow. Arabella was the calmest of the three. Sarah knew Rollo was puzzled by the attention given to his former roommate, she could also see he wouldn't budge from the front of Clancy's shed.

On the eighth night, Sarah awoke to her phone. Bob shouted Ara was in labor and Obert was on the way. Ach! Sarah thought, I almost heard him without the phone. Is this where I boil water? She hauled herself out of bed, went to the kitchen, and pushed the button on the coffee maker.

Once dressed, she hurried to the corral and saw Obert's truck turn into the driveway. Ara, still on her feet, had an introspective look about her. She dropped her head as a labor pain rippled across her flanks.

Bob said, "We should call Malcolm. He said to call when she started labor. Don't you think we should call?"

"Bob, how long have we been raising cattle? Need I remind you that calves don't appear after the first five minutes of labor? This may take hours."

Obert leaped out of his truck as Arabella had another contraction. "We need to call Malcolm. She's in labor. Both calves could present simultaneously?"

He rubbed Ara's forehead and whispered words of comfort. The cow looked at him as if he were daft.

Sarah rolled her eyes. "Listen, you both know better. Let's see how she gets on, it's the middle of the night. We can call Malcolm in an hour or two. She's not in trouble, her contractions have just started.

Two hours later, Arabella went down, gave a mighty bellow, and began to strain. Another bellow and several more heaves produced two feet and a twitching nose.

"Perfect!" Bob exclaimed. "The calf is alive, with two feet out." Obert joined Bob. They crouched behind the straining cow. Arabella's legs stiffened, she bawled again and pushed the baby's shoulders out. Two more contractions and a small red heifer flopped on the ground. Bob cleared her airway. Obert rubbed her with an old towel.

Sarah glanced at her watch. "Well, it's five o'clock, Malcolm has started his day. I'm calling him. Let's see where he is. It's Saturday, Sam may be shadowing him. I hope she is, she'll be excited to see the babies." She pulled out her phone and made the call. "We're lucky bums today. Malcolm is finishing work at the Von Bergs, he'll be here shortly. Samantha is with him."

The newcomer was making determined efforts to rise. Arabella refused to get up. She knew a second calf had to be delivered. Obert pulled the calf in front of her and the cow licked her baby.

Obert said, "They're both fine. Ara may take a break before she goes back into hard labor."

Bob nodded. "I agree, Sarah's right, it'll be good for Mal to look at them. You and I will feel better."

Sarah headed for the house. "Coffee? Breakfast? Both men fidgeted, looked at their feet, hemmed and hawed. "I can't believe you two. You don't want to leave her? Fine, I'll bring food and beverages. Ara may want a drink. I reckon you can put a bucket under her nose. She is likely very thirsty."

Bob, Obert, and Sarah were having breakfast, using the hood of their truck as a makeshift table, when Mal drove into the yard. He and Samantha hurried toward Arabella and the newborn. Samantha patted Ara and knelt by the calf. She couldn't contain her delight over the tiny bovine.

"Dr. Malcolm, she's beautiful. The image of her mum. Ara, you should be proud. I reckon her unborn sibling will be just as gorgeous."

Malcolm examined the baby and looked at Arabella. The cow flipped her ears at the vet but wouldn't rise. Malcolm said, "All right Mummy, you rest. Don't get up." Laughing, he got on his knees and inspected Ara's nether regions. "All's well back here. She's taking a break before she starts to push hard. The red heifer struggled to her feet and tottered to Arabella's enormous bag. She tried to nurse. Since Mum was lying down, the calf had to work before she latched onto a teat.

Sarah said, "That poor baby may as well be standing on her head. Honestly, Ara, you are a big, spoiled brat. Get up so your baby can eat."

Bob and Obert jumped to the cow's defense. "She's tired! Poor thing just produced a fine calf! She is smart enough to know she needs her rest!"

"Sarah put up her hands. "All right, all right, I stand corrected. Mal, what do you think? Is she okay? "

"Yes, look at her flanks. I see ripples, they're small contractions that will soon turn into powerful expulsive efforts."

A droning sound filled the air. Rollo had left Clancy's shed and was standing near the gate. The big carnivore stared at the calf. Booming purrs rose from him.

Samantha went to him and rubbed his forehead. "Look, Rollo, isn't she cute? Guess what? Arabella has twins, the second one will be here soon." Rollo peered at her and then focused his attention on the calf. Full of milk, she flopped in the straw.

Arabella turned and mooed a greeting. She remained on the ground. Her daughter heard the purring, pricked her brand new ears toward the sound, rose, and took a few wobbly steps toward Rollo. She reached through the fence and grabbed a mouthful of his mane, chewed, found it not to her liking, and attempted to nurse on his chin. She gazed into the lion's eyes. He purred, she drooled.

Obert slapped Bob's shoulder. "History repeats itself. Look, Ara relaxed. She knows her baby is in good hands…erm…paws."

Samantha rubbed Rollo's head, declared him to be the best boy ever, and said, "Rosie! Let's name her Rosie. She's the right color, and she has a disposition to match her coat."

Sarah agreed. "Perfect, Sam, you've done it again. It's a perfect name for this little one."

Arabella lurched to her feet, paced in a circle, and flopped down on her opposite side. She snorted, stiffened, and bore down.

Malcolm said, "Here comes act two. She re-positioned herself and is going back into hard labor. I'll bet the second calf will be an easier birth, providing it's positioned correctly. We don't need a head back."

Sarah and Sam cuddled Rosie. An agitated Rollo stood and watched his Arabella groan and thrash. He turned to Sarah. Sarah rubbed his ear. "It's okay, big guy, Ara is having another baby. Don't be scared. Malcolm is here."

Arabella had two violent contractions. The third produced the calf's head and feet. Two more expulsive efforts and the baby slid onto the straw. Malcolm cleared the airway and waited. Arabella gave another heave and produced the afterbirth.

"Atta girl," Malcolm said, "Let's look at this baby. The vet cleared membranes from the calf's nose to assure an airway. He lifted a rear leg.

"Another heifer, what luck! This one is coal black. Isn't the bull black?"

Sarah knelt by the calf and rubbed her with a wisp of straw. "Yes, all black with no white markings. His daughter is the same. I don't see a speck of white on her."

Samantha, entranced by the babies, said, "Aunt Sarah, this little girl's color reminds me of Mummy's necklace with the black Onyx stones. Shall we name her Onyx?"

"Obert saluted and cried. "Bravo! You've done it again. Both names are spot on."

Malcolm examined Arabella and her twins. He pronounced all three healthy and advised rest for the mum and babies. He cautioned Ara might not have enough milk and that her humans should be ready to bottle-feed if needed.

Sarah threw back her head and howled. "Mal don't worry about these two going hungry. I'm sure my husband and Obert will live with them. If the babies look distressed, these two will attend to them.

✸ Rollo ✸
Chapter 51

Stampeding wildebeests! It's been an exciting time! Clancy began to heal and eat well. Sarah's idea about ground meat was brilliant. The old fellow swallowed panful's of meatballs and gained strength. We knew his time with us was short. He didn't know what made him walk onto our property or how he got separated from his pride. I suspected his mind was not functioning correctly because one of the few things he did recall was his mum calling when he was a tiny cub. He made that sound. My human pride members were happy to see an improvement in Clancy, but I could smell death on him. I knew it wouldn't be long before he left us. He knew he was dying and grateful to be in a place of peace and safety. I appointed myself his protector. Michael also helped with Clancy's care. At sunrise, Michael would drive into the yard and join me. Together, we would sit and wait for the old fellow to awaken. When Michael heard him bumbling round, he would open the door and begin the morning ritual. Michael would speak words of encouragement in Maa. Clancy would align himself with his nose touching my flank. He knew his vision was poor and relied upon me to be his eyes. Michael would walk on his opposite side. He would place a hand on Clancy's back and we would do a slow stroll round the paddock. The old fellow had few other needs. His morning walk satisfied him and he returned to the shed for breakfast and a nap. Sarah or Bob would prepare his meal and make sure his bedding was clean. The hens and I would do morning hyena patrol and settle on the porch. I positioned myself at the top of the steps so I could see Clancy's shed. The weather had mercifully cooled.

Arabella returned to us. Obert brought her home after she weaned her first cub. She joined her pride but always came to the fence for a visit.

I'm so stupid! I couldn't understand why she kept getting bigger, and bigger, and bigger. Good pasture, I reasoned, she's on lush fodder. Clancy was here for a week when Malcolm arrived to examine him. He chose to leave our old lion alone. That was fine with us, we didn't want our patient upset. I suspected Malcolm knew he would die soon.

Anyway, Sarah asked Malcolm to check on Ara, and he obliged. Bob and Obert had built a small pen for the cow near the house. Why did they want her near them? I reckoned they wanted to talk to her. Obert liked to groom and bathe her, so it made sense to have her available. I also thought they wished to confine her to limit her eating. Perhaps this was a diet. I'm so stupid! Malcolm examined her and proclaimed she was carrying twins. Twins! She had two cubs in that huge belly. Well, Bob and Obert were ecstatic at the news. Malcolm guessed she would deliver in two weeks. Those two silly men drew up a schedule to ensure someone was near round the clock. Sarah, the voice of reason, tried to talk common sense into them. She failed. At night, either Bob or Obert would sleep in the truck bed. Sarah didn't take part in cow-watching duty.

Several nights later, I awoke to a racket. Bob was shouting into that odd thing the humans carry with them. The house and yard were lit up. Sarah hurried down the stairs. Within minutes, Obert's truck pulled into the driveway. It was still dark, but I knew dawn was fast approaching. Well, I wouldn't miss whatever would happen next. I'm too nosey. I strolled to the lawn. Poor Arabella was flat on the ground. She was making dreadful sounds. Her legs were stiff and her eyes had a glazed expression. Why isn't someone helping her? I got close to the fence and purred, but

I was sure purring wouldn't help. Her belly was heaving, and after one enormous contraction, two hooves and the tip of a nose protruded from her rear end. In moments, the calf was born. So tiny! It thrilled Bob and Obert that the baby was female. They made sure the little one was breathing properly and let her rest. She was the same shade as Arabella, a rich, red color. Within minutes, that little mite was making determined efforts to rise. She impressed me. We lions are born blind and helpless. We can barely haul ourselves around to find Mum. Not this newborn. She stood on shaky legs and butted her mum's enormous bag. Arabella wouldn't get to her feet. Obert and Bob steadied the baby while Sarah groaned and rolled her eyes. I sided with the men. Poor Ara, she had put forth a tremendous effort and was exhausted. I reckoned she was conserving her strength for the second delivery. The little redhead nursed and collapsed in a heap on the clean straw. Samantha named her 'Rosie'.

Delighted with her, I boomed a greeting. That minx hauled herself upright, tottered over, and yanked on my mane. She didn't like that and tried to nurse on my chin. Obert was pleased the cub acted like her mother. Me? Not so much. I remember Arabella as a baby. She was mischievous, just like Samantha. She was also a slob. When she wasn't chewing on my mane, she was drooling on my face. This new baby was cute and friendly. I could have short visits through the fence. The sun turned the world into colors when Malcolm and Samantha arrived.

Arabella rose and went flopped on her opposite side. Malcolm predicted the second cub would soon appear. That poor cow! She gave another strangled bellow, lifted her tail, and strained. That Malcolm! We've had our differences, but he's such a good animal doctor and advocate. Within minutes, another cub was deposited on the straw. This one, another female, was jet black. Malcolm made sure the baby was breathing and waited. That little black cub was struggling to her feet while still attached to her mum. She shook her head and bleated hello to everyone. Malcolm laughed and freed her from the birth membranes. He steadied her while her mum rose and began a thorough examination of her new baby. Rosie hauled herself to her feet and joined her sister. I thought Obert and Bob would injure themselves, they were so excited about these two cubs. Everyone agreed the three would stay confined. Ara needed to produce twice her milk volume. Bob and Obert were prepared to bottle-feed if necessary. Bah! The twins thrived, Ara had enough milk for them. Obert insisted they needed to be confined for a month. Bob agreed. Sarah said they were being overprotective.

The men allowed them onto the access road, the cubs loved it. I spent part of the day watching them frolic in the larger space. Like all cubs, they would collapse and sleep for several hours after a play session. They were part of my pride, I would protect them. Prides give us strength and solidarity, we must protect the youngsters. My pride is odd, but I'm dedicated to it.

Chapter 52

Sarah and Bob trotted down the stairs. Bob said, "Our babies are three months old. Can you believe it? Obert's idea to allow them into the access road was brilliant, It gives Arabella and her twins more room but keeps them close to us."

"Bob, you and Obert would like to see those bovines in the house."

"Well, Obert is Maasai, they keep their cattle close to them."

Sarah glanced down the driveway. "Ach! Where's Rollo? He's usually in front of his tray by now."

Bob answered, "I see Michael's bakkie, parked in its usual spot. Maybe Clancy's sleeping in this morning."

Sarah entered the outside kitchen, selected Rollo's breakfast, tossed it in the cart, and moved across the yard. Frowning, she put the meat in the tray and looked toward Clancy's paddock. There was no sign of Rollo. "Bob, something's wrong, Where are they?"

"I agree with you. I've got a bad feeling about this."

As the Aimtrees approached the shed, they heard Michael singing softly in Maa, Sarah grabbed Bob's arm. "Clancy has left us. I know it in my bones."

Bob nodded. "I think you're right."

The two looked into the shed. Rollo sat near Clancy's head. He was purring. Michael knelt behind the dead lion and stroked his back. He sang in the language of his people.

"Michael," Sarah whispered. "We're here. We'll help you carry your grief. Please, let us help you. "She went to Rollo and tugged his mane. "My beautiful boy, you knew this was going to happen. Your breakfast is waiting. Let us take care of Clancy."

The lion followed Sarah. She locked him in his paddock and returned to Clancy's shed. Bob called Obert. He was coming with the backhoe to dig the grave.

Sarah knelt and spoke to the grief-stricken Michael. "I'll get an old quilt. We'll wrap him for burial"

Bob placed a hand on Michael's shoulder. "Your brother is coming. We'll dig the grave and gather large stones from the back pasture. We'll make sure Clancy rests in peace."

The men selected the grave site while Sarah found the quilt. Halfway through the excavation, Michael gestured to Obert to stop the tractor. He traded places with his brother and continued to deepen the hole. Sarah returned with the quilt and all three people slid Clancy into it. They hauled him to the gravesite. Sarah provided heavy twine and wrapped him in the covering. She trotted to the outside kitchen and returned with a bag of meatballs. Once the grave was dug, they all placed three long ropes round the shroud. The first, at Clancy's shoulders, then midsection, and finally his rear quarters. He was carefully lowered, and the ropes were removed. Sarah handed the three men meatballs. They all tossed them on Clancy's body.

Wiping her eyes, Sarah said, "I wanted to give him a good send-off and some snacks for his next journey.

Bob headed toward the tractor. "My turn, folks." He began to fill the grave.

After finishing that, they placed large stones on the site. Michael and Obert put their hands on the stones and sang another tribute. Bob and Sarah joined them in spirit.

A subdued Sarah and Bob struggled through the rest of their day. Sarah's heart broke for Rollo and Michael. The lion stayed near the grave until dusk. He plodded toward the house, got his meal, and went back to Clancy's final resting spot. Just before bedtime, It pleased Sarah to see him on the stoep. She and Bob drank a glass of wine and watched him settle in front of the stairs.

Sarah asked, "Do you think we should lock him in the paddock tonight? I don't want him to wander, trying to find Clancy."

Bob shook his head. "I think he knows exactly where the old fellow is resting. I vote to leave him be."

"Done and done. Let's get some sleep."

Hours later the two people jerked awake to sounds of loud screaming. Sarah gasped. "That's an elephant. It sounds close, maybe on the lawn."

"I beg to differ. It's plural, elephants, and it sounds like they're in the kitchen, never mind the lawn. Can you hand me my boots?"

Sarah scrambled for her own footwear and, pajama-clad, hurried through the house. She flipped on the yard lights and goggled at the scene on the lawn. Rollo sat, surrounded by Tumaini, Freddie, and the two young matriarchs, Njeri and Gasira. All four gigantic animals were patting Rollo with their trunk tips.

Bob joined his wife and exclaimed. "Good lord, Tumaini has grown tusks. He's huge!"

"He isn't the only one who has grown. Look at the two females! They tower above Tumaini and Freddie."

"Umm, do you think they remember us? What I'm really asking is if it's safe to join them?"

"I do." Sarah hurried down the stairs and stood next to Tumaini. "Look at you! You're all grown up. How did you know we were sad tonight? How did you know Rollo needed comforting?"

Tumaini rumbled. He wrapped his trunk round Sarah's neck and snuffled in her hair.

"Oh, Bob! Do you remember? He did this when he arrived. Remember how fragile and sick he was?"

"Ah, yes, well, he's fragile and sick no more. Geez! I can't believe how big he is! Tusks! Look at his tusks!"

Bob joined his wife on the lawn. The four elephants wrapped trunks round their shoulders. They rumbled and flared their ears. Rollo stood and leaned against Tumaini. Head down, the lion seemed to be comforted by elephant.

Sarah, murmured, "Oh Bob, remember? Tumaini would cuddle against Rollo when he was tiny. It seems the roles have reversed."

Bob wiped his eyes. "It sure does, Sarah, I'm a bit overcome here. I'll sit on the stairs until I get my bearings."

Gasira stepped forward. She lowered her head and wrapped her trunk round Bob's neck. Statue like she waited. Bob burst into tears. Sarah joined Gasira in comforting her husband. Rollo stood and braced his face against Bob's knees.

In a shaky voice, Bob said, "Sarah, this is amazing? I'm being comforted by two different species."

"I feel this is a holy moment for us."

Bob sniffed, and replied, "Peter always tells us how intuitive his big orphans are. I admit I didn't really believe him."

"And now? I know I'm a believer."

"My dear wife! I could go on the road as a salesman for elephant ESP."

Sarah patted Bob's knee. "Your sense of humor is back. I vote to sit here and see what happens next."

Twenty minutes later, Tumaini gently touched his three caregivers. He flared his ears, trumpeted, and swung to face the driveway. His three fellow orphans fell in behind him as he paced toward the river and disappeared into the darkness. Over the next two years, the four would visit. Always nocturnal, several more herd members accompanied them. They stayed in the driveway. Two humans and one lion would visit until the enormous animals took their leave.

✸ Rollo ✸
Chapter 53

I awoke to silence. It was hours until dawn, but I knew Clancy had left us. His snoring breaths had stopped. Distraught, I sat up and shook my head. I hoped he would find Uncle Sid. When my time came, two familiar faces would greet me. Too upset to sleep, I paced round the paddock. An hour later, I saw shapes, then, the sun chased the night away. I waited for Michael at the gate. He took my face in his hands and murmured in Maa. We went into the shed. Michael checked Clancy. I reckoned he wanted to be sure the old boy wasn't breathing. We sat and grieved, each in our own way. Michael sang songs of tribute and praise. Me? I managed a feeble purr and knew I would sorely miss this creature. Don't get me wrong, my pride of humans, hens, cows, and elephants is important to me. I'd give my life for them. But Clancy was a lion.

Bob and Sarah walked across the driveway. Grim-faced, they also knew Clancy was gone. Obert arrived with the tractor. It took hours to dig a hole deep enough to assure scavengers wouldn't dig and desecrate Clancy's body. By scavengers, I refer to those loathsome hyenas. Clancy was wrapped in a cloth and carefully lowered into the grave. Sarah, bless her heart, gave meatballs to everyone, and they tossed them on the shroud. I admit to thinking it was a waste of perfectly good food, but I understood it was part of the ritual. Sarah slipped me a couple of those delicious treats. I felt terrible, but not terrible enough to ignore them. The men took turns filling the hole. They placed large rocks on the grave. A splendid idea! They were another deterrent to scavengers. After dinner, I lay by the grave until dark. Lonely for my pride, I joined

Bob and Sarah on the stoep. The hens joined us and settled behind the fern.

I fell into a troubled sleep. Poor Clancy, I hoped he'd found Uncle Sid. Several hours later, I lurched to my feet. Elephants! Elephants were trumpeting! They were on the lawn. I peered round the stoep railing and blinked in astonishment. Four enormous elephants stood at the bottom of the step. Tumaini? Was the behemoth on the lawn Tumaini? Could this be the bratty cub that lived with us for two years?. He raised his trunk, flared his ears, and made a soft sound. He frightened me, but I couldn't help walking down the steps. I looked up at this gigantic creature. He gently tugged my mane with his trunk tip. He had tusks! It was Tumaini. I purred a greeting. For reasons I couldn't explain, his presence was a comfort to me. Three more monsters approached. Glory! As Obert says, Freddie, Najiri, and Gasira patted me with their trunks and did that odd elephant rumble. I sat and let their compassion and sympathy wash through me.

Sarah and Bob joined us. The elephants comforted them. Trunk tips patted faces and hair. Sarah stood next to Tumaini and touched one of his tusks. Those tusks! Let me tell you, I never considered he would grow them. Poor Bob, Clancy's death upset him, usually not emotional, he sat on the steps and wept. Gasira and Sarah consoled and comforted him. After an hour, Tumaini turned and led the others down the driveway. How did they know we were sad? How did they know we needed comfort and support?

Over the next two years, the elephants would visited us. They always came at night. We would gather on the lawn, Sarah and Bob would receive as many pats as I. The huge beasts would rumble, snuffle in our hair, and tug on my mane. At a signal none of us recognized, the four would join the small herd in the driveway and return to the river.

Chapter 54

"Ach! Bob, the elephants are here. Gad! What time is it? They sound anxious. The hair on my neck is raised."

"I agree, let's get out there. Something's wrong."

They threw on clothes and hurried through the house. Bob flipped the yard lights on. Sarah, halfway down the stairs, stopped and gasped. "Bob, I think the ellies injured Rollo. Look, he's lying in front of them. Is that blood? Get your phone. Call Malcolm."

Bob disappeared into the house, returned, and joined his wife. "I can't believe they hurt Rollo. I'm wondering if we should approach them. Let's call Peter, we need his expertise."

Sarah shook her head. "I'm going to him, can you get some towels? He has several slashes on his side and chest. Until help arrives, I'm going to put pressure on these bleeding wounds. I can't believe the ellies hurt our boy."

Bob made the calls and joined Sarah. They applied pressure to Rollo's wounds and waited for Malcolm. The lion was unconscious, his breathing shallow.

Sarah looked up and said, "Call Obert, Michael, and the Von Bergs. Rollo may not survive this. I want his friends here"

"Already done, everyone is in route. Sam can assist Malcolm. She's been his helper for several years."

Sarah glanced at the forest of elephant legs that surrounded them. "It's the usual suspects, isn't it? Tumaini, Freddie, Najiri and Gasiri, the rest of the herd are in the driveway."

"We'll soon know, I saw headlights swing off the road onto our property." Bob watched the lights veer off the road to the right, then left. He couldn't be sure, but they appeared to stop. "I think your prediction was correct. There's an obstruction in our road."

Obert and Michael parked and hurried to the lawn. Obert said, Glory! Your driveway is full of elephants!"

Both men hurried to Rollo and knelt to help Sarah. Michael whispered words of comfort. The elephants patted humans and lion with trunk tips. Another set of lights appeared in the driveway. Malcolm parked on the verge and hurried toward them.

"Did you know your driveway is full of elephants? Ah! Your lawn is also full of elephants. What the hell happened to Rollo?" Malcolm began his examination."

Sarah said, "We don't know. I hope the ellies didn't injure him. Peter's on his way. He knows them better than anyone."

Malcolm grunted. "I don't think elephants did this. These are slashing wounds, likely inflicted by another predator. Possibly, lions, or hyenas. Those brutes would attack a solitary lion. Did you hear a fight?"

Sarah shook her head. "No, we heard the elephants. The sounds they were making told us they were upset. We knew something was wrong."

Two more sets of headlights jerked up the drive. Peter flew out of his vehicle and joined them. "He spoke to the four orphans. "Did you lot save our lion? By the Gods! I wish you could talk." He knelt next to Rollo and patted his mane. "Malcolm, what can I do to help? Tell me what to do."

"Keep your bloody elephants from trampling us. Did I hear that the Von Bergs are coming? I could use Samantha. She knows where everything is in my truck."

Sarah answered, "They're on the way. Should we get more towels?"

"Yes, let's roll him over and check his other side. We need to treat the worst wounds first."

Before careful hands rolled the injured animal to his other side, Sarah placed clean towels on the ground. "Mal, can you tell how badly he's injured?"

"Not yet, I see the wounds on his sides are equal in severity. He's bleeding, but I doubt any major vessel is lashed. Whatever animal attacked him tried to rip his belly open. Thank God they weren't successful. We would be putting him down. My guess is the ellies intervened."

Car doors slammed. Sarah watched her young friend fly out of the truck. Samantha said, "Aunt Sarah, your road is full of elephants. Oh, Dr. Malcolm, poor Rollo. What do you need? Your headlamp? Suture material? Irrigation fluids?"

"All the above, Sam. Don't forget gloves."

Sam hurried to the truck. It took her only minutes to assemble items on a metal tray. Gloved up, she rejoined Malcolm.

Sarah hugged a distraught Felicity. They listened to Brandon. "Hey, old man, it looks like you tangled with a chainsaw. Not to worry, we'll put you right. You've got expert help and all your friends are here."

Malcolm told the group he needed to give Rollo a short-acting sedative. "I know he's unconscious, but I can't have him waking up while I suture him."

Sam returned with the tray, gave Malcolm the syringe, and knelt beside him. When the sedative took effect, Malcolm flushed the worst laceration and sutured the wound. Sam was an extra pair of hands for him. She gave him supplies before he asked, clipped sutures, and blotted the bleeding wounds. The group turned Rollo onto his other side. Malcolm sutured more lacerations. Tumaini grabbed Malcolm's cap and held it aloft. Sam frowned, held her hand out, and demanded the hat. Sheepishly, the enormous animal gave it to her. When the wounds were sutured, Rollo was gently rolled onto the sling and the group transported him to the mattress in the den.

Peter said, "I'll bring two mattresses, I know you'll be with him night and day. I can't control the ellies. They'll move when they're ready. They may be here for hours."

Sarah muttered, "I hope they don't walk through the fence."

"We can't stop them. I hope they'll be respectful."

Samantha leaned against Tumaini's front leg. She tugged his ear and said, "I know you're all worried. So are we. Rollo needs to rest now. Please be quiet. Don't upset him, he'll soon be awake."

The four elephants flared their ears, rumbled, and walked to Rollo's den. They stood in front of his bench.

The people enter the den and waited. Rollo's eyes fluttered. He groaned and managed a weak, wheezy purr. A determined effort brought him to his chest. He blinked, looked around at his friends, and tried to rise.

"Rest old man, "Malcolm said. He placed his hand on Rollo's shoulder. Sarah let's get a bucket of water. I need to see if he'll drink."

Sam dashed to the stoep. "I know where the buckets are kept. I'll get one."

Rollo drank, groaned, and put his head down.

"That's good enough for now. Don't feed him until morning. Humph, it is morning. Offer him food this afternoon. I'm assuming one of you will stay with him."

Sam said, "Mummy, can I stay? I'll fetch water, clean towels, or whatever is needed."

Felicity nodded. "Of course, Sarah, do you object?"

"Nope, we're glad to have you. Let's get our sleeping gear."

The four elephants turned and walked down the driveway. The next morning, Sarah saw vultures circling by the river. She sent Bob and the brothers to investigate.

When they returned, Bob said, "Sarah, The river path is strewn with torn branches. Three dead hyenas are lying in the mud. I think we were right. Rollo wandered to the river, got attacked, and was saved by the ellies. Thank God they were near."

She nodded. " Rollo went to greet his friends. Our poor simba. I doubt he would have ventured this far from home if he hadn't heard his friends."

"I know this sounds awful, but I'm glad those vicious brutes got stomped into jelly."

Humans and Rollo struggled for the first three days. He was clearly hurting and reluctant to walk. He tottered off the mattress only to relieve himself. His caregivers provided water. Sara and Sam made buckets of meatballs and held them under Rollo's nose. The lion devoured them. Malcolm visited daily to inspect and clean the wounds.

Ten days after the attack, Malcolm sat back on his heels and told Sarah, "I'm pleased with the healing. None of them are infected. Look, the skin's pink and healthy. He'll be back to normal soon."

She heaved a sigh of relief. "Everyone has been worried about him. This is wonderful news."

Rollo, sprawled on the mattress, purred in agreement. Three

days later, Malcolm looked in on the Aimtrees. He found Sarah, Bob, and Samantha with Rollo. Sam held a pan of water, and Sarah waited with meatballs. Bob brushed the animal's mane. King-like Rollo allowed his pride to serve him.

Malcolm's eyes narrowed. "What're you lot doing? Why isn't he on his feet to eat and drink?"

Sarah blushed and stammered. "Erm, um, he enjoys our attention. We're not sure he should walk."

Malcolm exploded. "Are you all daft? He's playing you like a violin. The wounds are healed. He gets up to relieve himself. Doesn't he?"

"Erm, yes, he does."

"Get rid of all this nonsense. He eats and drinks on his feet. Are you still giving him meatballs?"

Samantha giggled. "We're grinding kilos of meat for him."

"For Pete's sake, there's nothing wrong with his jaws. Feed him a regular meal."

Rollo sighed, put his head down, and whimpered.

Malcolm shook his head. "Don't try that with me, you big faker. You're back to your normal routine."

✸ Rollo ✸
Chapter 55

I woke to the sound of trumpeting elephants. The wind blew their sound and scent to me. Delighted to know my friends were coming, I made a foolish decision. I would surprise them by greeting them at the river. Crossing the road made me nervous because of the passing vehicles. I'm aware of how to watch for cars. It was the middle of the night, I knew there would be little traffic. I padded down the driveway and paused at the spot where Clancy had collapsed. I'd never been further than this spot. Not on foot. I hurried across the road. Good! In seconds, I was on the path. The worst is over, elephants would accompany me back to the house. Bah! I was wrong. The riverbanks were covered in thick brush. Trees leaned over the water. Fascinated, I followed the fast-moving current. The water danced and sparkled in the moonlight.

Where were the ellies? I wasn't paying attention, the wind shifted, and their scent diminished. The ellies were upriver, and I had followed the current downstream. The brush rustled, and a pack of hyenas hurtled out of the foliage. Snarling, the leader faced me, while several of the spotted devils moved to my sides. I knew they were building the courage to attack. I roared and leaped at the largest one. The rest swarmed onto me. I fought them off, but they overwhelmed me. Ears flattened against their ugly heads, they overpowered me. I went down and felt slashing wounds on both sides and my chest. I saw glimpses of their spotted coats and lethal teeth. They whooped with victory, sure they had a meal secured. Before I lost consciousness, the ground shook. I'm going to see Uncle Sid and Clancy. Maybe the ground shakes when a creature leaves this earth.

Drifting in and out of consciousness, I'm being half carried, my paws are dragging the ground. I'm supported by rubbery things round my chest and belly. Is this how we get to heaven? How very odd. I imagined flying through the air to arrive. Elephants, elephants are screaming. Did they come with me? Uncle Sid and Clancy will be surprised. I hope they have enough room for us. Did I hear Sarah and Bob? Am I on the lawn? There is cool, moist grass underneath me. Well, there may be lush lawns in heaven. What are Sarah and Bob doing here? Is that Malcolm? I'm confused and in pain. How could I be hurting if I'm in heaven? Am I dead? Ouch, Malcolm just stabbed me in the behind. I'm not dead, I'm home and my friends are helping me. Uncle Sid and Clancy won't see me tonight.

Malcolm's medicine put me into a deep sleep. I awoke on the mattress, my human pride members were with me, and I could smell and hear ellies near the fence. Malcolm made sure I had water and Sarah supplied meatballs. My wounds throbbed, I couldn't lay on my side. It was too painful. So, I sprawled on my chest and groaned. The next three days were terrible. Malcolm arrived every day to examine my wounds. Sarah, Bob, Obert, and Michael catered to my every need. It was a treat to be pampered. Sam helped with my food. She and Sarah decided I shouldn't have to chew, they made meatballs for me. A week later, I felt better, my wounds were healing, but it was nice to have people waiting on me. I couldn't resist playing the invalid role. Groaning or looking distressed got me food, water, or a careful massage. All right, all right, I took advantage of the situation. I couldn't resist being pampered. Malcolm exposed me, he said my wounds were healed, and I was acting like a spoiled brat. Well, it was wonderful while it lasted.

The hens and I resumed patrol. For the first three days, the stairs weren't easy to climb. My sides were stiff, and I had to move slowly. Once on the stoep, my bed awaited me. Those bloody hyenas nearly killed me. Sarah worried I would wander again. Not too bloody likely! I'll let the ellies come to the house. That's what I should have done, but I didn't think hyenas lived that close to us. Once on the path, the rushing water fascinated me. I wasn't paying attention when the brutes ambushed me. I'm lucky to be alive and thank my giant friends and human pride members for saving my life.

Chapter 56

Sarah pocketed her phone and looked at Bob. "That was Malcolm. He has a request I don't think we can honor."

Bob put down his newspaper. "Really? What's he asking?"

Sarah glanced at Rollo, snoozing under the fern. "Erm, I'll tell you in the house."

"What? Why? You've an odd expression on your face. What it is?"

Sarah stood and walked indoors. Bob trailed behind her. She sighed and sat at the kitchen table. "What do you know about striped hyenas?"

"Striped hyenas? They exist, that's what I know. Why do you ask?"

"Malcolm wants us to foster a striped hyena cub. It'll be for a few weeks. He said–"

"Are you daft? A hyena? The beasts almost killed Rollo six months ago. What's Malcolm thinking?"

"Spotted hyenas attacked Rollo, striped ones live north of us."

"Spots, stripes, who cares! How can Malcolm request this of us?"

"I know but listen to this story. We don't have to do it. Striped hyenas live in Northern Africa. Some are in Kenya and Tanzania. People who deal in bush meat and other illegal animal products shipped a mother and her three cubs to our part of the world. Their transport vehicle smashed into a tree, rolled several times, and caught fire. This cub is the only survivor. There's a strong market for certain parts of the striped hyena."

"You mean like rhino horn?"

"Yes, the powdered skull is used by certain indigenous tribes for medicinal purposes. Their unique pelt is valuable, some people consider the meat a delicacy. Parts of this animal are supposed to be powerful aphrodisiacs. The traffickers would raise and slaughter the cubs. The mother might be used for breeding."

"Sarah, this story is terrible, but how can we have a hyena on the property? Rollo may go berserk and attack it."

"Striped hyenas are on the near-endangered list. Unlike their spotted cousins, they're shy, solitary creatures. This surviving cub has a broken right front leg and a broken left hind leg. She has a cracked pelvis. The vet school has set her broken bones and put pins in the pelvis. They can't find a sanctuary that'll devote enough time for rehabilitation. She's female, her broken legs are in casts. The vets estimate her age between four and five months. She'd be nursing if her mum was alive, but she's old enough for solid food."

"You want to foster her? What about Rollo? Need I remind you, the only time he showed aggression was toward hyenas."

"He won't harm a defenseless creature. I'm not arguing with you, I know it's risky. I feel we have to help this baby. We must both agree because she'll be a labor-intensive project."

"Rollo has always been your boy, if you think he'll tolerate her, then I agree to help."

"Ach! I'm not sure he'll tolerate her, but he won't tear her limb from limb."

"We've forgotten he's an immense apex predator, we can't control him if he decides to hurt her. We'll be lucky to save ourselves."

"I know, I've considered that. I still want to help her. Don't say yes to appease me."

"I don't trust my decision and I don't trust Rollo. I trust your opinion and judgment of his behavior in this matter. Call Malcolm and tell him we'll take her. Michael and Obert will be aghast."

Sarah smiled, "Can't you hear Obert? Glory! A hyena! Are you daft? Here?"

Sarah made the call. Malcolm told her the cub would stay at the vet school for a week. He suggested barricading one end of the stoep with a small barrier, perhaps a baby gate.

Sarah knew Rollo understood her, he also read her body language. On their next walk, she saw him glancing at her, a perplexed look on his face. She couldn't bring herself to tell him.

Six days later, Malcolm arrived with their patient. Inside his truck, a pathetic creature cowered in a crate. The cub had two legs in casts, and a plastic cone buckled round her neck. It prevented her from chewing the casts, it also restricted her vision.

Bob took one look and cried. "Good Lord, the poor thing. Mal, how much pain is she in?"

"The surgeons stabilized her broken legs, I'm not sure about the pelvis injury. That fracture could be very painful. Malcolm looked at the straw-covered section of the stoep. "This is a perfect spot for her. I'll apologize in advance for your sleep loss. This animal is nocturnal, but she's lost her family and has terrible injuries. She'll cry most of the time."

Malcolm deposited the hyena in the pen. She struggled to rise. Hampered by the casts and cone, she sprawled in the bedding.

Malcolm looked over the railing. "Where's Rollo? On patrol?"

Sarah nodded. "Yep, he'll be here shortly."

The object of the discussion padded up the steps. Wrinkling

his nose, he snarled and bared his teeth at the familiar scent. He looked into the small pen, lowered his head, and slunk down the stairs. He disappeared into the paddock. The cub wailed. The hens squawked in displeasure and flew into the trees.

"That's that," said Bob, we know how he feels."

Sarah said, "I'll talk to him later and explain why she's here. He'll ignore her."

"Let's hope he ignores her."

Malcolm adjusted the cone. "I'm worried about you getting in his way, should he attack her. We've forgotten how powerful he is."

Bob said, "I was prepared to hate her. I can't, she's too small and frightened. What do we feed her? Do the casts require maintenance?"

"I've formula from the school. Offer a bottle and Sarah's famous meatballs. Remove the cone and feed her on the lawn. She needs help to relieve herself. She can't squat. One of you steady her with a towel round her belly, the other can hold her shoulders."

Sarah asked, "Does she have a name?"

"Nalangu, a Maasai word, it means from another tribe."

"That's spot on!" Bob said, "She's a foreigner. Sarah told me why she and her family were shipped from their home. Why are humans so cruel and ignorant?"

Malcolm shook his head. "If I knew that answer, I'd be a rich man. People can be horrible to each other and animals. Should I take her back to the vet school? I don't want you injured. I'm having second thoughts about this."

Sarah shook her head. "Rollo won't hurt her. He's annoyed and sulking, but let's see how we get on. We'll try for a week. Let's see if we can provide specialized care for her.

Nalangu fretted in her pen. Without help, she struggled to rise, the cone hindered her vision, it extended beyond her muzzle to prevent her from chewing the casts. She flailed and cried until Bob carried her to the lawn. The cub leaned against the towel to relieve herself but refused the bottle. She ate one meatball.

Sarah rubbed Nalangu's neck. "Missy, you need to eat. Your broken legs won't heal without nourishment. We know you're in pain and lonely. We'll help you heal."

Bob put the cub in the pen. Sarah handed him the cone.

He grimaced and said, "I already hate this thing. I think she's more upset about restricted vision than her broken limbs." He buckled the device round the hyena's neck.

"I agree, she's a lost soul. I'm more worried about her appetite."

"What appetite? She's eaten one meatball."

"We'll try again in two hours. Meanwhile, I'll talk to Rollo."

Over the next five days, Nalangu whimpered all day and howled all night. She ate a few meatballs when the cone was off but refused her bottle. She wasted away in front of her caregivers.

Malcolm arrived to examine her. "You both have dark circles under your eyes. No offense, but you look awful. All your hard work isn't helping. This creature can't survive much longer. I think she's given up and will starve to death. Let me take her to the school for euthanasia, we need to end her suffering. They may want to do an autopsy."

Sarah glanced at her husband. He'd bonded with Nalangu the way she had bonded with Rollo, the way Michael bonded with Clancy. "Bob, what should we do?"

"I don't want her to die. She's a mess because stupid people made terrible decisions. Can we try for another week? Mal, can we do that?"

"Of course, soldier on for another few days."

Bob asked, "Mal, can you put her to sleep here? I'd like to bury her near Clancy."

"Sure, call when you're ready."

Six nights later, Bob and Sarah returned to the house after another futile attempt to feed Nalangu. The animal refused Sarah's treats and lay in her pen, a picture of misery. Exhausted, they got into bed and prayed for two more hours of sleep.

Sarah's eyes flew open. There was light in the room. She tapped Bob's shoulder. "Bob, it's dawn. Let's check on her. Brace yourself if she's left us."

Sarah clattered through the screen door, Bob on her heels. They both stared at the sight on the stoep. Rollo lay against the small fence. Nalangu, sound asleep, lay close to him on her side of the barrier. The lion heard the screen door slam, Startled, he jerked to his chest and looked at Sarah with an embarrassed expression. She knew the animal had planned to leave before dawn. He'd fallen asleep next to the hyena. She also knew his purring and warmth comforted their patient.

Wisely, she carried on with the morning routine. "Bob, I'll meet you on the lawn, let me feed Rollo. Come with me, big boy, it's breakfast time."

Bob removed the hated cone and carried Nalangu to the lawn. Sarah joined them with her meatballs. The cub did her bathroom duties. She ate the meatballs.

"Sarah, look at this! Should I get the bottle?"

"Sure, let's try it."

Nalangu drank half the bottle of formula, yawned, looked at

Bob, and opened her mouth in a huge hyena grin. She yipped and wagged her stubby tail.

"Sarah, has our boy worked his magic again? Did he seem normal to you?"

Sarah snorted. "I struggled not to laugh at him. He's mortified about getting caught sleeping with a hyena."

"Let's hope he's not too embarrassed to join her again. It's never occurred to me that he's as sleep-deprived as we are."

"That's my hope, I miss him. We're used to his snoring presence."

Later that day, Sarah sat at the stoep table, immersed in paperwork. Rollo padded up the steps. Nalangu sensed him and whimpered. She lurched to the barrier and peeked over the top. Rollo touched noses with her, sighed, and lay down next to the fence. Delighted, the cub pitched on her side and scooted next to him. Sarah knew her boy would comfort the cub until she left. Several more weeks passed, and the youngster, calmed by Rollo, slept and ate well.

One morning, Malcolm arrived and took Nalangu to the school for cast removal and X-rays. He'd found a sanctuary that would take her.

"Sarah, I've no right to ask for more, but I'm asking. Could you keep her for a few more weeks? She needs brief, frequent walks on a leash. Her muscles are atrophied from the casts. The sanctuary needs to know her mobility status before they accept her."

"Sure, since Rollo stepped up as a babysitter, she's no trouble. I can't wait to see her without casts and the dreaded cone. We know she's disoriented because she can't see or walk normally."

"I agree, let's remove these things. I'll return her this afternoon."

Malcolm deposited a liberated Nalangu on the lawn. She tottered to Rollo, touched noses, and flopped between his front legs. He purred and sat, she grinned her hyena grin and snuffled in the grass.

Malcolm blinked in astonishment. "I thought you were joking. When did they become pals?"

Bob gave Malcolm the short version of Rollo's behavioral change. "Sarah's convinced he was trying to calm her so we could get more sleep. I agree and thank God it worked. We can exercise her, what's the program?"

"She needs to build muscle in her legs, use the lawn, and don't allow her on the stairs. Releasing her is out of the question, she doesn't know how to hunt. Her mobility may be an issue. The sanctuary folks warned me she may have to live in isolation. Hyenas, like all predators, won't tolerate weakness. If she's too crippled, they'll kill her."

Three weeks later, Malcolm watched the youngster walk. Her gait was abnormal, far from sound, she drug one back leg. With Sarah's urging, she managed a stiff, slow trot.

Malcolm shook his head. "Her gait is too abnormal for her to live with the pack. The sanctuary will isolate her. Has she mastered the stairs?"

Nalangu answered Malcolm's question by following Rollo to the stoep. They settled on his bed.

Bob rubbed his eyes and said, "I don't like that idea. She'll be lonely. Sarah, can we keep her? I know it's another creature to feed, but she deserves better than solitary confinement for the rest of her life."

"My only concern was Rollo. That's a non-issue. He's accepted her. She's respectful and quiet. She's accepted the hens. Last week, Pearl hopped on her back. Nalangu grinned at that ancient hen and went back to sleep."

Malcolm said, "The school has no objection. This is a better home for her. Are you sure about this?" He glanced at the lion.

Rollo walked to Sarah, he purred and gently tapped her leg with an enormous forepaw. She tugged his mane and asked, "My boy, do you want to live with this odd-looking beast?"

Malcolm laughed, "That's how I read his behavior. Lord, he doesn't need to talk to communicate. One last thing, the professors may use their reproductive technology to get her pregnant. They can inseminate her and do a C-section."

Bob stared at him. "How the hell do you get semen from a male hyena? And don't say, 'very carefully'. How can they do that? Wait! Forget I asked, I don't want to know."

Rollo sat up and stared at Malcolm. He looked at Nalangu, then Sarah. His eyebrows waggled. He snorted and flopped onto his bed.

Sarah said, "We'll discuss that next year. Rollo, how do you feel about baby hyenas?"

✱ Rollo ✱
Chapter 57

THERE IS A HYENA ON THE STOEP! Now I know why the humans are acting odd. Sarah couldn't meet my gaze. Bob, Malcolm, Obert, and Michael appeared to be hiding something. All of them would stop talking when I was present. I'm used to their irrational behavior, but this was a puzzle. What were they hiding? Bah! I found out this afternoon. A hyena, Malcolm brought the beast and deposited it in the new pen. I couldn't understand the need for that space. Bob put straw and shaving on the floor. He and Obert built a fence on one side of the stoep. The girls and I were halfway up the steps when the reek of hyena filled my nostrils. A small whimpering creature cowered in the pen. Hyena! That's a hyena. I growled and bared my impressive canines. Sarah, Bob, and Malcolm stood in front of the little fence. I couldn't attack my pride members, they saved my life. I slunk down the stairs and disappeared for the day. That night, the beast howled loud enough to wake us. Sarah and Bob took the creature to the lawn. What the heck were they doing? It's the middle of the night. Again, my curiosity will be the death of me. I shoved the girls into the straw, slunk into the yard, and hid behind my bench.

The beast had a device strapped round its head. Two limbs were encased in a white, stiff material. I saw it needed to squat but couldn't. Bob steadied its hind limbs. Sarah spoke to it and then offered food. A bottle! How could it be so young? What happened to it? It didn't resemble the hyenas that tried to kill me. This one had stripes on its body and legs. I don't care if it's every color of the rainbow. Bob called it by name. 'Nalangu', that's Maasai, the word means from another tribe. Oh, too bloody right,

I'll say it's a foreigner, and female, wonderful, that's all I need. What if she stays, grows, and reproduces?

The next few days and nights were awful. That damaged creature made more noise than Tumaini. Several times a night, Bob and Sarah worked with her. Malcolm arrived one afternoon to discuss the cub's future. I pretended to be asleep in the den. Nalangu wasn't eating, she had two broken limbs and a damaged pelvis. Though unsure of its function, I learned the cub needed an intact pelvis to walk properly. Malcolm said it was best to put her to sleep. She was suffering, she wouldn't heal if she wouldn't eat. Bob asked for more time. Malcolm agreed to another week.

That night, the caterwauling started after dusk. I had a plan. After the humans visited her, I would make my move. If Malcolm wanted to put her to sleep, I would assist him. We're tired of sleepless nights. After their third visit, I crept across the lawn and onto the stoep. Nalangu heard me, she struggled to her feet and came to the barrier. She propped the cone in the straw and braced against it to get up. It was a clever move. My plan was to put her to sleep permanently. She put her face up and tried to touch noses with me. I looked into a pair of black eyes filled with pain, loneliness, and terror. Sighing, I obliged her. Then I lay down close to the fence and purred. I can't hurt her, she's small and broken. She pitched on her side and scooted next to me, and went to sleep I'd return to the den in a few hours, so Bob and Sarah wouldn't see me. I closed my eyes for a moment. The screen door slammed. Aghast, I looked up to the sunlight streaming over the railing.

Sarah and Bob stared at me. Wonderful! They'd caught me comforting a hyena. I'll never live this down! Well, this creature isn't a threat, she can't walk or see well. Sarah, bless her, sensed my embarrassment and carried on with the morning routine. I returned to the stoep that afternoon. It's cooler there and I was tired of sulking. I also missed my pride members. Nalangu settled and slept next to me. Four days later, a new dog bed appeared on the stoep, next to her pen. Good, I'll be pampered while comforting this cub. She's leaving in a few weeks, I'll tolerate the situation.

A month later, Malcolm took Nalangu to the vet school. When he returned, he put her on the lawn. Free of casts and cone, she looked much happier. As Malcolm predicted, her gait was terrible. She limped and her rear end tipped sideways with each step. Bob was fiercely optimistic we could heal this baby. I knew Sarah and Malcolm had doubts, as did I. Bob and Sarah began with slow, frequent strolls round the lawn. Nalangu sniffed and rolled on the cool grass. She explored Sarah's garden. Butterflies fascinated her. When the gauzy creatures fluttered near the flowers, Nalangu sat and stared at them. Sarah removed the little fence. Nalangu never left me so we didn't need it. A month later, she accompanied us on patrol. She could climb the stairs in a slow, halting manner. Malcolm was correct in his original assessment. Nalangu was too damaged to join her pride.

One night, the elephants visited. I hoped to join them without Nalangu, but she woke and followed me to the lawn. Oh boy! Tumaini and Freddie caught her scent and sounded the alarm. Terrified, Nalangu dove underneath me. The girls strode forward to assess the situation. Gasiri blew and stomped, head high, she sniffed the air. Sarah and Bob hurried to help me but it was unnecessary. The mini-matriarchs recognized this hyena was no threat. They also saw I comforted her, just like I comforted Tumaini. These giant animals are so smart. They all remembered Tumaini's behavior. In minutes, Nalangu peeped round my legs and stared at her new friends. Four trunk tips examined her striped coat. Najiri sniffed her crooked pelvis while the young bulls patted her face. Nalangu gave them her best hyena grin. My human pride members sat on the steps. I reckon they were relieved that we hadn't been churned into mush.

Several days later, Malcolm came to see us. The hens and

I were dozing under the fern. Nalangu slept on her back, her limbs propped against my side. She snored in whistling breaths. Malcolm described a sanctuary for striped hyenas. The people were dedicated and knowledgeable about these animals. Nalangu would live alone. She was too damaged to live with other hyenas.

The humans didn't want her to live alone. Nor did I. What is happening to me? Do I want to live with a hyena for years? I sat up, and stared at Sarah. It was another of those rare times when I wished I could talk. Startled awake, Nalangu squawked, rolled under me, and peered at the humans from between my front legs. She yipped and thumped her tail. This cub loves and trusts me. She doesn't know she's a hyena and I'm a lion, and we're supposed to be mortal enemies. Going to Sarah, I leaned against her and purred to express my decision. This cub can't live alone, she'll be sad. I want her to stay. She deserves a peaceful life. Besides, she's a member of the pride. I helped resolve the matter, she would remain here. On his way down the stairs, Malcolm mentioned a possible pregnancy. Pregnancy? Wait one minute. Baby hyenas? Here? Bah! They'll be like the chicks, into everything. I'll have no peace. Nalangu crawled out from beneath me, propped her front legs on my chest, and licked my face. Ah well, perhaps I could assist in cub rearing. After all, I'm experienced in these matters.

Rhino Tears Winery

Launched at the end of 2014, Rhino Tears has already raised almost R 2 million to be used in the war against rhino poaching within South Africa's National Parks. The funds raised are used to purchase equipment and train rangers on the front line of the anti-poaching war, as well as special projects such as the Kruger National Park canine training facility.

The idea for the wine came about when Mt Vernon MD, John Hooper, spent a couple of days with the field rangers at the Kruger Wilderness Experience bush camp in the Kruger National Park. It was here that the idea for a wine that could raise money for anti-poaching efforts was born.

http://www.rhinotears.co.za/our-story/

Team Lioness

In 2019, the tenBoma wildlife security team created Team Lioness: one of the first all-women ranger units in Kenya. Chosen based on leadership, academic achievements, and integrity, the team of eight young Maasai women are defying constraining social norms and creating new opportunities for women.

Based under the Olgulului Community Wildlife Rangers (OCWR) on the border of Tanzania and Kenya, Team Lioness protects the traditional community land that surrounds Amboseli National Park. The rangers serve as the first line of defense against the poaching and retaliatory killing of elephants, lions, giraffes, cheetahs, and other iconic wildlife who frequent the land's wildlife corridors.

https://www.ifaw.org/projects/team-lioness

Acknowledgments

I have many people to thank for assisting me in this first time project. Linda Bello-Ruiz helped me craft a cohesive story. She showed me how to navigate Word and gave me countless suggestions to improve the tale. Stacey Dennick and Joel Neuberg instructors for my creative writing class also helped with patience and knowledge. I wish to mention all my pals in the class for their constructive and positive feedback. Their suggestions helped to streamline the story.

My heartfelt thanks to my five friends that slogged through the first draft of Rollo: Wendy Wiley, Annie Douglas, Theresa Wistrom, Debbie Miramontes and Jean Fox. Thank you for your feedback.

A huge thanks to Luana Cowan for catching all my typos and grammatical errors.

Last, but certainly not least, a huge thanks to my husband who let me hog the computer and bought reams of paper and gallons of printer ink. Paul, I love you.

Carol Livramento

Author Carol Livramento graduated from the University of California, Davis with a degree in Animal Husbandry. She grew up in a rural area of Northern California where she had horses, dogs, cats, rabbits and sheep for friends. Her love of animals is evident in this book, Rollo, where she explores the world of an African lion and his pride members. Always fascinated with African wildlife, the story came to her in a dream. A retired laboratory technologist Carol continues to live in Northern California with Paul, her husband of forty years. She is currently working on her second book, *Maudie and Me*, about one of her horses.

Printed in the USA
CPSIA information can be obtained
at www.ICGtesting.com
LVHW062206201024
794170LV00021B/304

9 798330 204618